PRAISE FOR MARIEKE NIJKAMP

"Thrilling, raw, and unforgettable. A story about humanity, resilience, and hope. Nijkamp at their best!"

—Kami Garcia, #1 *New York Times* bestselling coauthor of *Beautiful Creatures*, for *At the End of Everything*

"A stomach-churning thriller that delivers prudent social commentary on the complicated reality of being a teen with mental health issues, and what it means to survive when no one cares if you live."

—*Shelf Awareness* for *At the End of Everything*

"A compelling story of terror, betrayal, and heroism... This brutal, emotionally charged novel will grip readers and leave them brokenhearted."

—*Kirkus Reviews* for *This Is Where It Ends*

"Love, loyalty, bravery, and loss meld into a chaotic, heart-wrenching mélange of issues that unite some and divide others. A highly diverse cast of characters, paired with vivid imagery and close attention to detail, set the stage for an engrossing, unrelenting tale."

—*Publishers Weekly* for *This Is Where It Ends*

★"With exceptional handling of everything from mental illness to guilt and a riveting, magic realist narrative, this well-wrought, haunting novel will stick with readers long after the final page."

—*Booklist* for *Before I Let Go*, Starred Review

"Immersive and captivating. Thrilling in every sense of the word."

—Karen M. McManus, #1 *New York Times* bestselling author of *One of Us Is Lying*, for *Even If We Break*

"The darkly twisted ode to self-discovery briskly whisks an intersectionally inclusive group through a reasonably stormy, emotionally charged scenario that considers the sometimes-steep price of growing up and growing apart."

—*Publishers Weekly* for *Even If We Break*

ALSO BY MARIEKE NIJKAMP

This Is Where It Ends
Before I Let Go
Even If We Break
At the End of Everything

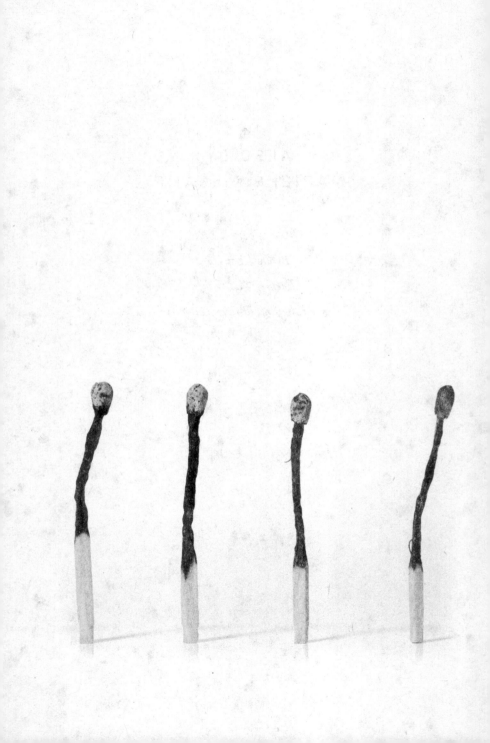

AFTER WE BURNED

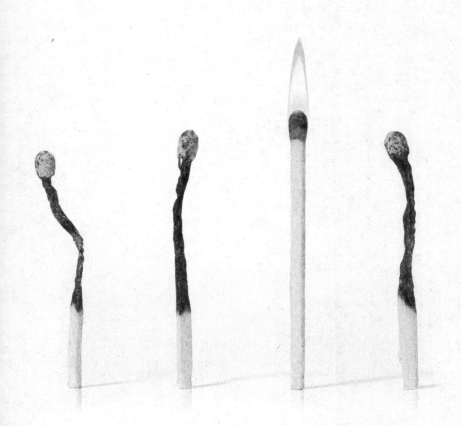

After We Burned

MARIEKE NIJKAMP

Copyright © 2025 by Marieke Nijkamp
Cover and internal design © 2025 by Sourcebooks
Cover design by Natalie C. Sousa
Cover images © Carmen Martínez Torrón/Getty Images, domnitsky/Shutterstock
Internal design by Tara Jaggers/Sourcebooks
Internal images © ThomasVogel/Getty Images, JamesBrey/Getty Images
Edge images © Tartila/Shutterstock, Ovacular/Shutterstock

Sourcebooks and the colophon are registered trademarks of Sourcebooks.

All rights reserved. No part of this book may be reproduced in any form or by any electronic or mechanical means, including information storage and retrieval systems—except in the case of brief quotations embodied in critical articles or reviews—without permission in writing from its publisher, Sourcebooks.

No part of this book may be used or reproduced in any manner for the purpose of training artificial intelligence technologies or systems.

The characters and events portrayed in this book are fictitious or are used fictitiously. Any similarity to real persons, living or dead, is purely coincidental and not intended by the author.

Published by Sourcebooks Fire, an imprint of Sourcebooks
P.O. Box 4410, Naperville, Illinois 60567–4410
(630) 961-3900
sourcebooks.com

Cataloging-in-Publication Data is on file with the Library of Congress.

Printed and bound in the United States of America.
WOZ 10 9 8 7 6 5 4 3 2 1

To the ones who fight for better days

Please be aware that this book deals with heavy topics including sexual assault and its aftermath, physical abuse, and parental neglect. Please proceed with caution and keep your own comfort levels in mind. If at any point this book becomes too overwhelming, there's no shame in setting it aside. Please be gentle with yourself, and if necessary, reach out to trusted loved ones for help.

CHAPTER ONE
EDEN

12:45 A.M.

I press myself against the brick wall and curse. My hair clings in wet strands to my face and rain seeps through my sweatshirt. We're not supposed to meet until one a.m., but if I stay outside any longer, I'm going to be soaked to the bone.

Theo would call this *thematically appropriate*. More than a dozen of my favorite comics start with a dark and stormy night, and now I've got one of my own. I can't escape this godforsaken place soon enough.

Lightning zigzags through the sky, illuminating the empty road leading up to the school. It leaves a purple glow in its wake, and when the darkness takes over again, thunder crashes, rattling the windows. The wind howls.

I pull at the straps of my heavy backpack, cinching it close.

Another flash.

There.

Ms. Thompson never completely closes her classroom windows. She thinks proper air circulation is important for understanding mathematical formulas, and one of her windows is slightly ajar.

I dash over to it and slide my hands under the sash, pushing it farther open. I toss my backpack inside first, then clamber in behind it. I've never been athletic, but I hate getting wet.

Once inside, I close the window enough to keep the rain from blowing in. It's dry in here, but that's all Pierce High School has going for it.

The classroom is dark. The only light comes from the narrow window in the door and the auxiliary lights in the hallway beyond. The silence inside is overwhelming. I hate it.

I hoist my bulky backpack onto one of the desks to make sure its contents—my clothes, comics, and wooden carvings—haven't been soaked. I grab my phone and shoot a quick text to my partner-in-running-away to tell her I'm waiting inside. The school is halfway between our homes, and there are no nosy neighbors to see us leaving together.

I shiver. The storm whistles through the building. It's uncomfortable to be here. The school feels so foreign at night.

In the distance, a door rattles. I snatch my bag and duck beside a desk, irrationally convinced I'm not alone. When I was much younger, I used to think that teachers lived at school, that they slept there after we all went home. Then I grew up.

Someone probably left another window open down the hall, but curiosity gets the best of me.

I edge toward the door. I place my hand on the handle and wait, gathering courage.

Then I open it, inch by inch by inch.

The hallway beyond is dim and empty.

Across the hall, next to the stairwell, the door to the computer lab swings on its hinges, slamming but not catching in the jamb with every gust of wind.

See? I tell myself. *No one.*

I prop open the door with my backpack so I don't get locked out and tiptoe to the computer lab—and freeze.

A large tree branch has smashed one of the windows, but that's not what's causing the draft. Another window stands fully open.

Muddy footprints stain the linoleum floor of the classroom.

Another thunderclap shakes the building, and then, directly overhead, there's a loud crash on the second floor.

I'm not alone.

CHAPTER TWO
PAYTON

A WEEK AFTER

The first time Eden and I kissed was in the car wash. It was the best and most clichéd thing we ever did. Eden was riding shotgun, and as the conveyor belt pulled us toward the brushes and bubbles, I noticed her window was cracked open, so I reached across to close it.

And she leaned in to kiss me.

It was my first kiss. She tasted like strawberries and chocolate and joy.

I leaned into her, and she pulled back slightly, her eyes sparkling. "I've wanted to do that for a while. You okay?"

I licked my lips. "So much better than okay." I brushed her hair out of her face, and we melted together.

For those few moments, it was only the two of us, the sweet scent of the cherry soap, and the bubbles popping against the windshield. The outside world ceased to exist. Everything was perfect.

Now, if I close my eyes, I smell only smoke and ash. It clings to me, even though it's been a week since the school burned.

We all wanted to see it, what was left of Pierce High School. The blackened skeleton of a once-proud building. By the time I showed up the morning after, dozens of students were crowded around the building. It was supposed to be the last day before spring break, but instead all our classes were canceled. The fire had been extinguished, and there was more of the building left than I thought there would be, but the air felt heavy with loss. It was hard to breathe, as if phantom smoke were wrapping itself around my lungs.

I claw at my chest.

It still feels impossible to breathe.

In a town named Fenix, someone should rise from the ashes—rise and get the hell out of this place.

But Eden won't.

Reverend DeVries stands at the front of church next to her coffin and tells us about the night the school burned and Eden died. She's the reason we're all here on a random Thursday. His sonorous voice guides Eden's family, her classmates, her teachers through their grief.

"We do not know why Eden was inside the school that night, and we may never know. What happened was a tragic accident. Lightning struck the building and ignited the flammable materials in one of the chemistry labs."

Reverend DeVries looks toward the first pew, where Eden's mother sits, dressed in all black. It makes the silvery strands in her auburn hair more stark and her skin sallow. She doesn't cry. I wonder if she's cried at all. Her latest boyfriend—Arthur, I think—has wrapped a big, muscular arm around her shoulders. He looks stoic.

"I have it from the highest civil authority that the safety systems worked properly," Reverend DeVries continues. "No one is at fault for this tragedy."

He glances in the direction of Mrs. Lewis-Walker, who sits in the row directly behind Eden's family. Not because she was important to Eden, but because she is important to Fenix. She's the CEO of Lewis Industries, the largest employer in the town, who—to the shock and approval of many—has come to pay her respects to a girl she likely never knew. I heard it in the muttering around me. Her presence exemplifies Lewis Industries' unique standing in Fenix. Her daughter, Oakley, sits next to her, her arms wrapped around her middle. Mrs. Lewis-Walker holds Oakley's wrist in a viselike grip.

"While we wonder why poor Eden was inside," Reverend DeVries says, "at the last, she tried to live. As we celebrate her life, let me impress that on upon you: This brave, vulnerable young girl's only hope of escape from the fire was through a second-floor window. If she hadn't landed on the concrete curb below, she could have lived. She *should* have lived. She wanted to live. Remember that when you think of her."

His words make me sick to my stomach, as if dying by accident is somehow the better option. I've heard the rumors. That she broke into the school to jump. That she set the fire herself. That she was there that night to end her life. That she got what she wanted.

None of it is true.

I wish I could tell them that.

None of it is true.

I wonder what it must have felt like for her. The fall. Those moments between window and ground.

If she'd been luckier, she could have survived it. Reverend DeVries is right about one thing: She *should have* survived it.

The thought wraps itself around me. My lungs are burning.

I pick at my nails. The ridges of blue where I didn't remove my polish properly. Flecks of red.

The reverend continues. "In these awful situations, I ask myself, 'What is God's plan?' It feels cruel, but He always has a reason."

I dig my fingers into the wooden pew. No, *Eden* had a plan.

She wasn't at school to jump. She was there to escape.

With me.

I touch my phone in my pocket of my jeans. A screenshot of Eden's last message sits in my photo gallery. I usually delete the texts I get, but I couldn't bear to delete this one.

EDEN:
> It's gross out. I'm waiting inside. Let me know when you're here.

Eden's plan was to get out of Fenix and leave all these people—who never cared for her in life and only pretend to care for her in death—behind. She didn't just want to live, she wanted to be happy.

Eden, who loved old-fashioned horror comics.

Eden, who was a wizard at woodworking.

Eden, who wanted to learn to ride a horse.

I didn't see her message until it was too late.

She deserved more than what Fenix, Colorado, could offer. She deserved a loving home. A future. But all she gets now is a hypocritical memorial service and a place in the cold, hard ground. She's stuck here forever, and so am I.

Reverend DeVries drones on about salvation, but I'm not the only one who seems increasingly outraged.

On the other side of aisle sits Theo, Eden's neighbor and other best friend. He glowers and mutters under his breath throughout the sermon, clearly as disgusted as I am. He has a right to be. He's one of the few who treated her well.

I imagine everyone else is here out of small-town obligation. Outside of the families who went away for spring break, most of Pierce High School's juniors are present, and several seniors are too. They all look uncomfortable in their own ways.

I scan the dozens of faces in the church. RJ and Mason, who used to delight in stealing Eden's wood carvings from her backpack, are both staring at the floor, and Mason is fidgeting with his tie.

Morgan and Nafisa, who were in Eden's art class, are right behind them. Morgan's eyes are red and watery, and they lean into Nafisa. From what Eden told me, the two of them were supportive of her work, admiring her carvings and including her in group projects. But they never had any sort of relationship—good or bad—beyond that. They didn't hang out after class. They didn't go shopping for art supplies together.

I guess sometimes the best we can hope for is comfortable neutrality, but it seems like they regret that they didn't try harder.

It's odd. The finality of death brings out everything we wish we had done differently. All the ways we wish we could have been better to each other. Perhaps that's the deeper meaning Reverend DeVries is looking for.

Well, he can take it and shove it.

The people of Fenix don't get to regret all the things they should have said, all the things they should have done. It's far too late for that. Regret won't change what happened. To any of us.

In the pew in front of mine, Kelsey Fink plucks at the neckline of her dress. She's one of the seniors. One of the popular kids. I don't think anyone quite understands why she's here.

When I lean back, I can see her face. She looks completely disengaged from everything that's happening around her, as though this Kelsey is a husk of a girl. It makes me uncomfortable, how empty and untouchable she looks. Like me, she's here alone.

As if she knows that I'm looking at her, she slowly turns and stares at me. Stares through me.

I look away.

At least her emptiness is more genuine than the expressions of the students who look pious and sad without having any claim to grief. Students like Zanna Lewis, who sits across the aisle from Kelsey and keeps throwing worried glances in her direction. Zanna isn't here for Eden. Zanna didn't exist in the same social universe as Eden. They only ever interacted when Zanna made fun of Eden's carvings, and Eden always kept her head down and steered clear of her.

But now Zanna sits in the pew alongside her father, and Mr. Lewis has an arm wrapped protectively around her shoulders. He is one of Pierce High School's most popular teachers. A son of Fenix's most prominent family. He runs several science programs for kids through Lewis Industries. He's *perfect*.

And it was *his* chemistry lab where the fire started, where Eden jumped.

Hot rage burns through me as he stares at the coffin unflinchingly. Does Mr. Lewis feel any guilt or responsibility that Eden died in *his* classroom? Does he care why she was there?

Does anyone?

Eden could have waited out the storm on the first floor, near where we were supposed to meet. If the authorities had done their jobs properly, surely they would have investigated why she didn't.

The "highest civil authority" deemed it an accident. But it makes me wonder—and not for the first time—who is the highest civil authority in Fenix? The mayor? The police? The school administration? Or Lewis Industries?

Is *anyone* asking the right questions?

Because Eden deserves justice, and I deserve the truth.

Eden was *mine*. My best friend. My love. The other half of my heart. The girl who convinced me there were other places to call home. She promised me there were people who cared and many ways to be a family.

I feel the emptiness of the seats on either side of me.

"The fact that we are here together," Reverend DeVries says, "is a sign that God has a better future planned for us all. One in which we take the comradery I see before me now, this shared grief, this shared *bond*, and use it to fuel our compassion and care for others. We—"

I stop listening and stare at the coffin at the front of the church until my eyes burn. Eden deserves more than tears and a spectacle of grief. At the very least, she deserves everything I should have said.

I love you.

I miss you.

I'm sorry.

Fuck.

I stand, ignoring the looks of shock and disapproval, and walk out of the church.

CHAPTER THREE
PAYTON

A WEEK AFTER

Outside, the cool spring breeze ripples through the young blades of grass and early wildflowers between the headstones. Somewhere, one of these graves is reserved for Eden. I can't spot any freshly dug earth.

I've barely made it off the path when a voice stops me in my tracks.

"Payton?"

With a slight squeak, the heavy church doors swing shut, and in front of them stands Theo, his hands pushed deep into the pockets of his slacks. His chin-length blond hair blows into his face, and he grimaces. His shoulders are pulled up to his ears, and his wiry body radiates tension.

"I know we haven't talked much. Or ever. But I saw you walk out, and I wanted to make sure you were okay. I know how much Eden cared for you."

His words rush out at a breakneck speed, like he's afraid he'll lose them if he doesn't blurt them out.

Despite the reflex to say I'm fine, I answer truthfully. "No."

"Yeah. Me neither. Do you want company? I could use some."

I don't, but when he runs his hands through his hair, he looks lost. What he said about Eden caring about me holds true for him too. I can't turn away from him. I owe her that much. "Sure."

"I'm not really a fan of graveyards," Theo says, "but I've always admired people who embrace the macabre without feeling like they're jinxing themselves. I dressed as a zombie for Halloween once. It gave me nightmares for days. I could barely handle reading Eden's comics, though she made me try."

I manage a small smile, nothing more than a twitch of my mouth, but at least I don't feel like screaming. He's nervous, and that makes me feel better. It makes me less nervous myself. I learned long ago that being afraid or anxious looks different in every person, but rambling and wringing your hands is harmless. Usually. It's the fear that eats you up from the inside, the fear that leaves nothing behind but a shell with no inhibitions, that's far more dangerous.

"Want to sit by the tree?" I point to the large cottonwood nearby.

Theo raises an eyebrow at the gravestones. "You think it's safe?"

I roll my eyes. "I don't think zombies are going to come out of the ground to eat your brains, Theo." I add, "Not during the day."

He smiles, a curious look on his face.

"What?"

"Eden could have said that. You know you meant a lot to her, right?"

"You meant a lot to her too," I say to deflect.

We walk past the oldest graves in Fenix, which aren't that ancient. The town is old enough to look run down, but not old enough to have character. Big enough to have its own local government, but small enough for it to feel like legal nepotism. Sometimes it is.

At the tree, I drop to the grass and pull my knees to my chest, leaning against the rough bark of the trunk. Despite the sunlight, the ground is cold, and the air feels sharp after the stuffy church. I clear my throat, "It seems like I should know you better. But keeping her worlds separate also meant a lot to Eden."

Once when we were hanging out at her place, Theo waved at Eden from the tree between their houses. She waved back at him and closed the curtains, never offering to introduce us.

I never asked. I was happy keeping Eden to myself.

Theo coughs out a surprised laugh as he perches on the grass. His green eyes take in every inch of me. "I think it felt safer for her. Like if she kept us to herself, she was less likely to lose us. But sometimes I wonder if we only got to see the parts of her that she reserved for us. Half of who she was. Half of everything."

I blink. I've never considered that.

Theo continues, "I know she wasn't happy at home, but do you think there's truth to what people have been saying? That Eden broke into the school to jump?" His voice grows soft. "Because I don't believe it. I would have seen it. I would know." It's almost a plea.

I lean forward, resting my chin on my knees, and consider how to respond. Can I trust him with the truth? It's such a fragile thing, truth. Give it to the wrong person, and they'll break it.

They'll break you.

Theo stares at the ground like he's afraid to meet my gaze. Like he's afraid *I* saw that part of Eden.

I pick at my nails again.

Theo mentioned nightmares. I've had them for the past seven nights. But they're not the ones I'm used to. I'm not running, chased by shadows. Not locked up, drowning, lost.

In these dreams, nothing happens. Fenix doesn't change. Eden is dead, and life goes on. No one cares, and no one investigates.

I'm screaming, and no one listens.

No one ever listens.

Someone needs to uncover what happened the night the school burned, and if the authorities won't do it, there isn't anyone better suited than Theo. He's liked at school in a way that Eden and I never were. People greet him, share lunch with him. They'll talk to him. They'll believe him. They'll listen to him. In some ways, they have to. He's the editor of the school newspaper.

Besides, he knows how to investigate a mystery. He found Pierce's long-lost mascot during the end of my freshman year.

The story was that a rival team had broken into the PE equipment closet a few years prior and stolen it, then buried the mascot head on school grounds. Theo followed the whispers and the rumors, until one dry spring day, he came to school with a shovel and an old blueprint of the school, and he dug up the half-decayed, unrealistically furry puma head.

It was the talk of the town for well over a week. Everyone treated it like a big scoop and a win for the school newspaper. *The prodigal mascot returns!* The puma head was even displayed in the main entrance during spirit week.

I just thought it was tragic. Every detail of it. No one cared about the story behind it, how the athletes' pranking had gotten out of hand. Everyone was obsessed with the old costume. What was left of it looked like half-rotten roadkill. Even the location where Theo found it was sad. It had been buried at the edge of the expanded parking lot, right at the edge of where the original sports fields and bleachers used to be.

But Theo impressed me. He never gave up, and he never shared who or what tipped him off about its location. Eden told me he got that from his mother, who is a journalist at a local TV station.

"One of the things Eden loved about you is that you're trustworthy and honest. That you're... What did she call it? Like a bloodhound when it comes to investigating for the school newspaper," I tell him. "She was so proud of you."

Theo pushes aimlessly at a blade of grass. His shoulders are tight.

I take a deep breath. It doesn't feel like oxygen actually reaches my lungs. "So you should know she didn't go into the school to jump." I pull out my phone, hesitate, then hold it out to him. "She went inside to find shelter from the storm. We were planning to run away. Together."

Theo takes my phone and reads the message. Once. Twice. Again.

When he looks at me, his green eyes seem to have darkened. "You were there when it happened."

It isn't a question. "I wasn't where I should have been." I nod toward the phone. "Clearly."

"Yeah." He hands me my phone back and pushes to his feet. He brushes his hands on his pants. He can't hide that they're trembling.

Then he screams.

CHAPTER FOUR
PAYTON

A WEEK AFTER

Theo's cry is feral and full of pain.

I startle. That same pain echoes within me too. "Theo…" He doesn't seem to hear me.

"I *knew* it. I *knew* it wasn't true. I knew Eden wasn't happy, but I knew she wasn't there to jump."

Suddenly, he crouches in front of me, and I flinch so hard, I think I sprain something. Theo doesn't seem to notice. "But if she was running away, if she was sheltering from the storm, why did she go to the second floor?"

"That's the real question, isn't it?" I ask, my heart racing.

He nods. "I have to know what *really* happened." He squints, and I can see a thousand thoughts bouncing around in his brain. He seizes on to one of them.

"Wait. Wasn't your father a cop? Or in the military? Or something like that? Has he heard anything about the investigation? Were there others inside the school? Is there a reason she went to the science wing? There has to be some evidence, some clue. Can you ask him?"

"No!" The word comes out far louder than I intended. I push my back against the tree to put more space between Theo and me. If I was Eden's quiet, contemplative half, he is loud and present enough for the both of us. "No," I say more evenly. "As far as I'm aware, he doesn't know *anything*. He can't be involved. He can't know we were running away. He can't know what happened. He *can't*."

The absolute last thing I want is to talk to my dad about Eden. Or the fire. There are reasons she and I planned to meet at the school that night and why we very rarely spent time at my house.

There are reasons why I can't be the one to tell this story, and Dad's one of them.

I need a safe way out first. I need to make sure that before the story gets told, I'll be gone.

Theo doesn't ask why. He doesn't push. "Then we have to figure out who does."

Underneath his bluster, he is a bit strange, a lot perceptive, and maybe even kind, though it's too soon to tell. Unfortunately, he's not quite perceptive enough to give me physical space.

He reaches for my hands.

I ball them into fists and wrap my arms around me.

That he notices. He grimaces. "I'm sorry. I didn't mean to make you uncomfortable."

I shrug. "Don't touch me. That's all."

The words sit between us. Our silence is broken only by hesitant birdsong in the tree above. Then a hymn from the church, faint enough that it simply drifts past us.

I glance in the direction of the double doors, but despite Theo's scream, no one followed us.

"No one believed me when I said it wasn't a suicide. I knew there was more to the story," Theo says.

He isn't just loud to my quiet, he's painfully truthful. I keep secrets like my life depends on it. Because it does.

"I knew Eden wouldn't leave me without saying something. I wish she'd told me about her plan to skip town, but I get it. It's okay. If she were leaving, she wouldn't have wanted anyone holding her back, and I know she would've been happy with you."

The words leave a lump in my throat. "She wanted to tell you. We had to get out first."

"I respect that." Theo looks toward the church. "Eden was the closest thing I've had to a sister. I've *hated* feeling like I didn't know her as well as I thought I did. That I failed her. But I didn't. I only lost her."

"How is that better?" I demand. "She's still gone."

He makes a face. "The alternative is that everything I thought was true between us wasn't."

I don't know how to respond to that. I squeeze my fists so tightly, my arms hurt.

"I'll make sure everyone knows Eden's truth too. I'll make sure her truth didn't die with her," Theo says with determination. He considers me. "We could investigate together, yeah? Find out why she went up to Mr. Lewis's classroom and what her final hours looked like."

"Aren't you afraid of what you may find?"

Theo shakes his head. "I want to tell the whole story. All of it."

The doors of the church open. Eden's coffin is carried out by her mother's boyfriend and five other men, seemingly picked at random. Theo should be there. *I* should be there. But we're not.

"Are you in?" Theo asks.

This is what I want. For someone to discover what happened the night the school burned. For someone to ask the right questions and come to the right conclusions. Why she ended up in that chemistry lab. Why she couldn't get out.

I want Fenix to see who's guilty and who's responsible.

I want someone to tell her story and the story of Pierce High School.

Because no one will trust me. Not in any way that matters.

And they shouldn't.

No one will believe my truth.

But Eden deserves justice.

And so do I.

I hold out my hand to Theo. "Yes."

CHAPTER FIVE
PAYTON

A WEEK AFTER

The house smells of cheap beer and burnt toast by the time I get home. Dad is snoring on the couch.

After following the pallbearers to Eden's grave, being home is a nightmare of a different kind. I keep trying to escape, but no matter what I do, I end up back in the same place: here.

I head for the kitchen to make a late lunch. I'm not hungry. Eating is a habit and a means of survival, not a pleasure. The fridge is nearly empty, with half a carton of milk, some moldy cheese, and eggs. I forgot to get groceries, and ever since the fire, Dad hasn't been in a good place. Not that I am either. But if I don't go to the store, neither of us will eat.

The pan is dirty from last night, so I scrub it out, then heat the stove. I take out the eggs, cut the mold off the cheese, and mix up scrambled eggs.

It's the strangest thing. That somewhere so familiar can feel completely different. Not because it has changed, but because you have. I said goodbye to this house, this road, the cracks in the asphalt, and the carefully maintained lawns the moment I got into my car to meet Eden at school. A week ago.

I said goodbye to buying food, to cleaning, to tiptoeing around to make sure I never made too much noise.

I drove out of the driveway, past the neighbors' houses. I turned the corner and left all of this behind.

Until I didn't.

I grab the bread out of the toaster and divide scrambled eggs over two pieces of toast. As I put the pan in the sink, I accidentally knock one of Dad's coffee mugs.

A roar comes from the couch at the noise.

I snatch my plate from the counter. If I'm lucky, I can make it to the stairs—

"Halt."

I freeze. It's a habit, like Dad's military voice is a habit.

He used to have a softer voice. He used to not be angry and tense all the time. Now he jumps at every loud sound, and I've learned to be quiet. But sometimes, like today, I'm clumsy. And sometimes I need to scream and hurt.

"Where have you been?" He reaches for an open can of beer from the end table next to the couch and downs it. His thin hair is plastered to his face, his eyes bloodshot.

"Come on. *Answer*."

"Funeral," I say, keeping my voice even. "A girl from school."

He doesn't get up, but he considers the words.

A part of me wants him to *ask*. Who was she? How am I? Is there anything I need? Once upon a time, after his first tour of duty, before Mom decided she couldn't deal with him, couldn't deal with *me*, he was kind and gentle. He taught me to ride my bike. He played basketball with me, both of us shooting balls at the hoop on the side of the house until it got dark. He told me bedtime stories he made up himself about a brave young adventurer named Payton who took on the world.

I look for that man now, and I don't see him.

After his friends died and he was injured by an IED on his second tour, he started drinking to deal with the residual pain, and most of his civilian friends abandoned him. Or maybe some of them left after he started drinking.

There are rare moments when something makes him laugh and I remember how we used to laugh together. For a long time, I held on to the hope that my old dad would come back. Except my dad went to war, and only the war returned.

He crunches the empty beer can in his fist and throws it in my direction. It's not aimed to hit me, not this time. It clatters to the floor.

Balancing my plate carefully, I scoop up the empty can and toss it in the trash.

When I turn, Dad's standing in front of me. His breath smells stale and sour, and he towers over me.

"I heard about that girl on the news," he says, slurring his speech a little. "She came here once, yeah? I thought she was strange. The whole story sounded strange."

He's been in this mood since before the fire. He sees threats and conspiracies everywhere. I don't want to argue with him, so I nod vaguely.

He grabs me by my shoulder. "They're liars, Payton. The lot of them."

Cold fear grips me. I want Dad to pay attention to my life, but not like this. I wish I could tell him what Eden meant to me. But if he ever finds out what happened, if he ever finds out what I did, he will *kill* me. "What do you mean?"

He squeezes painfully tight. "Others were there. She wasn't alone. I went there. I saw the school with my own eyes. Do you think a building like that would burn down due to a simple storm? If you ask me, it was an act of arson. Someone tried to blow up the school. It's only a matter of time before the school's security camera footage proves I'm right."

I tense. I didn't know there were security cameras at school, though I guess it makes sense.

I try to stay as calm as possible. "Nothing's come up in the investigation so far."

Dad pulls me close. The smell of beer and unbrushed teeth is overwhelming, and I have to force myself to keep from holding my breath. "I know it's not an *accident* that it was Mr. Lewis's chemistry lab either. It's the same people who were behind the protests at Lewis Industries. There are forces out there who wish to destroy the Lewis family, Payton. Trust me."

Dad has always had a strange fascination with the Lewis family. After he was discharged, he attended veteran events organized by and at Lewis Industries headquarters. He still goes there on occasion, though it's been several months since he last went. I wish he'd go more often—it's one of the things Lewis Industries gets *right* in Fenix. Those nights meant a lot to him and to other families. He came home *smiling*. At least, he smiled until I inevitably messed things up again. Or until he cracked open a can.

He continues, "That investigation was a *sham*. These young cops don't understand that they have to *fight* to protect this town and everything this community has built. There is danger everywhere." He coughs, and the sour scent curls on my tongue. "But I told them. They need to widen their search. Get security footage of the parking lot, of all the roads leading up to the school. That will show them."

"Dad." My throat constricts. What do I tell him? That not everything he sees around him is a cover-up? That not everything has to do with the Lewis family? "My friend *died*."

Part of me desperately hopes for some compassion. Some care.

But he's too caught up in the tangled web of his own paranoia. "If I find out you're involved, Payton…"

I carefully take a step back. "Why would I be?" I ask flatly.

My nails push into my leg.

"Derek will uncover the truth once and for all," he slurs. "I told him to come see me. We'll make this town safer. No one targets the school, our community, Lewis Industries, without punishment."

Derek—Officer Farlander, as he makes me call him—is Dad's former best friend and fellow soldier turned small-town cop. He used to calm Dad and redirect his anger and paranoia. He tried to help him get a job at the precinct, but Dad couldn't keep it. The work, the people—they overwhelmed him.

It's been almost a year since Derek's last visit. He calls, but he keeps finding reasons not to *be* here. He last time he came over, Dad jumped from one conspiracy theory to the next. He ranted about the environmental protesters at Lewis Industries and how they were paid by some shadowy elite. He complained that the police went too soft on them, that they needed to stop worrying about public opinion. That there were nefarious forces everywhere.

By the end of it, Derek looked exhausted and pissed. He shook his head, got to his feet, and told Dad, "You can't keep doing this, Tim. You have to find a way to move on, or your anger will destroy everything around you."

He saw me at the door and winced. "I'm sorry, kid."

I didn't know what to say. They were empty words.

It's my job to calm Dad now. If no one does, he'll keep going until he's torn through all the pieces of the story, real and imagined.

All the pieces of me.

"What if there isn't anything to uncover?" I try, very carefully, to steer him away. Eden deserves the truth, but not like this.

He grabs me by my collar. "I know what I'm talking about."

I jerk forward, and the plate slips from my hands. Eggs and toast splatter on the floor as the plate shatters into a thousand pieces.

Dad's face twists, and his eyes flash. He snarls something. I can't make out if he calls me useless or a disappointment. I know it will hurt more if I brace myself, but I do, just before he slams me hard into the wall.

THEO:

> Hey. It's Theo

> I found a way into the school

> You need to see this

> It's from Mr. Lewis's classroom. There's graffiti.

CHAPTER SIX
EDEN

12:51 A.M.

I shouldn't be here. I should leave.

It's the best option. It's the most sensible option. Stay quiet, don't attract attention, and get out of here.

But curiosity wins out over self-preservation.

Whoever's inside with me shouldn't be here either.

Is a teacher squatting? Did a student break in to change a grade? Maybe it's students from Wyvern High, our sportsball rival, trying to steal something after that mascot story.

I check my phone. No texts from Payton, only a warning symbol where the reception bar should be. Of course. It's not the first time a storm has taken out one of the cell towers.

I look out the front window, but I don't see any headlights.

I do see my own soggy footprints leading from the window to the hallway. Hiding isn't an option anymore.

I listen for movement as I head for the stairs. The rain lashes the windows like it's trying to get my attention. A crack of thunder makes me jump.

The auxiliary lights flicker, and darkness rolls through the school before the hall lights snap on again. I feel exposed and vulnerable.

Halfway up the stairs, I reconsider my daring plan. Maybe Theo is right. Maybe I could do with a little more self-preservation. My takeaway from no one protecting me should be that I learn to protect myself.

I take another step and another.

Wind and rain rattle the building. The safety lights above me buzz. Someone could be sneaking up on me and I wouldn't hear them.

I toy with the gold bracelet around my left wrist, running my thumb along the chain.

I glance at the stairs below me.

Empty.

After three years, you'd think I'd know this school by heart. But all buildings are creepier when they're empty. My imagination isn't helping either. If someone is following me, I will hear footsteps. If I stare at the shadows long enough, they'll move.

It's not what *is* here but what *isn't* that makes being here scary.

Another crack of thunder.

The lights blink out.

Somewhere on the second floor, someone screams.

CHAPTER SEVEN
KELSEY

SEVEN MONTHS BEFORE

My shoulders cramp. My head feels hot and heavy, like I've brought the last of the summer's heat inside.

I wish I had the courage to fail and laugh about it. Like Cameron. He holds up his chem test, marked with a bright red F. He points at the sad face in the upper corner and mimics it.

People laugh. Next to him, Luis smacks his shoulder, telling him to pay better attention, while Elijah proudly—and a little smugly—shows off his B+.

Cameron keeps his eyes on me, but I can only offer him a wan smile in return. My own test paper is face down on my desk in front of me. I can't look at it. It may not be a failing grade, but my D is a black hole, and I'm helpless in its gravitational pull.

"Don't worry," Cameron mouths. "It'll be fine."

He's lying. He has to be. He has to feel the pressure of senior year. There are college applications to work on, constant reminders that whatever we do, we don't work hard enough. *Your sister is at Columbia. Kelsey, what are* you *going to do?*

I have to be as good as her. I have to be better.

If I want to get into college, go to vet school, I have to find a way to *not* be terrible at chemistry. To get in all my undergrad course requirements and *not suck*. But this year everything feels impossible. My grades are plummeting. I love biology, but any science beyond that is too much.

Mr. Lewis pauses at Taylor Miller's desk in front of mine. He leans in to point at one of the questions. "You forgot to balance the oxygen here."

Taylor looks up at him and flushes. "Thanks."

Mr. Lewis offers her a kind smile. He lingers for a few seconds longer, placing a hand on her shoulder. He lowers his voice. "I know you've been having a rough time with your father being ill, but you've always been one of my brightest students. If you need my help, don't hesitate to ask."

Taylor's dad was diagnosed with Parkinson's over the summer, and she flinches every time someone brings it up. But when Mr. Lewis takes a step back, she nods. "I will."

She won't. She's one of those girls who wants to fix all her problems herself. We have that in common.

Mr. Lewis turns to Cameron and clears his throat. "I'll have you know, Mr. Jenkins, that I've made it my personal goal to help you get *one* passing grade this year."

"You're welcome to change this to an A," Cameron shoots back, his words sending a ripple of laughter through the room.

Mr. Lewis shakes his head. "You'll earn it fair and square, just like everyone else."

Cameron tips up his chin, grinning. "Challenge accepted."

Whatever Mr. Lewis wants to say next is cut short by the bell and a dozen students shoving their books in their bags.

I take my time, pretending to look for my tablet, in the hopes that I can catch Mr. Lewis alone. I need a way to fix this grade. Instead, when I look up, he's back at his desk and deep in conversation with Luis, and it doesn't look like they'll be done talking soon.

The problem is, Mr. Lewis is one of those teachers who cares about his students, and as a result, he is most students' favorite.

At the end of every year, Mr. Lewis treats his senior classes to a creative science program sponsored by Lewis Industries, his family's business and the multimillion-dollar aerospace company that employs more than half the town. It's the highlight of the year. Everyone spends the day watching pyrotechnics and making fake gold bars and dry ice volcanoes. Lewis Industries—where Mr. Lewis sits on the board—gives out scholarships to the top science students. The seniors who go come back giggling, wearing fake jewelry, and snacking on astronaut ice cream. And every other student at Pierce wishes they were them for a day.

Mr. Lewis is kind and gentle.

Besides, his daughter Zanna is one of my best friends. I've been to their home, where he's just *Zanna's dad*. (He tried to get my friends and I to call him *James*, but we immediately decided we would *never*.)

At the end of summer, when we were lounging at Zanna's family's pool—she's one of the best swimmers on the school's team—he cornered me. He put his hand on my arm and told me, "I probably shouldn't bring up school yet, but I overheard you girls talking. If you're worried about chemistry at any point, come to me. I'll help."

Anxiety rushed through me, and the words tumbled out. "Do you think I won't be good enough, sir?"

He shook his head. "How often do I have to tell you to stop being so formal around here? No, I do not think that's the case at all. But I don't want you to be worried that the material's challenging when you have such a bright future ahead of you."

He squeezed my arm. "Okay?"

I tried to shove away my discomfort. I nodded. "Thank you." I grinned. "Sir."

He'll be understanding if I ask him about extra credit assignments. I just don't want to ask him when others might hear. Not when word may leak back to my parents or—somehow worse—my sister. The thought alone claws at my throat.

So when Cameron pops his head back in impatiently and

complains, "Kelsey, hurry *up*. Lunch is too short as it is," I grab my bag and sling it over my shoulder. I smooth my skirt, then walk by Mr. Lewis's desk and try to ignore his questioning gaze.

In the hallway, I sigh. "I hate people who are naturally good at chemistry."

Cameron gives me a look, and I groan before he can say anything. "I know, I know, you're *naturally excellent at other kinds of chemistry*."

"Girls *love* my chemistry."

"Gross. I don't."

He slings an arm across my shoulders and pulls softly at my hair. "Come on, Kels. You worry too much. One bad grade won't mess up the rest of your life."

"You don't worry enough," I grumble. "You're never going to get into college like this."

He laughs a little bitterly. "No one here believes I could cut it anyway."

Cameron has always had a reputation for as long as I can remember. He used to punch bullies in middle school and broke the unofficial Pierce High School record for most detentions in his freshman year. He argues, talks back, and doesn't care about showing up to class if he doesn't understand why what we're learning matters. He is most teachers' problem student because of that independence and passion.

His moment of glory was when he got roped into pulling off the senior prank last year, despite still being a junior himself. Word is his gaming friends realized they could make good use of his weeklong suspension. No one but Cameron could have found a way to get the principal's car parked inside the gym and filled with Ping-Pong balls. So this year he's infamous—and he loves it.

I think.

"I believe you can," I protest.

He squeezes my shoulders. "That's why we're friends. But after I graduate, my educational career is done. Matteo will let me work in the restaurant, and I will never have to look at a textbook again in my life."

"You could do something more—"

"Stop," he cuts me off. "I can't think of anything more valuable than feeding people and making them happy, so don't even try."

I bite my lip. "I didn't mean…" My voice trails off. I *did* mean it like that. Like the only thing that matters is getting the best grades, getting into the best college, getting the fanciest degrees. I meant it exactly like that. "Fuck. I'm sorry."

Cameron smirks at me. "You're starting to sound like your parents."

I gasp. "How dare you?"

But the corner of my mouth tugs up into a smile. Cameron has always been able to make me laugh. Ever since we were kids at church and other girls teased me about the ribbons I'd unsuccessfully tried to braid into my hair, he's stood up for me. Most of Fenix assumes we'll end up married with 2.3 kids and a dog, but I don't think of him like that. Or of anyone. Not yet, anyway. Maybe not ever. Cam is simply the brother I wish I had.

He deserves for me to take his plans seriously, for me to take him seriously—even when it feels like my entire brain is consumed by fear of *not being good enough*. "I'm proud of you, you know that?" I say. "You're following your dreams."

"You'll get to chase yours," he says, like there's no question about it.

When we walk outside, the summer's warmth is dissipating, and the air is crisp with the promise of fall.

Zanna and Oakley are already waiting at one of the picnic tables. Oakley's dark brown curls dance when she laughs at something Zanna says, and when she turns to wave at us, her eyes sparkle.

Oakley is one of those girls who is effortlessly popular and earns straight A's. I'm liked, sure. I have friends. But she is *loved*.

Zanna is more aloof. She hides behind her long bangs, and her smile is sharp and sardonic.

But whether by luck or Zanna pulling strings, the four of us have always had the same lunch period, our own little bubble away from grades and worries and expectations.

Well, somewhat.

By the time we sit down, Oakley is ranting about the pop quiz her French teacher sprang on them, which she's certain she failed, though we all know she's never failed a test in her life. When I harrumph at her, she grins and blushes, making her lingering summer freckles a little darker. "I just don't want to give CEO Mom any more excuses to keep me here this summer."

"It's September," Zanna reminds her without looking up.

Oakley shrugs. "Better to be prepared."

Zanna leaves her lunch untouched on the table. Instead, she toys with two different bottles of nail polish, one plum and one grass green. After a moment, she discards the plum.

Despite the pungent smell of nail polish hanging around us, I soak in the familiarity. Some days, Cameron hangs out with the football team or his gaming friends during lunch. Sometimes Zanna is away for swim meets or sits with the church choir. In the spring, Oakley ditches us for the soccer team every now and again. But usually, *mostly*, it's the four of us together, here or doing homework in Oakley's mom's gigantic study or chugging caffeine at Bean There or going to the movies together.

It's the four of us against the world, and I wouldn't want it any other way.

Ten minutes later, I can *breathe* again. The late September sun warms the courtyard and my face. My friends are gathered around me. This is happiness. This is what senior year should be like.

I'm not failing at friendship.

Oakley has retrieved Zanna's plum nail polish and is painting her toenails. I lean against Cameron's shoulder, stealing a bite of his cold cheese pizza. His stepdad makes the best pizza in town, so Cameron's lunch usually far outshines anything we pack or anything Pierce High School has to offer.

"Hey!" He swats me away.

I elbow him. "I've been thinking, we should get matching Halloween outfits next month."

Across from us, Oakley looks up sharply, and I roll my eyes. Oakley has been my best friend since pre-K. Before I met Cameron, before her mother inherited Lewis Industries and became the boss of three-quarters of the town. Back when she was simply the girl who lived three doors down from me and spent most of her afternoons coloring in my room. She'll always be my better half. But for some reason, she's never stopped being jealous of how comfortably Cameron and I get along. Like she thinks he's a threat.

"All four of us," I clarify. "It's our last Halloween together. It'll be like old times. Remember when we all dressed up like vampires freshman year?"

Zanna raises a perfectly sculpted eyebrow at the suggestion. Despite her being Oakley's cousin, I didn't really get to know Zanna until the summer before high school, when the three of us went to the same summer camp.

Vampire night cemented our friendship. Sure, Zanna thought dressing up was childish then, and she probably thinks it's childish now, but I want to do something fun.

"Are you saying we should trick-or-treat too?" Zanna asks.

If I thought we could get away with it, I would. "Maybe. Oakley, can we steal your baby brother?"

"I love you, but no," Oakley says, not missing a beat to consider the brilliance of my plan. "You've never seen Freddie on a sugar high. He's a menace. It's enough to make me feel old and decrepit."

"He's not even five yet," I scoff. "It's not like he'll stay up all night." When he's around me, Freddie is an adorable preschooler who takes my hand and stares at me with his bright green eyes and does nothing wrong, ever.

Oakley pins me with a haunted stare. "He *would*. You haven't seen what I've seen."

"Fine," I give in. "Only the Halloween dance, then. A special memory for the four of us before next year when everyone is off to"—I catch myself and change what I'm about to say without so much as glancing at Cameron—"whatever it is we do next."

The truth is, even if he stays in town, the rest of us won't. I hope to get into Colorado State. Zanna wants to go east, ideally to New York. Oakley has her eyes set on Europe, though she isn't sure how or where yet. Her mother dreams about her daughter following in her footsteps. She admitted once that she just wants to get away from the pressure of being the heir apparent to Lewis Industries. Besides, Zanna wouldn't mind being second in line to the aerospace throne.

"Maybe we should go as witches." Zanna picks a grape from her lunch, holding the fruit between two long, green nails. She narrows her eyes and looks past the grape at a nearby picnic table, where a junior in an oversize tie-dye shirt and baggy pants is whittling away at a small block of wood. A cruel smile flashes across her face. "We can ask the weirdo to carve our wands."

I sigh. "Don't be like that, Z."

Zanna scowls. "That girl makes me uncomfortable."

"I think it's awesome that Eden goes her own way," Cameron puts in, smoothing the conversation. "And I like witches."

He waggles his eyebrows at her, and Zanna snorts and blushes. "Whatever."

For all his rebelliousness, Cameron is the calming presence in our group of hotheads with sharp edges.

Eden doesn't give any indication that she has heard us. She's intently focused on what looks like a small wooden fox. She's one of those people who's forever a bit out of place. Her clothes are too big, and she might've cut her hair with the same tools she uses to carve wood. I don't think I've ever seen her talk to anyone except the other art kids. If it wasn't for the bell calling us back to class, I think she'd probably stay here, focused and lost to the world, until dark.

"We'll figure something out," Oakley promises. "Unforgettable outfits for all four of us. Everyone should come by my place after school."

Cameron shakes his head. "Restaurant. Sorry."

Zanna shoves her stuff into her bag. She groans. "I can't either. Dad wants us to visit Gran. He volunteered us for groceries and cleaning. I wouldn't hate it, but ever since her knee surgery, she's been in a foul mood, watching TV, gobbling up weird political conspiracy theories, and then ranting about them."

"Oof." Oakley winces. "I'm glad Mom hid behind her CEO duties and sent a gift basket. Though she did offer to hire help."

"Don't worry, Gran will rant about that too. She expected *so much better* from her eldest daughter and grandchild, but kids these days don't care about their elders anymore, so now she's stuck with me." Zanna pitches her voice to sound old and curmudgeonly.

Oakley snorts. "Uh-huh. Give her my love."

Zanna gives Oakley the finger instead. "Do it yourself, coward."

I grab my bag. "I'll come by, but I have to see Mr. Lewis first. I need to figure out how to raise my grade." I nibble at my lip.

Cameron nudges me. "Don't worry. It'll be fine. You have a whole year of tests ahead of you."

Anxiety tightens my chest. "It will be, won't it? He'll help, right?"

"Everyone loves you," Oakley puts in. "It's not a failure to ask for help. It's a brave thing to do."

As always when Mr. Lewis comes up in conversation, Zanna keeps quiet. She hates being the teacher's kid and avoids seeing her dad in school as much as possible. She told us freshman year that she refuses to get stuck between her friends and her father. She won't mediate. She won't ask him for anything on our behalf or the other way around. And she has stuck to that.

She looks away now.

Cameron, on the other hand, nods furiously. "Oakley is right, Kels. If he can threaten me with a passing grade, he'll help you too. You know he's one of the good ones." He means the teachers who see us as people and not just as obstacles on the way to the weekend.

Yeah. Okay.

I clench and unclench my hands by my sides, and Oakley bumps my shoulder gently. "He'll get it."

Oakley glances at her cousin again as the lunch crowd funnels back into the school. A grin curls on her lips. Some days the two of them hardly talk. Others they bicker like siblings. On rare days, they go in claws out. "Speaking of Uncle James, last week I overheard some of the juniors gossiping about the *mysterious* and *gorgeous* Mr. Lewis. They called him a silver fox."

Zanna gags.

"He's a teacher," I say. "That's disgusting."

"He's also my *father*," Zanna points out. "I don't want to think anyone considers Dad hot, least of all people my age or younger."

Honestly, me neither.

Cameron shakes his head. "No, thank you."

As we enter the school, Oakley laughs airily. But underneath her laughter is something cold and sharp, vulnerable in a way I've never seen before. She pretends she has to rush to her AP psychology class. "See me after school!" she calls.

"Good luck," Cameron says before he dashes off too.

"I've got this," I mutter. "I've got this."

"Kels." Only Zanna could fill one syllable with such scorn. "He knows we're friends. He won't let you fail." It's a rare display of gentleness, but coming from Zanna, it means the world.

So I nod.

He won't.

I'm doing the right thing.

I hope.

CHAPTER EIGHT
KELSEY

SEVEN MONTHS BEFORE

Sunlight fragments off the many bottles and beakers in the lab. Mr. Lewis is collecting materials that have been left out on desks and lab tables when I knock.

He looks up at me and smiles. "Kelsey, what can I do for you?"

I produce my chem test, which I'm holding so tightly it's wrinkled. "Um." I never ask for help. I hate admitting that I need it. "I messed up this test, and you told me, um…"

The hallway is quiet. I glance over my shoulder, like I'm admitting to some kind of crime. In my family, failing might be a felony. With every test, with every report card, for as long as I can remember, our parents have been telling Alice and me about the importance of a good education. Dad is fond of reminding us that if we want to succeed at anything later in life, we have to succeed *now*. Mom is big on personal responsibility, insisting that the choices we make as teens and young adults will impact the rest of our lives.

So, you know, no pressure.

They'll be proud of my choice to improve myself. I think.

Mr. Lewis beckons me inside. "Come on in."

I sit in the seat next to his desk. He spins his own chair to face me. "Tell me what's wrong," he says gently, taking the test from my hands.

"I need to get into vet school." The words spill from me. I knew I wanted to be a vet from the first time Dad took Alice and me to the Fenix Riding Club for lessons. I was seven, and I was sold. I did everything I could to care for the horses, even though I was barely big enough to hold a saddle. As soon as I could, I started volunteering at the Fenix animal shelter too. Every after-school activity, every choice I've made, has been with the same goal in mind.

Flunking chemistry simply isn't an option. I tell Mr. Lewis about the prerequisite courses I'll need as an undergrad. I tell him that I can't afford to tank my GPA while applying to college, but I also can't drop chem. I want to understand it. I *need* to understand it, otherwise I'm just delaying inevitable failure.

Mr. Lewis chuckles at that, but when I glare at him, he schools his expression into one of contrition.

"This may not be the most responsible thing for me to say, but high school and college aren't the same, Kelsey," he says. "I'd like to think I'm quite good at what I do, but college will challenge you, and your teachers will inspire you. I know plenty of students who had a hard time in high school who flourished in college—even your sister. A different learning environment can do wonders, and if I know one thing about you, it's that you're willing to work hard. I respect that in a girl. Don't sell yourself short because you're struggling now."

I barely hear those last words. I'm stuck on what he said about Alice. "My sister never failed any of her classes," I say in an almost accusatory tone, then add a belated, awkward "sir."

"You are unfailingly polite, aren't you?" Mr. Lewis leans forward and gives me a half smile. "Alice had her difficulties, Kelsey. But like you, she knew what to do to succeed."

He's a bit too close for comfort, but I don't move away. I appreciate the reminder that I'm not the first teenager navigating pressure and anxiety. He understands my fears. And I understand why so many students and alumni are fond of him, because for the first time today—honestly, for the first time since I started chemistry—I feel like maybe things will work out after all.

"It's my dream to specialize in equine medicine," I say. "I don't mind extra work. I just don't want to disappoint myself."

"You wish to pursue your passions." Mr. Lewis nods. "It's admirable. When I was a little older than you, my parents insisted that I follow in their footsteps and take on the family business. Your parents both work for Lewis Industries too, right?" He shakes his head. "I wanted to teach. To mold the minds of future generations. I also didn't want my genius sister's unattainable reputation. We have to make our own choices."

I breathe. He *gets* it. He does. "Exactly. But I don't want to disappoint my parents either." I'm the only one in the family who seems to suck at science, except for biology. "I'll do anything to fix my grade so they'll never find out."

Something flickers in Mr. Lewis's expression.

I wait for him to tell me not to let the pressure to succeed hold me back, or that it's important to enjoy my senior year, or whatever else adults think is helpful advice.

But instead, he simply—quietly—says, "Good."

He stands. He takes a beaker from his desk and carries it to the cupboard. On the way back, he shuts the door, then locks it with a *click*. "So we're not interrupted," he says with a smile. "I'm sure we can find a way to work this out."

It's against school policy for a teacher and a student to be alone in a closed classroom, but I don't say anything.

He takes his seat once more and leans in. "You know, I love a girl with dedication."

The words lilt teasingly, but I'm not quite sure how to take them. Mr. Lewis is close enough that our knees are touching.

"I—" I try to scoot my chair backward, but his foot is hooked around the leg, keeping me close.

He must not notice.

I mean, it's not like he's doing it on purpose.

"Thank you." I clear my throat. Somehow, this classroom feels more oppressive than it did this morning, when that bright red D sucked all the air out of the room. "Anyway, I'd love to talk about extra credit? Extra assignments? I will do whatever you need me to do. If you need time to figure it out—I mean, I—I can come back later."

Mr. Lewis continues to stare at me. "I don't need time, Kelsey."

I cross my arms without meaning to.

"You know you can trust me," he says.

It isn't a question but a statement of fact. A reminder.

During spring break last year, Oakley and I slept over at Zanna's house. We stayed up late watching horror movies. By three a.m. I was so keyed up, I slipped down to the kitchen to make myself a cup of coffee. Some nights when my brain is too loud, caffeine is the only thing that calms me.

Suddenly, he was there. I nearly jumped out of my skin. In the quiet, he looked at me. I very nearly *screamed*, and he laughed.

"Here I thought *you* were the intruder in *my* house." He rubbed my arms and massaged my shoulders in an effort to calm me down, because I was trembling all over.

"I'm sorry," I said. I told him it was the movies that had made me jumpy. "I didn't mean to wake you up. I just got—"

He pushed a wayward strand of hair out of my face and turned me toward the coffeemaker. "Don't worry, you can trust me. I won't let anything happen to you."

Suddenly the classroom looks unfamiliar. Like I've never been here before. Like the man in front of me is a stranger instead of "call-me-James" Mr. Lewis. Every alarm bell in my mind starts ringing, screaming at me to get away, while another part of my brain reminds me that this is my teacher, my friend's father. He's one of the good ones. He's going to help me.

"Don't worry," he says. "No one needs to know about this."

He places his hand on my bare knee.

I freeze, torn between disbelief and terror.

He cups my chin with his other hand.

This time, I push back. But his foot keeps my chair in place. His fingers slide up my leg, and he shakes his head like he's disappointed that I don't seem to understand this simple assignment.

"Don't worry," he says again. "I won't let you fail."

He holds me tight enough that I have no escape as he leans in to kiss me and his hand drifts upward.

I always thought I would be the type of person who fights.

Despite my anxiety over grades and school and being good enough, when faced with injustice, it's like another part of me takes over.

I speak up when I hear people being cruel.

At the stables, I'm the first to run at rowdy horses.

When someone dumped three neglected, starving kittens on the doorstep of the animal shelter, I chased after the truck that peeled out of the parking lot. The young man behind the wheel almost ran me down as I yelled after him, and Juliette, who runs the shelter, was nearly apoplectic. She's so gentle and patient with all the animals, but that day, she screamed at me that she'd much rather never know who dropped off an animal than risk losing me to make a point.

She was *afraid*.

I wasn't.

I've never frozen in fear before.

So I thought I would fight.

I don't.

I can't.

Turns out you never know how you'll react to something until it happens.

When his hand drifts upward, I can't even whisper in protest.

—

This isn't happening. I try to convince myself of that.

There's a wad of gum shaped like a flower on the ceiling. I've never looked at the ceiling before.

It's strange to see this unintentional bit of decoration.

The edges of the flower blur, because I'm staring at it like it's a lifeline. This gum is the one safe thing I can look at, so I focus on the shape of it, burning it into my retinas.

Someone knocks on the door and tries to open it.

My breath catches.

I don't look away from the ceiling until Mr. Lewis moves away to wash his hands.

My hands are balled into tight fists, and I don't know how to relax them. My nails dig deep into my palms. My muscles are all knotted up.

My body doesn't feel like mine. It's been fifteen minutes, twenty at most. But this is another life. I am another girl.

I tug down my shirt and fumble with my skirt. I lick my lips, and I want to vomit.

Another knock.

Whoever's outside won't leave us alone. I should be grateful, but—

"Dad?" Zanna's voice cleaves through me.

At his desk, Mr. Lewis picks up his leather bag and slides our chemistry homework into the biggest compartment. "One moment, please, Zanna," he calls out. "We're wrapping up a conversation. Can you meet me at the car?"

She doesn't answer. I imagine her on the other side of the door, tapping her phone with her long green nails. I imagine one of her trademark long-suffering sighs. "Whatever."

If she'd been here ten minutes ago…

Still, I could call out to her, ask her to help me, please help me.

I draw breath—

The words escape me.

He's her *father*.

Does she know? She can't possibly.

Did I say something—anything—that makes this right?

Did I make him think I wanted this?

Desperation bubbles up, and I clamp down on it.

I try to get to my feet, but I waver. I reach out to steady myself on the desk, but with every movement, I'm fragmenting. I'm losing pieces of myself. There's a growing void where *I* should be.

Mr. Lewis leans in and traces my jaw. "I feel honored that you trust me with your concerns, Kelsey."

Trust? I nearly laugh and I choke on his words, all at the same time. *My concerns?*

I pull away. I force myself to look at him, the monster that he is. But when I do, all I see is the same Mr. Lewis who explains the periodic table to us. One of my best friends' dads, who orders pizza or cooks for us when we're over to study. The teacher who tells us to come to him with anything if we ever need the help of an adult.

I thought I *could* trust him.

"I meant it when I promised I won't let you fail. I'm here for you."

"Do you really believe that?" I manage. My voice sounds like I haven't spoken in days.

He swings his bag over his shoulder and comes to stand in front of me. He cups my cheek. "Kelsey, *Kelsey*, don't forget that you came to me. You needed my help. You *wanted* my help."

"I didn't want—"

"You told me so yourself," he interrupts me. "You're willing to do *anything* to succeed. You want to keep this a secret, just between us."

I cast my mind back, but it's like trying to look through a distorted mirror. Did I say that? Did I imply it? Did I somehow make him believe that I consented to any of this?

He powers through. "You're a determined young woman, and I'll make sure you don't have to worry about your chemistry grade. I'll take care of you."

I—

I—

I hate him.

I—

I didn't *want* this.

I want to get out. I need to get out.

He's between me and the door.

I force myself to inhale, but there's no oxygen. I breathe deeper, but it doesn't help. My lungs burn. I keep trying to draw in air, but it's harder and harder, and my breath grows shallower and shallower.

Mr. Lewis grabs my shoulders and massages them, like he did that night during spring break. "Kelsey, you're hyperventilating. Calm down."

Ever the considerate teacher.

I hate how he says my name like it gives him power over me.

I should have run.

I should have told him no.

I should have—

I should have…

He shouldn't have.

"Open the door." My voice is louder and harsher than I expect. I grab my bag from the floor and hold it like a protective shield in front of me. "Let me out."

He waits long enough to remind me that he is in control, and it's effective. He turns the lock but keeps hold of the door handle. "You're a bright young woman, Kelsey, and everyone at this school wants to see you succeed. I know you will do much better on your next chem test."

"Let me out!"

He opens the door.

I run. Down the hallway. Out of the STEM wing. Through the mostly empty school.

I don't know whether to be grateful or disappointed that no one sees me. That Zanna isn't waiting outside the door. That Oakley didn't offer me a ride.

I wouldn't know what to tell them, anyway.

Did I say anything…?

I don't stop until I reach the girls' bathroom, where I lock myself into one of the farthest stalls and puke.

CHAPTER NINE
EDEN

12:53 A.M.

The clattering of rain sounds like footsteps all around me. The wind howls through the open windows downstairs.

I try to decide on my next steps. I may be curious and brave and foolish, but I'm not rational under pressure. Not like Theo, who needs to understand a situation first, or Payton, who goes cold and calculating. Push me too hard and I snap. Three of my mother's boyfriends can attest to that.

I will myself to be calm. I breathe in as deeply—and quietly—as possible as I head up the last few steps to the second floor. I pause and peek around the doorframe.

No one. The second floor appears as empty as the first.

In the distance, one stubborn safety light flickers on and off.

Every year, Principal Young tells us *this* is the year they're going to modernize the uncomfortable building with its high ceilings and squeaky floors. *This* is the year they'll swap the old equipment for shiny new materials and technology. I'm not sure that anyone believes it anymore. It's not like the school doesn't have funding—it's a charter school, so it gets some money from the state and relies on the district and on Fenix for the rest.

And Fenix, Colorado, is solidly *middling* at everything. The average person in this not-quite-small, not-quite-large town is middle class and has moderate politics, moderate test scores, and middle-of-the-road opinions about anything that could be construed as divisive. At least on the surface.

Still, the one thing everyone agrees on is that education matters and that it's *the* ticket to a successful future. Thankfully for the school, most parents are willing to invest in that, as is Lewis Industries. No one in town would dare to question Lewis Industries, and in return, Lewis Industries takes good care of Fenix. So the school has funding, but the board chooses to spend its money on sports teams and STEM classes, not on updating our facilities. Tough if you happen to like history or art and need new resources or paints. Or if you need the emergency generator to work during an outage.

I scan the space, trying to figure out where the sound came from.

One of the classroom doors opens on the far side of the hallway, and someone steps out, shoulders pulled up to his ears, head down, staring at something in his hands.

I back toward the stairwell entrance.

The figure stops and straightens.

I hold my breath and make myself small, certain that sudden movement will give away my presence.

I wait and listen for the squeak of footsteps, but the rain drowns out all sound. I count to ten, then to twenty, but nothing.

Click.

I bite my lip and peer into the hallway again.

The figure stands in profile. He holds the tiniest flame between his hands. It snuffs out and he flicks the lighter again. Then again. On. Off. On. Off. On.

In the safety light overhead, I can make out his features. Messy, wavy brown hair peeks out of a gray hoodie. His nose is upturned. It's Cameron Jenkins.

If there's one other thing everyone in Fenix agrees on, it's that Cameron is bad news. He got kicked out of school for assaulting a teacher right before Christmas break. He's tried to prove himself every since, but he's lost jobs at a car wash, Safeway, and Bean There. Eventually, his stepfather let him back into the restaurant, but everyone knows Matteo was furious.

Cameron Jenkins used to be the Pierce High School football team's most talented bench sitter. He could've been a starting player if only he'd gotten his head on straight. Now he's Fenix's most famous senior fuckup.

If he's here in the middle of the night—

Well, Cameron is never up to any good.

CHAPTER TEN
THEO

NINE DAYS AFTER

I close the messenger app after texting Payton and shift my attention back to the room in front of me. I don't want to stay any longer than necessary.

I'm not supposed to be here at all, of course. Crime scene tape circles the school. Although it seems the police are finished collecting evidence. Aside from a single patrol car hanging out in the parking lot beside the school—the officer inside spending more time looking at his phone than looking out—there's no one here to stop me.

I hope.

I never intended to break in. I just need to know what happened. Payton confirmed that Eden didn't break into the school to jump, and even though the texts on Payton's phone—the evidence that she was planning to run away—leave a hole in my chest, I have to push through. Mom taught me that the most important thing in life is the truth. Truth breeds trust and community. Truth is the foundation of every friendship, every relationship. The truth demands that we all be a little vulnerable, that we don't hide ourselves from one another.

Truth is why Mom is a reporter and why I want to be a journalist too. She wouldn't approve of me sneaking into the school today, but she'd understand it. Even without the school newspaper as an excuse, I would be here. For Eden. As far as I'm concerned, that friendship hasn't ended because she died. I couldn't do much to protect Eden in life, not from the shitty boyfriends her mother kept bringing home or the stares at school, but I can look out for her now.

I pull the scarf I wear around my face a little higher, trying to keep the smell of fire out of my nose, and take pictures of what remains of Mr. Lewis's classroom. This room sustained the most damage.

The police determined that Eden was here based on the burn marks and residue left on her clothes and in her hair. It was, they said, a tragic accident.

From the doorway, I can see where the explosion blasted through the room. Charred chairs and lab benches look like they were tossed around in a tornado. There are half-burned posters of the periodic table and chemical formulas on the walls. Everything is covered in soot and drowned in water and foam. It's been a week, but the acrid smell of fire is still heavy in the air.

It's hard to imagine that only eight days ago, students took notes in here and joked about homework, sporting events, and spring break plans. No one could have foreseen this.

This level of destruction makes no sense. Not for a regular thunderstorm. The teachers are meticulous about safely storing flammable and combustible materials. Could a lightning strike really do this much damage?

The longer I think about it, the more questions I have.

There's nothing of substance left in this mess.

With my phone, I zoom in on the remains of a textbook that miraculously survived the destruction, on the scars left by the fire, and then, finally, on the graffiti on the walls.

I made out the first word, and letter by letter, the others too. The same three words, over and over again, in bloody red against the blackened walls.

Criminal.

Pervert.

Rapist.

They're accusations aimed at Mr. Lewis. They must be. Cries of outrage or cries for help. Bold letters in bright red that claim he hurt someone.

"Fuck, Eden." The words slip out and echo in the empty room. "What did you stumble into?"

Pervert.

Criminal.

Rapist.

The words must have been spray-painted on the walls right before the fire, because if anyone had seen them, everyone at Pierce would be talking about it. Rumors and stories spread like wildfire at this school.

Some stories.

Apparently not all.

Pervert.

Criminal.

Rapist.

Someone must have done this after the school was cleaned and locked up for the night. Who else was here? Were they here when Eden died? Did she walk in on them? Is that why she died?

It *couldn't* have been her. She never had Mr. Lewis for chemistry. She *hated* science. She preferred to be, in her own words, *not terrible* at social studies. She barely squeezed by in Ms. Thompson's math classes, and we celebrated when she managed to make it through Algebra 2. She took biology to meet her lab requirement.

I had Mr. Lewis as a teacher. He was amazing. Funny, kind. He did experiments with us that made science *almost* fun enough to take an extra class. He worked hard to make sure none of us failed. When he saw someone teasing me in the hallway, he intervened. Afterward he told me that if anyone bullied me, he would take care of it. He wanted me to thrive. It was nice to feel like I had someone looking out for me.

And not just me, either. Every story I've ever heard about Mr. Lewis makes him out to be the cool teacher. This doesn't add up.

The only strange story I've ever heard about him is that one of his seniors got expelled earlier this year after getting into a fight with him. Theoretically, he or his friends could have done this.

Pervert.

Rapist.

Criminal.

My mind races. I read the words a hundred times. If this is a prank, it's a cruel one. If it isn't...

I don't want to believe it. But that doesn't mean I shouldn't. Why would someone go to these lengths if it wasn't true?

It can't be true.

Can it be true?

The truth is, I wouldn't know, would I?

I've never noticed.

I never get noticed. Not anymore.

The men who leer at girls don't see me. And it's not that boys don't get assaulted. They do. But I'd be lying if I didn't admit that passing makes walking the hallways at school or the streets at night less intimidating. People at Pierce don't know me as anyone other than Theo. Sure, there are assholes who see me and make assumptions. But I don't constantly have to calculate how safe people are like I did before we moved here five years ago. My button-downs and slacks offer me a level of protection.

The girls at school have other privileges—but they don't have that luxury.

The thought makes me sick.

Pervert.

Rapist.

Criminal.

I shake myself. If I'm going to be a journalist, I have to stay unbiased and do my research. These are the facts I have, assuming this is no prank.

Fact: Whoever painted these words wanted to make themselves heard. That's the only thing that makes sense to me, the only reason these words are so loud and bright in their red paint.

Fact: No one has spoken up since the fire. This graffiti was intentional, but everyone talks about the events of that night as an accident. It's been a full week, and no one has brought this up. Will they try again? Will they stay silent? Mr. Lewis is many things: chemistry teacher, parent, member of the PTA, part of the Lewis dynasty. This changes things.

Fact: Eden died on the same night these words appeared. Those two things aren't necessarily connected, but the chance that they aren't is infinitesimal.

Fact: This isn't just about Eden anymore. She deserves for the truth to be told about what happened the night she died. But she isn't the only one.

Whoever did this deserves for their truth be known too. I wonder if the police are keeping this graffiti from the public as they build their case. Even if they think the explosion was an accident, surely they have to be investigating this. Don't they have an obligation to keep others safe as well? Don't people need to know that there might be a predator in their midst?

I scan the room, taking in all the details. There is so much debris, I almost don't notice a mangled can of what looks to be spray paint. The metal is blackened. The top looks like it exploded. But if I can figure out where it's from, perhaps I can figure out whose it was.

I take a careful step in its direction, and the floor creaks in protest. Another step, and there's a loud *snap*.

I leap back toward the doorway, and part of the floor breaks off and falls into the classroom below.

No wonder the school is cordoned off. It isn't only about the investigation. The building isn't structurally safe. My heart leaps into my throat. Did the floor just shift underneath me again?

I have to get out of here.

I zoom in and take a picture of the can before I step back. The flooring sags.

Gently, I make my way back toward the staircase. The hallway seems less affected by the fire, but I didn't pay close attention to the cracks and empty spaces before. Now it feels like I'm balancing on the bare bones of what used to be a school.

A gust of wind makes the building groan like a wounded animal.

I hurry down the stairs toward solid ground as fast as I can.

The first floor looks the same as ever, aside from smoke and water damage from the sprinkler system.

If I breathe in, the pungent smell of the fire mixes with other familiar scents. The rubber-and-sweat smell of the linoleum. The metallic scent of the lockers, where the paint on the doors has flaked off. It looks like school. Call me a nerd, call me lucky or ignorant, but I loved it here.

Perhaps I was the only one.

I check my phone to see if Payton has replied—she hasn't.

I push outside and stare at the double doors for a second.

How did Eden get in? She couldn't have walked through the front door when the school was closed.

I stuff my hands deep into my pockets and consider the lawn that spreads out in front of the school beyond the bus circle. With the dusk sky growing darker, the grass looks bluish green. The road beyond that is empty. The police car is probably still sitting in the parking lot where Eden and Payton agreed to meet. Eden must have broken into the one of the classrooms on the first floor.

Did the police check all those classrooms for clues too?

It's dangerous to go back inside. I know that. But if I go home now and miss something important, I wouldn't forgive myself.

I circle around the school toward where Eden most likely would have entered, staying as close to the building as I can. I don't want to walk past the curb where Eden fell. I know it's cordoned off. I know it's *cleared*. But I…can't.

Instead, I peer into every room. The darker it gets outside, the harder it is to make out any details. What am I even looking for?

This may be pointless.

As I reach the math classrooms, the police car turns on its headlights, and its idling engine roars to life. I jump.

One of the windows is open, and I act without thinking. I hoist myself up over the sill and crouch under the window.

The car's headlights shine inside, illuminating part of the classroom. I hold my breath and watch, waiting for it to pass. Only then does it occur to me—

Why is this window open?

I scan the room. On the floor, half hidden by the door, is a dark shadow. A green backpack. *Eden's* backpack.

I crawl toward it, staying low. The room is waterlogged and smells of mildew.

As soon as I'm within reaching distance, I scoop up the backpack and pull it onto my lap. I unzip the largest compartment.

Clothes. Eden's shirts, which fell in two categories: brightly colored and baggy or black with the collars cut out.

Half a dozen soggy comics clumped together.

One night last summer when we were both sitting in the tree between our houses, she told me to go get snacks, and she got a stack of comics out of her room. We read them by flashlight, and they were horrifying—all monsters and nightmares. She *loved* them. She reveled in them.

I jumped at every strange noise as we turned page after page.

"They're just stories," she teased me.

"No thank you," I said. I pushed the snacks in her direction.

She grabbed a candy bar and smirked. "Horror isn't scary, Theo."

"Are we reading the same thing?"

"They're stories of survival," she said with such determination. "Survival against all odds."

I leaned back against the trunk of the tree, and she leaned against me. I felt her shiver despite the warmth.

"You can survive anything," I told her.

She didn't respond.

I wish she had.

I continue to rifle through her bag. Her wallet, a muddy envelope, and a leather cord with a carved and polished apple on a branch.

I bring my hand up to my throat, to the necklace she made for me. A cluster of grapes. She didn't have a good reason for carving fruit charms—none that she told me, anyway—but I know how much they meant to her. A small heart is carved into the branch with a *P* and an *E* inside it. I wish she could have been happy far away with Payton. I want it so badly it hurts.

I pull out her woodworking kit, which she never let anyone else touch.

No spray paint cans, nor is there any room in the backpack to carry additional items. It isn't definite proof that she wasn't the one who did the graffiti, but it makes me breathe easier all the same.

Finally, I move one of her tightly rolled shirts, and my breath catches. It loosens around a finely designed wooden horse. One of the legs has been glued on. Her father made this for her. It used to stand on a narrow shelf above her bed, along with the carvings she'd made that she was particularly proud of, a collection of German fairy tales that her parents used to read to her, and a photo of a baby Eden with both of her parents looking at her adoringly.

She planned to leave, and she hoped for something better than this.

That night in the tree, she told me she loved that Mom and I had moved in because it made Fenix a little more bearable. Still, she wanted more.

I promised she'd have it one day. We were going to be juniors. Graduation wasn't that far off. The whole world was out there waiting for her.

That conversation haunts me now. Could I have helped her?

I zip the backpack and swing it over my shoulders, then work my way back to the window. I'll crawl out as soon as the police car continues on its rounds.

She never made it out.

I will.

CHAPTER ELEVEN
THEO

NINE DAYS AFTER

It feels like forever before I can climb through the window unnoticed. By the time I get home, it's dark, and even though it's the weekend, Mom is working at the dining table. She takes one look at me, and I must look as rattled as I feel, because she brings out a tub of chocolate chip cookie dough.

"Do you want to talk about it?"

"I do," I admit, "but I need more information first."

"Is it dangerous?" she asks.

I scrunch up my face. "It's important."

"Hm."

In most families, sneaking out and coming back looking haunted would probably be cause for concern, but Mom never leaps to conclusions. When I was younger, when Dad was alive, she was a war correspondent. She doesn't scare easily.

"You know I trust you to act responsibly, Theodore. Promise me that you'll ask for help when you need it."

I always have. I trust that she'll always have my back.

Until I met Eden, I naively thought all parents were like that. When I started paying attention, I realized how lucky I was to have a parent who loved and supported me unconditionally.

"I promise," I say. "Of course."

She smiles and hands me a spoon. "Good."

Before I go to bed, I stand at my window.

Eden and I met the day Mom and I moved into this house. I went to explore my new room and found a girl in the tree outside. She was reading a faded comic, edges torn from wear, and she was utterly engrossed.

I opened my window and she *gawked* at me. She shielded the comic and looked to be on the verge of scampering out of the tree.

"We're new here," I said quickly. "I'm Theodore. But everyone calls me Theo. I've never actually climbed trees before. Can I join you?"

I climbed out the window and reached for the nearest sturdy branch. The tree was old and big enough that it stretched all the way to my room, and though I'd never been much for climbing, I tenderly tested if the branch would hold my weight. I took a step forward and then another, holding on to the leafy branches around me. "I don't think I'm very good at this." I wore one of my dad's old vests, and it was slightly too big for me. As I scooted toward the center of the tree, the fabric caught on twigs and rough bits of bark, and the leaves tickled my arms and neck. I flinched and pushed them away.

Eden stared at me with big wary eyes. But then she placed the comic to the side and laughed. It was the brightest sound in the whole wide world.

"I'm Eden," she said. "Welcome to my tree."

We started to meet there to hang out. I got better at climbing. She read gruesome fairy tales to me, and I shared Mom's cooking with her. She listened to my plans for the school newspaper, and I watched her carve and make magic. She made me laugh. I made her wonder. The shadow that clung to her everywhere else fell away.

I miss her.

I miss her.

I miss her.

I thought I'd grown used to mourning after Dad died. It turns out the pain is as sharp this time, as breathtaking all over again.

Grief is an old friend, but Eden was my *best* friend.

After a weekend of precious little sleep and too many thoughts, my alarm goes off at six thirty a.m. At eight, the school message system reminds us, we're supposed to gather at Fenix Middle School for an update on our classes and the aftermath of the fire.

Mom grumbled that the school should have held an assembly immediately after the fire and provided grief counselors for all of us, but I didn't mind that they took the week of spring break to get their act together. It was hard enough seeing Eden's room every day and knowing that she wasn't there anymore. I keep expecting her to lean out and wave at me. I didn't want to be at school and see her absence there too.

All of that changed Saturday night.

I still taste soot on my tongue, but I have a purpose now. My head is pounding with a dozen urgent questions.

I have a desperate need to talk to Payton. I texted her again yesterday, but she didn't reply. I want to show her the backpack. I want to tell her what I found. I want to tell her that the truth—the whole story—has gotten a lot more complicated. I want to investigate the rest, and I want her to be involved. Together. Like she said she would be.

I know so little about Payton, but I know Eden would want me to be there for her.

I dress comfortably and stuff pens and a power bank into my pockets. My phone is fully charged in case I need to film anything.

Given that it was a classroom that was defaced, I've decided that the people responsible must be students. They'll probably be present at the assembly. Will they act suspicious or guilty? If I'd known about the graffiti earlier, I would have paid attention in the church too.

I also wonder if the school will acknowledge that there's more to the story than they've told us. Surely they can't sweep accusations like these under the rug.

I fill a thermos with coffee before I grab my backpack and head out the door. By the time I reach the middle school, I've nearly drunk it all. My hands are trembling, but not from caffeine.

The parking lot is filled with Pierce students' cars. Like Pierce, Fenix Middle School was closed last week for spring break, and it's supposed to be back in session today. Hosting all of us here today is probably a headache for the administration, but it's not like we have another school to go to. They need to figure out what to do with us.

Not that any of the students around me seem particularly concerned. They chatter about their spring break adventures. About their plans for prom. It's as if nothing has happened.

Once I get to the gym where we're supposed to gather, I try to find Payton in the mass of people. I finally notice her in the farthest corner, her shoulders set. She stares ahead.

With the teachers herding kids to sit, going up to her will have to wait until after the assembly. I find a seat and take out a pen and my notebook.

When I was eleven and wanted to start a newspaper at my middle school, back when we lived in Flagstaff, Mom bought me a small black leather-bound notebook for my writing. I filled it up. Then another one. Then another. Those notebooks became my thing, like I'd imprinted on the first one. Dad bought me a sparkling blue notebook for my next birthday, but I barely even touched that. Last year, Mom ordered sixteen leather-bound notebooks for my sixteenth birthday. I'm only halfway through the third, but something tells me that is set to change.

The assembly begins. First to speak is Principal Young. As usual, she's dressed in a sober, dark gray skirt suit and her brown hair, streaked with white, is pulled back into a bun. Her makeup can't mask the dark circles under her eyes. She gives us empty platitudes and clichéd life lessons, reminding us that we need to cherish every moment together and that the best thing we can do is support each other through these trying times.

She impresses upon us that grief can be alienating and overwhelming and that we will have access to grief counselors if we feel the need to talk.

It seems to be a well-rehearsed speech, and she manages to completely avoid naming Eden. She's been reduced to "our fellow student" and "a girl whose life was tragically cut short." It feels as impersonal as Eden's funeral. It's a painful reminder that most of Fenix never tried to get to know her. Not really.

Students mutter and grumble around me.

"I didn't even know her. Why should I talk to some shrink?"

"Man, if they're going to keep on like this, I might jump too."

"Dude, you can't say shit like that."

"Do you suppose we'll get the rest of the school year off? What will happen to prom and our sporting events?"

The last comment comes from Siobhan Jones, a petite, dark-haired girl who looks like she still belongs in middle school.

She gets her answer when Principal Young cedes the stage to Mr. Llewellyn, who is there on behalf of the school district. He's wrinkly and white with a bushy mustache and slicked-back brown-and-gray hair. He wears a black suit and looks appropriately grave when he tells us, "The school district is committed to ensuring that you can return to the building at the earliest possible opportunity. We will rebuild. We will come out of this stronger. We are in talks with Fenix Middle School about allocating space to us, and until that is resolved, we will offer classes virtually."

His comment is met with boos and shouts of disappointment.

It's like a bucket of snow has been dumped on me. Payton and I are grieving Eden. Maybe some of her art class friends are too. But for the majority of the school, this is all an inconvenience. They miss school and their regular schedules, not the girl who lost her life.

I don't see any guilt or leads around me, only impatience.

But across the way, Amaya Hernández is listening closely too. She catches my gaze, and there's concern in her eyes. She knows Eden and I were close.

I give her a small smile and lift my notebook. She gives me a thumbs-up. We're both on the newspaper, and she's seen me in *figure out this story* mode before. I'll have to get her, June, and Jalen up to speed on what I've found.

Mr. Llewellyn passes the microphone to three teachers: Coach Mills, PE teacher and coach of the girls' field hockey team; Mx. Sousa, who is the most intimidating history teacher you'll ever meet as well as our *Puma Press* adviser; and Mr. Lewis.

It's strange—a part of me breathes a little easier seeing him onstage. The school administration wouldn't let him be part of this assembly if there were a chance he was guilty, right? It's like I expect him to fix everything that's happened. It's the same part of me that hesitates to believe the allegations on his classroom walls because he was *kind* to me.

Mr. Lewis looks grayer than usual. Instead of slacks, he wears jeans and a button-down shirt, and his hair is unruly. Still, he smiles, and he looks so comfortable that I wonder if he even knows about the graffiti at all.

What *does* he know?

"In addition to grief counselors," Coach Mills says, projecting her voice like she's on the sideline of a game instead speaking into a microphone, "we want to remind you that you can always come to any of us. We are here for you. You are valued and valuable, and you are not alone, even if it sometimes feels like it. The loss of Eden Randall is heartbreaking, and I want you all to know that you have multiple avenues for help, should you need it. We're happy to talk.

And you know I'm always happy to run laps with anyone who needs some company."

Her joke is met with laughter, and for the first time since the assembly started, the mood eases.

"But Coach," one of the girls calls out from the back row—I can't make out who it is. "That's your solution to everything! Worried about grades? Go for a run. Thinking too much about college apps? Go for a run. Sick and tired of running? *Go for a run.*"

"Physical fitness stimulates the brain, Julia," Coach Mills replies like it's a common refrain. Julia must be on the field hockey team.

"If you don't like running," Mr. Lewis puts in, "you can come to Mx. Sousa and me." He smirks. "I'm always happy to help figure out the right *solution* to your problems."

His words are met with groans and a few laughs. Luis Serrano and Elijah Kane, two seniors who are sitting in front of me, shake their heads and grumble. They were friends with Cameron Jenkins, the senior who got expelled after getting into a fight with Mr. Lewis.

Then a voice rings out.

"This is such bullshit."

Around me, everyone shifts. The voice continues, rising and cracking with emotion. "What's the point of all of this, anyway? Eden Randall is dead. The school burned. Everyone is *happy to talk*, but we're all going back to business as fucking usual. It's like none of this matters."

I can't place the voice. It must be one of Eden's art friends. But when I turn and locate the girl, it isn't someone from Eden's art class.

It's Kelsey Fink, a senior, one of the most popular girls in school.

As far as I know, Kelsey wasn't friends with Eden. They never crossed paths, unless you count walking the same hallways at school. But she seems genuinely, overwhelmingly upset. I wonder if her outburst is really about Eden.

Oakley Walker, who's next to Kelsey, holds her arm tightly and tries to soothe her.

Kelsey bursts into tears.

I sit up.

Whispers ripple through the gym.

"What is happening?" someone asks. "Is she okay? I didn't know she cared."

I didn't either. I don't know what to make of this behavior. Is it guilt? Grief? I scribble down a few notes.

Onstage, the three teachers confer briefly, and then Coach Mills pushes Mr. Lewis in Kelsey's direction. The microphone picks up her voice saying, "She's one of your students. Get to it."

At that moment, I am certain these teachers don't know Mr. Lewis's classroom was defaced. They can't know about the words on the walls.

But the principal must.

I glance over to the side of the gym where Principal Young stands, her arms folded and her brow furrowed. What is she thinking? What have the fire department and the police told her?

I glance back at Kelsey. Her breath comes in rasping, wrecked gasps. She's hyperventilating. Oakley is trying to calm her as the kids around them part to make way for the teacher.

Mr. Lewis reaches out a hand to Kelsey. "Kelsey? Let's get you out of here. You need to breathe. Breathe for me."

Kelsey jerks backward violently.

Oakley *hisses* like a feral cat at Mr. Lewis. At her *uncle*, I realize.

"Leave her be. Don't *touch* her." Oakley rises to stand protectively in front of her friend.

Everyone around me is talking now. The gym is a sea of sound and concern, the volume flowing through the room like waves. But Kelsey, Oakley, and Mr. Lewis exist in a bubble of angry silence.

Mr. Lewis stares down Oakley. "Do *not* fight me on this, Oakley Walker. Your friend needs to get out of this crowd and get some air or it will only get worse. Help her or sit down so someone else can. I have no patience for you making this worse. Take her to the nurse's office."

I expect Oakley to push back. All her hackles are up. I've never seen anyone react to Mr. Lewis like this. The only reason she would, I assume, is because she knows about the graffiti on the walls. The teachers may not know, but Oakley Walker and Kelsey Fink do.

And what's more, they believe the accusations.

Oakley clenches her jaw and nods. She throws a disgusted glance in the direction of the teachers and administrators, then helps get Kelsey—who is sobbing and breathless—to the exit.

When the doors close behind them, silence descends. Discomfort too.

I scribble in my notebook, which I've been steadily filling with observations from this morning.

There's a lot of tension between Oakley and Mr. Lewis. I wonder if Oakley and Kelsey will talk to me. It's a lead. It's a start. Part of me wants to follow them out, but while Principal Young tries to regain everyone's attention, I look over at Payton. Her face is pale and panicked. I don't know how to reassure her in gestures, so I grab my phone and text.

> I'm here for you. I'll find you after.

CHAPTER TWELVE
THEO

ELEVEN DAYS AFTER

After assembly, we are released from the gym—and from school for the day. Principal Young told us to keep an eye on the school messaging system for more information on the start of virtual classes later this week. Between the destruction of part of the science wing and the water damage to books and computers, she explained that it would take our teachers several days to transition to remote learning again.

That comment was met with cheers.

I may be the only student who *wants* to go back to school, back to some hint of normalcy when everything around me has stopped making sense. But I don't mind not having to face school without Eden yet. And this gives me more time to dive into this story.

By now, Kelsey and Oakley are all anyone is talking about. Eden's death is yesterday's news. Kelsey's breakdown is today's. And Oakley and Kelsey are nowhere to be found.

Sometimes I wonder if this is all anyone in Fenix cares about: the next bit of gossip. It's strange to think that a girl dying and a girl hyperventilating are so easily interchangeable.

But then I think about the words on Mr. Lewis's walls, and I look around me, wondering how many of my fellow students have stories and secrets they *don't* share. I think about all the scoops I've discovered for the school newspaper, in light of all the truths I may have missed.

"T?" Amaya's voice cuts through my thoughts. She appears next to me, placing her hand on my arm. "I haven't seen you since the fire. I know you were close with Eden. How are you holding up?"

"I'm…" I don't know what I am. "It all feels pretty surreal. Like, I expect her to climb into our tree to hang out. Or rant about her Spanish class. Or get excited about a new carving she's started." I wasn't intending to share so much, but the words spill out. It feels good to talk about her.

"I know everyone thought she was weird, but she was…" *Protecting herself? Desperate to find a place to belong?* "She was my friend."

Compassion settles in Amaya's warm brown eyes. "You should write an in memoriam for Eden. Tell us about who she was. It won't make up for so many of us not knowing her in life, but it's better than not knowing her at all, isn't it?"

"I'd like that." I swallow against the lump in my throat before I get emotional in public, and I smile at her. "I don't know how or when we'll be able to publish the next issue of the *Puma Press*, but I also want to make sure we do a full article on the fire and on what happened at the assembly today."

Amaya tilts her head. "Kelsey Fink's outburst?"

I glance around to make sure no one is within earshot. "I think there's more to the story."

Amaya frowns. "What do you mean?"

I contemplate telling her what I've seen. But I broke into the school illegally. I don't want to get her involved until I know for sure that I won't get her in trouble. Amaya is off to Seattle University's prelaw program next year. I don't want to get in the way of that. Not until I know what to say. So I tell her, "Call it a hunch for now. I'll tell you when I have something solid, okay?"

Her perfectly manicured eyebrows come together in a way that makes her look just like my mother, and I squirm uncomfortably. But she nods. "You know why I wanted to be part of the *Puma Press* crew? I hate how much of what happens at Pierce and in Fenix happens behind closed doors, off the record. I know we're not changing the world, but writing about our community gives words to what might otherwise stay unspoken. We create a record. You can't change patterns you don't see." She squeezes my arm. "So I'm here when you need me and when you can tell me. June, Jalen, and I—we've got your back. We'll dig up those ghosts with you."

I smile at that. The three of them aren't the friends you call to bury a body—they're all too curious and committed to the truth. But they *are* the friends I'd call in the middle of the night to dig up a decomposing mascot head. "I'll hold you to it."

Out of the corner of my eye, I see Payton exit the school. I don't want to lose her, but I don't want to ditch Amaya either. "I'm good. I promise you I am. I'll tell you everything when I can. Let me just figure out what there is to tell."

The last bit is a white lie, but some of the worry lines fade from Amaya's face. "Good. Text me."

I nod. "Thank you."

Eden once told me I was lucky to have them. My mother. My friends. A safety net. She was right, and I didn't appreciate it until now. If I ever have to jump, I know I have people who'll catch me.

I feel Amaya's gaze lingering on me as I dash after Payton. I have to jog to keep up. She has her head angled down so her hair hides her face. Today must have been hell for her. I hated it, but taking notes gave me a purpose and distraction during the assembly. She had to sit there and recognize how few of the teachers and students cared about the girl who loved her.

"Hey," I call out.

She jumps, bringing her hand to her chest, breathing hard. "Fuck, Theo. You scared me."

Heat spreads across my cheeks. I saw how she reacted when I tried to touch her in the graveyard. I don't want to make her uncomfortable, even by accident. If she was running away from Fenix, she had a reason. "I'm sorry. I didn't mean to scare you. Are you okay?"

She scoffs. "No. Are you?" She pushes her hands into her pockets, and she's so tightly wound that I'm afraid to get too close.

"Did you get my texts?" I ask.

When she sighs in what I think is an affirmative way, I push on, though I carefully leave out details. I don't want to risk being overheard. "What I saw is a sign that others were there that night. I want to find out who they were and what they have to do with Eden's death."

Her jaw works, and she looks away from me. "Dad says there'll be security footage."

"Oh." I haven't considered that, but it's a good point. There might be. "That's good. That would make it easier to prove she wasn't alone." I pause. "I have theories I want to talk to you about. And I found something you should see."

For the first time during this conversation, Payton looks straight at me. There are shadows under her eyes like she hasn't slept in days. Is it possible she looks thinner than she did at the funeral? She looks like she's fading. But her eyes spark with curiosity—and relief. "I'm sorry I didn't reply to your text. I couldn't. I—You found something?"

"Can I show you?" I gesture toward the parking lot. "It'd be better to talk at my place. I could drop you off at home afterward if you don't have your own car."

She manages the ghost of a smile. "I walked. The middle school isn't too far from our house."

If I remember where she lives correctly, it's at least two miles, but I guess fresh air helps clear my head too.

"I can drop you off here too," I offer.

She visibly relaxes. "Yeah, thanks. Okay. I can go with you. I can do that."

It sounds like she's reassuring herself more than confirming. I shift the focus by pointing. "My car is over there."

We walk together. She doesn't speak, and she tenses at every sound. When a thrush comes bursting out of the bushes, carrying a stick and making an impressive racket, I wonder if she might faint.

Instead, she laughs humorlessly and coughs. "Fuck, I'm tired."

Before I can reply, she continues, her voice flat. "I know a lot of people joke about the idea of safe spaces. Or they think they're a sign of weakness. But Eden was that for me. She was the person I could go to when everything felt overwhelming. She didn't judge me. She didn't try to change me. She never made me feel like I wasn't good enough. She never laughed at me or pitied me. Some days, she was the only person who saw me as me. She was my safe space. Without her..." She shakes her head.

I wait for her to finish the sentence, but she doesn't.

"I feel lost without her," I say.

She nods. "Yeah. Me too."

When I pull up at home, Mom's at work, so I take Payton up to my room. Framed prints of newspapers from pivotal moments in history decorate the walls, surrounded by articles I've written. Most friends stand and stare. But she walks directly to my window, the one that looks out on Eden's room. She drinks in the view.

I push my desk chair aside, toppling a stack of hoodies and binders, and pull Eden's backpack out from under my desk, where I'd hid it. I should probably hand it over to the police, but I don't want them to ask where I found it or for it to end up in some kind of evidence locker to be forgotten. I'd rather give it to Eden's mother.

That is, if I can gather the courage to talk to her. We've never interacted much before. She was a character in Eden's tales. Now she is so full of pain, I don't know if I have the words. After the news broke about Eden's death, Mom and I went over to offer our sympathies and drop off a home-cooked meal, but I hung back during the exchange.

Facing her makes Eden's loss more real.

And anyway, I want to show this to Payton first.

"Payton?"

She tears herself away from the window, and when she does, she *gasps*.

With two big steps, she crosses the room and drops to her knees next to the bag. It still smells of smoke. She runs her hands up and down the fabric. "Where did you find it?"

"Ms. Thompson's classroom," I whisper. Suddenly it's hard to keep my voice steady. "When you showed me her text message, I realized she had to have been waiting on that side of the building."

Payton smiles, though her voice trembles. "Like a bloodhound."

Color rushes to my cheeks. "It was common sense."

Payton slowly unzips the bag, careful not to jostle its contents. "You know, one night when I stayed over at her place, she pointed out your room to me. She told me, 'My best friend Theo is going to be a world-famous reporter. And someday, I'm going to convince him to tell me how he found that disgusting puma head.'"

I choke on a laugh. Eden said the same thing to me. "I always told her that a good reporter doesn't betray his sources."

"Yeah," Payton says. "I like that about you."

She pulls out the carved horse, and her hands shake. Her voice is raw and pained as she says, "I hate this. It hurts so much. There were so many things I didn't tell her. I should have told her I loved her. I should have said that a thousand times over, again and again and again."

I can't look at her because it feels too private, so I fiddle with the wooden quill and ink jar Eden carved for my sixteenth birthday. I should have told her that too. I should have said I loved her. That she was my best friend. That she made me want to live up to her faith in me.

I know better than to not tell the people I love that I care about them every chance I get. Yet it's still so easy to forget.

I glance over. Payton is going through the woodworking kit. She clings to one of the tools so tightly, the carving tip cuts into her palm. Blood drips down her fingers.

I clear my throat and point at it, and she stares, surprised.

"Oh. I didn't notice." She swears, but I think she's feeling more emotional pain than physical pain, seeing this part of Eden without seeing her.

I toss Payton a clean handkerchief to wipe away the blood. I point to the envelope. "Do you know what that is? Or was?"

Payton cleans her hand. "It was an old letter from her grandparents. Her father's parents. They have a farm in Wyoming, and that's where we were going." She holds the paper gently. "She didn't know them well, but she dreamed about horses and orchards full of fruit trees. She wanted it to be her home. If you plan to show this bag to Eden's mother… I don't think she needs to see this."

"She deserves to know the truth," I counter.

Payton shakes her head. "Sometimes the truth hurts more than gentle lies."

"No," I say. "The truth may hurt, but it can also heal. Maybe it will help her understand Eden. Maybe it will help her to—one day—find closure. It's not up to us to take away people's choice to know."

I spot the apple charm Eden carved and pull it out of the bag. I turn it around so Payton can see the little heart that Eden included. "Besides, the truth may be cathartic too." I hold it out to her. "She made it as a reminder that you were headed for a new life," I say. "She knew you loved her."

Payton takes a deep, shuddering breath. I think she won't touch the necklace. Then she reaches for it and cradles the charm. She whispers, "You said you had theories?"

She looks fragile and overwhelmed, but despite the crack in her voice, her eyes are hard and determined.

I reach for my phone. "I told you I went to the school. Well, I went up to Mr. Lewis's classroom, because that's where the damage was, where they said Eden got caught in the fire." I pause to choose my words. "There were allegations on the walls. Graffiti beneath the soot."

I show her the pictures. *Pervert, criminal, rapist.* I continue, "It means others must have been inside the school at the same time. That must have been why she went to the second floor."

Payton swipes through the pictures. There's a question in her eyes. "Do you believe what it says? The graffiti?"

"If I'm honest, it's surprising. You had him too, right? Did you ever notice anything strange? Inappropriate? He's always been so kind to me. Do you think it could be a prank gone wrong?"

"The fact that he's been kind to you doesn't mean he doesn't have the capacity to be horrid to others," she points out sharply.

"True," I acknowledge.

My mother has always taught me to believe survivors. There's nothing to gain by falsely accusing someone, she said. So I find it hard to admit that I don't *want* to believe *these* accusations.

I say, "Today during assembly, when Kelsey Fink freaked out,

Oakley Walker nearly bit Mr. Lewis's head off. What do you think they know? Were they involved?"

An emotion I can't read flashes across her face. "I imagine Mr. Lewis would have been told," Payton says. She passes back my phone. "Maybe the whole Lewis family knows."

Yeah, maybe. They're the most powerful family in town. It wouldn't surprise me. It *does* surprise me that Oakley is seemingly so willing to believe the allegations because I naively expect family to support each other. "I could try to ask Oakley, but I'm not sure she'd want to talk to me. Not without proof. She has no reason to trust me."

"Not if you don't believe what the graffiti says."

"It's not that I don't believe it, but I don't want to leap to conclusions. You have to admit there are two options. It's true or it's not. It could be a cruel prank. But if it isn't…"

I flick through the pictures again and take myself out of the equation. "Who did Mr. Lewis assault?"

The words are heavy.

Payton shudders.

"Mr. Lewis assaulted students," she whispers.

I rub at my eyes. "If it's true, why is it the first we've heard of it? Why didn't anyone say anything before? Why wasn't he reported?"

Payton gets to her feet and walks over to the window. "Who says he wasn't?"

"Without rumors spreading throughout the school?" I counter.

Maybe it's arrogant to think I would have known, but—"Someone on the *Puma Press* crew would have heard."

She shrugs. "I think you should believe whoever wrote that."

Her voice gives me pause. "Payton?"

She doesn't turn. "Yes?"

I try to find the right words to ask the question I don't *want* to ask. "Do you think Eden was a part of this? I know she never took any of his classes, but…did he…was she…do you think he did something to her?"

Payton runs the necklace through her fingers and rocks on the balls of her feet. "No." She shakes her head. "They barely even crossed paths. I'm sure of it. She had nothing to do with this. She was there by accident."

She got caught up in it. That must be it. "What if it was someone she knew? Maybe she was there to help?"

I glance at my bedroom window. At Eden's tree. She carefully kept her friendships with Payton and me separate. Maybe she held more secrets.

Payton's face twists into a sick grimace. "It doesn't matter what I *think*," she says, and it sounds almost like a plea. "It matters what the truth is. It matters that someone is brave enough to tell it." She faces me and holds out the necklace. "Here. This belongs with the rest of her things. I don't deserve it." She looks utterly heartbroken when she adds, "I have to go."

She pushes past me toward the door, and I scramble to my feet. "Wait!"

She pauses, hand on the doorknob.

"We can tell the truth together," I say. "For Eden."

Tension lines Payton's shoulders. Panic settles in her eyes. "I wouldn't know where to start."

"You don't have to do it alone. Stay. We'll figure it out."

But when she glances up and meets my gaze, she has that same lost and lonely look that Eden sometimes wore.

I get it. It's a lot to deal with. The idea of Mr. Lewis hurting anyone makes me sick. Eden's death compounds it, makes everything a hundred times worse. I get that it's too much for Payton right now. "Let me give you a ride home, then?"

Outside, a car door slams. Payton flinches at the sound. "Don't worry. I'll walk."

Before I can say anything else, she opens the door and flees.

CHAPTER THIRTEEN
THEO

ELEVEN DAYS AFTER

Payton is right: What I think doesn't matter. It matters what the truth is. Someone needs to be brave enough to tell it. And if it's too hard for her, I'll do it for the both of us.

I know I'm missing many details, but I do have words on a wall. A can of spray paint. A mother who's a reporter. And access to the Pierce High School alumni server.

The spray paint is the only tangible clue pointing to whatever happened the night the school burned.

While it's entirely likely that whoever bought it did so online, maybe—just maybe—I can find the breadcrumbs in Fenix.

So first, I go to the big-box store. They sell cans of spray paint, locked behind plastic windows, but when I walk the aisles, the packaging and shape are all different from the one I saw in the classroom. I don't want to linger. It feels like everyone is looking at me, even though the store's busy with shoppers.

I drop by McKenna's Craft Store next, and after a lap through their paint aisles, I ask where they keep their spray paint. McKenna squints at me over her oval glasses and says she doesn't carry it anymore, because "kids these days" used to buy it for "mayhem and mischief, like vandalizing the fountain in the park with lewd imagery."

I faintly remember hearing that story. "Didn't that happen, like, a decade ago?"

She scoffs. "And anyway, it's illegal to sell to minors now. Good."

For my final destination, I stop at Fenix Hardware, which has been owned by the same family since the town was founded. It smells of rust and varnish and petroleum spirits. It's the only other place I can think of that might sell spray paint.

The door jingles when I open it, and Old Man Adams looks up from his place behind the counter. His long white hair is tied back in a ponytail, and his broad shoulders stretch his shirt.

"You're Eden's friend, right?" he greets me. "What do you need?"

When my eyes adjust to the low light inside, I take in the long rows of racks and shelves, several of which are leaning against each other. It's entirely too claustrophobic for me, but Eden used to come here to buy supplies for her carving. She loved it here.

"I'm researching a piece for the school newspaper," I say. "Do you sell spray paint?"

Old Man Adams chews on a toothpick and nods. "Aisle five."

He points me in the right direction, and when I check out aisle five, I go warm and cold all at once. These are the same cans. The same brand, in all different colors, including the same bright red I found on the walls. I'm on the right track.

I return to Old Man Adams. "Did you sell any recently?"

He gives me an unreadable stare. "Plenty of kids from your school buy it. With their parents or other adults present, of course. I told the police that too." I want to feel relieved, but then he leans in closer like he's admitting to a secret and adds, "I know I shouldn't have, but I also sold some to Eden. It's a tragedy what happened. I'm gonna miss that kid around here."

"Yeah," I say. My head feels light, my arms heavy. "It's a nightmare."

Maybe it's a coincidence, a voice inside me says. She never crossed paths with Mr. Lewis. Maybe she needed the paint for her art. Maybe that's it.

Maybe.

Maybe.

Fuck, Eden. What did you stumble into?

—

Eden always wanted to know how I solved the mystery of Pierce's missing puma head. I wish I could go back in time and tell her. It wasn't nearly as exciting as she thought it was. I categorized the information I had. The tall tales. The urban legends. The stories about how the head had been stolen by Wyvern High. The rumors that the head was haunted. All the previous searches. The articles from old newspapers.

But as it turned out, the most useful information was on Pierce's online alumni community site, the Puma Boards, which I managed to log onto with a bit of creativity. Most graduates stop using the Puma Boards once they get to college or only keep up with school reunions. But a small, dedicated group of graduates who never made it out of Fenix has opinions on *everything*.

Since the school's IT system is dodgy at best, I only needed a made-up email address to log in and search the archives for mentions of the mascot. Once I discovered that the rumor that the head was buried came from *before* the school built a new parking lot, Amaya and I mapped out its location on older school maps. It was an educated guess, but it paid off.

Sometimes, all you need to find the truth is to figure out which details to add up.

Sometimes the truth is best found in what isn't shared out loud.

Maybe there are details to add up about Mr. Lewis too.

I look at Eden's carvings next to my laptop, and I log into the alumni site for the first time in years—my old fake password still works—and begin the search.

My screen fills with posts. Pictures of Mr. Lewis's Creative Science days dating back a dozen years. A former student who got his PhD in biochemistry posing with Mr. Lewis at his graduation ceremony, thanking him for an introduction that got him a job. A conversation about the fire.

> [MESSAGE] I can't believe it started in Mr. Lewis's classroom. He must feel terrible, even if he isn't responsible.
>
> [MESSAGE] Truth be told, I think that girl destroyed his room on purpose. I used to see her around town, and she's always been odd.
>
> [MESSAGE] You think she meant to blow up the school?
>
> [MESSAGE] I think she craved attention.
>
> [MESSAGE] Her poor mother. But that girl should have been reported to child welfare services long ago.
>
> [MESSAGE] Because she was lonely?
>
> [MESSAGE] Because she was a threat to herself and others.

Further on, a discussion about Mr. Lewis getting into a fight with a student.

> [MESSAGE] It's that boy from the Italian restaurant, isn't it? He's always been troubled.
>
> [MESSAGE] No respect for authority. Incorrigible.
>
> [MESSAGE] I heard it was at Mr. Lewis's request that the school

didn't press charges. Maybe it would have been better for that boy to learn discipline the hard way.

[MESSAGE] He said he did it to protect a friend.

[MESSAGE] From Mr. Lewis? Can you imagine?

[MESSAGE] Yes.

I narrow my eyes at that last entry, but when I try to find the username, all the system says is *account deleted*.

All the other messages are in support of Mr. Lewis.

[MESSAGE] No.

[MESSAGE] Absolutely not.

[MESSAGE] I wouldn't fancy being a teacher these days when the wrong word with the best intentions will put you on someone's blacklist.

[MESSAGE] Students should be able to trust their teachers and feel supported by them, and if there's one teacher who supports his students, it's Mr. Lewis.

[MESSAGE] Without Mr. Lewis, without his family, none of us would be where we are now. You may not remember what poverty looked like in Fenix, but I do.

It goes on like that for another two pages, and I can't find any more criticism. No one even mentions receiving bad grades or just not getting along with him. But that simple, small *yes* nags at me.

I take a deep breath and click on the button that says "new post," and I type.

> [MESSAGE] I don't think the girl who died was in Mr. Lewis's classroom by accident. I think there are secrets no one wants us to know. Has anyone else heard about him not treating (female) students well?

I stare at the message for a second and then press send. It's blunt, but for once, I don't want to be nuanced. I want someone to tell me I'm wrong.

Or right.

Mom comes home late from the station again, and she brings pizza from Matteo's, which is a clear sign that she's annoyed. She digs around in the fridge for something that counts as a side salad and grumbles, "I can't believe the school doesn't have a plan in place for a smooth transfer to virtual classes. Amateurs."

"I don't mind," I say, grabbing a slice. "I don't think anyone could have planned for this."

She eyes me. "How are you holding up, kid?"

I shrug and smile weakly and stuff my mouth to avoid having to answer.

"Hm." Mom forgoes her quest for a side salad and joins me instead.

When I stay silent, she talks to fill the void. She complains that she saw one of my teachers out shopping instead of preparing lessons. She tells me about the goings-on at the station and how her intern has been navigating his first solo assignment. It's comfortable between us as we share stories and the feeling of home.

By the time we've finished the pizza, I've gathered up my courage, and I set in motion my last bit of information gathering. "Mom? Have you ever heard any stories about Mr. Lewis?"

She stills. "Mr. Lewis, your chemistry teacher? What kind of stories?"

"That he isn't as perfect as people seem to think he is?" I know I need to be clearer, but there's a difference between anonymously asking a question on a message board and asking it out loud, face-to-face with my mother.

She narrows her eyes. "Theo…"

"Stories about him crossing the line with students?" Immediately I add, "Not me. I…heard rumors. It's for our newspaper."

Mom sits back hard. "Rumors about one of your teachers assaulting students? If that's the case, the administration needs to be informed immediately. They have a duty to report and investigate. If they don't, that's a Title IX violation." Her fingers twitch as though she's itching for a pen and notebook. "Who's the Title IX coordinator at Pierce—"

"I don't know if anyone reported anything," I interrupt her.

"Mom, please don't go into problem-solving mode immediately. I'm just trying to figure out what happened."

The more I think about it, the more I can't help but wonder if Mr. Lewis being, well, a member of the Lewis family is part of the reason no one has mentioned this before. More than half of the people in my class have parents who work for Lewis Industries. Lewis Industries invests heavily in the school and in Fenix. They donate to local political campaigns. They're Fenix's version of royalty. Who would dare to get on their bad side?

Mom considers me. "Does this have to do with the fire too? And why you were out the other night?"

I pick at the empty pizza box that stands between us on the dinner table. "Maybe."

Mom's worry radiates off her in waves, but to her credit, she keeps her voice level. "I haven't heard anything from any of the other parents, but—"

"If you're not the first to find out, you're the last. Yeah." She explained that to me once. People have a hard time talking to reporters for all kinds of valid reasons. I frown. "And you shouldn't ask around without a plan. You might spook people who aren't ready to come forward yet."

She hesitates, then says, "You never cease to amaze me, Theo. But you're a *kid*. Some problems aren't yours to shoulder, let alone fix."

I shake my head. "Someone needs to. No offense, but adults make a mess of things as much as teens do. If school isn't safe and the people in charge won't make it so, someone has to fight to make it better. I know you get that."

That's why I trust my mother with this. Other parents would never allow their kids to do what I'm doing. But Mom knows I won't lie to her. I know she trusts me. That makes everything easier, even if she grimaces like she wants a good excuse to tell me *no*. "Don't you have contacts with the local police? You can tell me if you hear something, right?"

"Theo... Mr. Lewis is both powerful and popular. That makes him dangerous. Men like him are all sharp edges, and the people who get too close end up being cut."

I know. "Too many people have been hurt already. I can't fix that, Mom. But I owe it to Eden to find out the truth. All I want to do is tell the story and do it justice. Promise."

I must have said similar things a dozen times during *Puma Press* meetings regarding far less serious subjects. The closest we've ever come to a story with anonymous tips, unnamed sources, and actual consequences was when we tried to report on a cheating scandal in Ms. Strong's sophomore music theory class. And that was three students breaking into her computer to steal a test.

This is real. It *matters*. Sitting across the table from Mom, it feels like we're not just mother and son but two real reporters comparing notes.

Until Mom clears her throat and surreptitiously wipes at her eyes. She reaches across the table to grab my hand and squeezes it so hard it hurts. "If at any point you feel like you're in over your head, you back out, and you come to me. Immediately. No delay. You come to me. If you get into any sort of trouble, I'm your first call." She shakes my hand. "You tell me what you're doing every step of the way. And once your story is done, I'm the first who reads it. Do you *promise* me?"

I squeeze her hand back. "Promise me you'll tell me what you hear too? Please?"

"Deal," she says.

"Deal," I repeat.

CHAPTER FOURTEEN
EDEN

12:55 A.M.

I know enough. My curiosity is sated. It has to be. Time to get back to waiting for Payton on the first floor. I don't want to get involved. I don't want to be involved in *anything* in Fenix anymore.

I don't want to get caught up in anyone's life ever again unless they actively want me to be a part of it. I don't want to be an accidental interloper or an afterthought. I don't want to be the girl who's always in the wrong place at the wrong time.

That's how I explained it to Payton when I confided in her. I'm done being seen as the nuisance who eats the leftovers from the fridge, who gets yelled at for where I leave my bike in the garage or for missing shavings when I clean up from my carvings. I'm done being an interruption in time my mother could be spending with her boyfriend. But I'm not running *away*, I'm running *toward* something.

It doesn't feel like much to ask for home to be a place where you belong, a place that isn't complete unless you're *there*.

I want my home to be a home, not somewhere I happen to live.

"Let me be your home," Payton said.

Those five words held heartbreak and hope, anger and longing.

"Come away with me," I suggested instead.

Being stuck is not for me. Neither is this.

I'm creeping down the stairs when someone laughs.

I recognize it immediately. It's Oakley Walker, unofficial queen of Pierce High School, heir apparent of Lewis Industries—and the girl I had my first crush on when I was a lowly freshman and she was a glamorous sophomore. Not that I think she ever saw me gaping at her whenever she walked by. People usually don't see me.

She used to be friendly with Cameron, and half the school shipped them in some kind of small-town Romeo and Juliet knockoff.

I can't help it. I glance back to look for her. Cameron is no longer in the hallway, but Oakley is walking with her best friend, Kelsey Fink, who would have a solid chance at prom queen if Oakley ever decided to move to Wyvern High. They're coming from the far side of the school, so they must have come in a different way, or they've been wandering around for a while. Probably the latter.

Despite the late hour and the storm, Oakley looks impeccable.

Kelsey doesn't. Her eyes dart back and forth. She's so on edge, she makes *me* nervous. A knit cap is pulled down over her ears, and she and Oakley are both wearing gloves.

"I'm *serious*, Oakley. I'm not sure about this." Kelsey pulls on the hem of her flannel shirt.

I hesitate. I shouldn't. Payton will be here soon.

But I do.

"Kels," Oakley says with a long-suffering sigh. "Come on. It's too late to back out."

"What if we get in trouble?" Kelsey challenges. "What if this doesn't change anything?" She gestures at the classroom and grimaces. "You know who'll be blamed for this, right?"

Oakley stops and grabs Kelsey's shoulders, forcing her friend to look at her. "Cameron knows what he's doing. *I* know what I'm doing. We're not going to back out now."

Kelsey sets her jaw, then looks away.

Oakley reaches out and gently, ever so gently, puts her palm against the side of Kelsey's face. "We all know what we're doing," she repeats. Her voice is tender and barely more than a whisper, but it carries to the stairwell. "We all know who we're doing it for."

I wonder if Kelsey notices that she's leaning into Oakley's hand.

Then she pulls away. "I know, but—"

"He needs to be stopped." Oakley speaks with conviction.

"I *know*," Kelsey says.

"If we don't do it, who will?"

Kelsey puts a bit of distance between herself and Oakley. She shakes her head, laughing bitterly. "No one will stop him. Not the principal. Not the school board. Not your mother. They all stand by and let it happen over and over again." She pushes an errant strand of hair out of her face, and her hand trembles. "How long do you think he's been getting away with this?"

My stomach drops. It doesn't take much imagination to fill in the blanks. I know this conversation. Every girl I know has had it, many of us more than once.

One night after a particularly bad breakup, my mother told me that talking and fighting and screaming together is the closest thing we girls have to the ability to keep each other safe. Even when no one else will listen, we can trust each other with our stories.

I never believed it was that easy. That night, she talked, and I listened.

Two days after that conversation, she and I-think-his-name-was-Bill were back together, and the space for us to talk was gone.

I've been lucky. My mother's boyfriends have never tried anything beyond wandering touches and drunk whispers—and that is still too much.

"I can't stand by," Oakley says. "Can you?"

Counting the doors to where they're standing, I figure they must be talking about Mr. Lewis. The chemistry teacher Cameron assaulted. One of the best teachers in the school, according to everyone. I don't know him well. I've only ever seen him in the hallways.

Kelsey's shoulders drop, and she sighs. "No, you're right," she says. "We need to do this."

She pats the bag she has over her shoulder and looks around. For an instant, I'm certain our gazes meet, though I am tucked into shadow. Pierce High School hides so many of its stories and secrets under the surface, and tonight I happen to be the monster under the bed who can see what's hidden in the darkness.

Oakley jumps when another loud crack of thunder rattles the school.

She yelps again when Kelsey reaches for her arm and pulls her toward the classroom. "Come on, let's go help them."

The safety light dims again, but not before it gives me one last view of Kelsey's twisted face, and her smile is so cold and sharp it scares me.

Her harsh words linger. "We have to take matters into our own hands."

CHAPTER FIFTEEN
PAYTON

TWELVE DAYS AFTER

There are days—rare days, but they do exist—when Dad's the one who cooks. When he sits outside and stares at the basketball hoop as though he's trying to remember himself. There are days when he truly sees me, and it's like bright sun after weeks of snow. He asks me about school. He tells me to get a job and promises that he'll learn to take care of himself.

One day in September, after attending a veterans' meeting at Lewis Industries, Dad cleaned the whole house. When I came home from school, the living room smelled of lemon, and there were no empty beer cans to be seen. He made himself and me a fresh pot of coffee. He downloaded college brochures to share with me, even though I was only a junior and college felt like it was ages away. He told me I should focus on the future and not get stuck in his past. For a whole glorious weekend, he tried to be there for me. His hands shook, and sometimes his gaze wandered, but he tried.

Until Monday morning, when I was preparing to leave for school. He told me I shouldn't go. He told me he needed me to stay. He shook me so hard my ears rang, and I fled. When I came home that afternoon, he'd already made his way through a six-pack.

Still, rare good days do exist.

Today's not one of them. I know it the moment I enter the house.

He sits watching the door, his arms folded. "Where have you been this time?"

At the school, staring at the black scars on the outside of the building, carefully staying away from the police car circling the parking lot. I can't say that, so I settle for, "Out, Dad."

"Don't take that tone with me. I expect you to let me know where you are." Unsteadily, he gets to his feet. "First you stay out all day after going to the school assembly. Then you disappear in the morning and don't come home until after nightfall. Where did you go?"

"I needed to clear my head."

"Do *not* lie to me."

"I'm not!" I keep my voice steady. My expression neutral. I know it doesn't matter, not when he's in this mood.

He corners me. I refuse to flinch. I don't want to be afraid any longer. But my body betrays me. My shoulders tighten, my hands clench into fists, my breathing grows shallow. "You're acting belligerently, and I will not stand for it. Young people need discipline, not aimless running around, causing chaos, destroying town property. Derek said there was another break-in at the crime scene. It's only a matter of time until the police discover who is responsible. If I find out you are involved, I'll make sure you regret it."

I raise my chin, and I wish I could tell him, *You won't.*

Maybe the thought slips out, because he grabs my shoulder, and he holds on tight. "What's that?"

"Nothing. Nothing, Dad."

"Don't talk back to me, Payton Davis, or I will remind you who's in charge here."

"Yes, sir."

"Are your friends tangled up in this?"

"My only friend *died* in that fire." I know I shouldn't needle him, but sometimes I want to. Sometimes I hope I'll get through to him and he'll see through my pain and my fear and my lies.

But his eyes are hard. "That girl destroyed the school. Tell me she didn't make you complicit in her criminal behavior."

I snap. "Just because your friends all deserted you doesn't mean mine are crimin—*aaargh*!"

His grasp tightens.

I don't want to, but I cry out. My knees buckle.

"Unlock your phone," he demands. He reaches for the phone in my pocket. I try to push his hand away, but his grip only tightens.

"There's nothing on it, Dad. What would there be?" I put my hand over my phone, but that only makes him more paranoid.

"As long as you live under my roof, I reserve the right to search your phone and belongings for any suspicious activity."

"I didn't do anything," I repeat.

He glances at his beat-up old laptop that lies charging in the corner of the room, and fear claws at me. Suddenly I'm afraid that Derek saw me at the school. That he told Dad. Even though today I was only there to think. To remember. It won't matter to him. He's already decided I'm guilty of something.

At that thought, something inside me *breaks*. With painfully sharp clarity, I realize that no matter what I do, Dad will never see me as his daughter, as someone to protect. I'll only ever be someone to accuse, doubt, question.

I have to protect myself, even from him.

With that, a cold detachment settles over me. "What do you think I did this time?"

He doesn't notice my change in demeanor. "Some coward posted defamatory statements about good James Lewis on the alumni boards. I already told Derek to investigate. I want to know you're not involved."

Ah, good James Lewis. Who showed up to Eden's funeral as though he had a right to mourn her. Who went back to work as if he isn't a threat to everyone around him.

Pervert. Rapist. Criminal.

I square my shoulders. Then I hold out my phone to Dad. "See for yourself."

I learned to be careful with my phone long ago. I also learned to be smart. I know what he won't find. I know what he will. Because I saved only one set of messages for this exact situation.

"Cameron Jenkins? You have got to be kidding me. What *exactly* is my daughter doing with a delinquent like him?"

Dad's fist slams into the wall next to me.

"I taught you better than that, Payton. That boy deserves to be in prison. Let's see what he has to say, hm? He wants to know how you're feeling after the other night? What did you do with that delinquent boy, Payton?!"

"Does it matter?"

This time, his fist connects with my jaw.

I refuse to cower. I reach up and snatch the phone from his hand. "I'm done listening to you, Dad. I'm done taking care of you. I'm done being your punching bag. I'm *done*."

With everything I have, all my despair and all my pain, I shove him backward, and he's shocked enough to stumble. Shocked enough that I say what I didn't say the night I planned to run.

"Goodbye, Dad."

CHAPTER SIXTEEN
PAYTON

TWELVE DAYS AFTER

"Payton, get back here!"

"Payton, come back!"

"Right now!"

No.

CHAPTER SEVENTEEN
PAYTON

TWELVE DAYS AFTER

I lean against the headstone opposite Eden's grave. Her grave has a temporary marker but no headstone yet. These things take time, apparently.

The ground is covered with small, colorful rocks, decorated with flowers and hearts and stars. I run trembling fingers over one with a miniature horse painted in blue and green.

Then there are the rocks with words. *We miss you. We should have been there for you. We're sorry.*

The same words echo through my head.

I'm sorry.

I miss you.

I failed you.

And,

You would be proud of me for standing up to him. Even if it came too late.

I bring my hand to my jaw, which is tender.

Dad usually knows better than to hit me where it shows. My bruises can almost always be hidden by long shirts and high collars.

My thumb hovers over the screenshot of Eden's last message. I should get rid of it. It's safer to.

I will remember her without it.

She'd want me to keep going and not look back.

Run.

But her message is the only reminder that I tried once. I tried to get out of here. Tried to believe that I deserved better. Once.

Run, Payton.

Trust me.

I do. I pull up my contacts and press Theo's name before I can stop myself. He picks up after the first ring.

"Payton?"

"I need help." I've never said those words before. I've never trusted people other than Eden to show up for me.

But Eden trusted him. And he did tell me I wouldn't have to do this alone. I have to believe him. I need to believe him, because if I don't, there's no one else.

"Where are you? What do you need?" Theo says, ever so simply.

"I'm with Eden."

I can almost hear him nod. "I'm on my way."

A beat before we put away our phones. A choice. I can tell him never mind, I made a mistake. He'll ask questions, but I can avoid those. I've done it before. I've learned to lie to everyone, including myself. I can push people away. I can run before he gets here. He'll follow, but I have time to make myself look good.

That's what I do. That's how I survive.

I drop my phone on the grass.

A little more than a week ago, I thought I had the courage to get away from this town, with its main street that fell into disrepair before the aerospace company repaved it, with its people who spend too much time judging others and not enough helping them, with its claws. Now I need enough courage to stay. A little bit longer, at least.

For Theo. For Eden.

I trace the colorful rocks on her grave. Last summer, I spent most days at Eden's place. We went to the park after dark to play hide-and-seek. We knew that in Fenix, bad things only happened behind closed doors, not out in the open. So we ran through the park, weaved through the trees, hid behind the fountain that Lewis Industries paid for, and laughed.

We hung out and dozed in my car afterward to avoid going home for a while. Eden curled up next to me and ran her fingers through my hair.

When Dad slammed me into a door because I'd forgotten to buy groceries and I ran, she tucked me into her bed and put on a playlist of cheesy songs from all my favorite old romance movies, and we pooled all our money together to order pizza from Matteo's. After dinner, I tugged at her hand—and we danced.

She saw all of me, and she made me believe I could be more.

"I should have listened to you," I whisper. "I should have trusted you."

"Payton?" Theo's hesitant voice comes from the path. I remember how uncomfortable he is amid the headstones.

I get to my feet and sway. Pain stabs through the side of my face, like needles trailing up from my jaw to my ear and head. "I'm here."

He approaches, using his phone as a flashlight. "Oh wow, that's..." He swallows whatever he was going to say.

I see his shock, followed by an emotion that's even harder to bear. Pity.

It weighs me down like an anchor.

Give me anger instead. Rage or compassion, but not pity.

My vision twists again, and Theo steps close, ever so gently placing a hand under my elbow to keep me standing.

I don't flinch. Falling would hurt more.

"Who did this to you?" he asks.

"I..." I don't know how to answer that. "Eden and I both had reasons to escape."

Theo narrows his eyes and understanding sparks. "Your father? Fuck."

"I'm fine. I just need a place to lie low for a while."

His hand is warm and steady. "Don't lie to me, please."

"Then don't look at me like I'm vulnerable," I snap. "I can't carry your sorrow too."

To my shock, Theo nods. "You're right. I'm sorry. I hate that this happened to you. It's not fair, and you don't deserve it."

I know, I could tell him. But he asked me not to lie to him. It's a hard habit to shake.

I have told him half truths. I've told him hidden truths. I'm afraid that if I tell him the whole truth, I'll lose him too.

That realization shocks me. When we were last here, I only wanted him to ask the right questions, to be the voice of reason Fenix could trust. I didn't expect more from him. In fact, I thought I'd prefer it if he hated me.

But hate is as hard to carry as pity. Besides, I have enough of it for the both of us.

"You can spend the night at my place," he continues. "Mom is still at work, but she won't mind."

"Are you sure?"

"Will it get you into more trouble?"

"Probably." I bring my fingers to my jaw. But then I look at him, *really* look at him. "But I know I'll be safe tonight."

That, at least, isn't a lie.

—

Two hours later, I'm sitting on Theo's bed, wearing an oversize T-shirt, looking at the newspaper articles on the walls. He got takeout. Noodles, because it hurts to chew. It's the best food I've had in a while. At home, we can't afford takeout. The money we have barely covers rent, utilities, food, and beer. And it's not like I have savings or spending money. I can't go to school, deal with and take care of Dad, and hold more than a summer job. So I make do with Dad's rare and infrequent allowances and the cards with cash that Mom sends whenever she remembers I exist. The last one—for my sixteenth birthday—said *Happy 14th!* and had a picture from some animated series I've never watched. The fifty bucks went to my car. A fixer-upper, because Dad thought it would teach me independence. A way for me to get back and forth from school easily. A way to do the shopping and drive him to VA appointments.

The car may fall apart and it's held together with duct tape, but he doesn't know quite how much freedom it gives me.

I consider texting Dad to let him know I'm staying with a friend before I realize I don't owe him my whereabouts. I don't plan to go home anymore. Not to stay.

I used to text when I stayed over at Eden's place. He never asked for specifics, so he couldn't get angry that I didn't tell him where I was.

Those nights, Eden and I would share her bed. Now, Theo has settled himself on the floor with blankets and a spare pillow.

"Thank you," I say softly.

He smiles. "Of course. Isn't this what friends are for?"

"Are we friends?" I ask.

I'm growing more used to Theo's pauses and careful considerations. After a moment, he responds, "I'd like to think so. If nothing else, the enemy of my enemy is my friend, right?"

My mouth feels dry. "Who's the enemy?"

"The fire. Mr. Lewis. The people who were inside the school that night." He hesitates, then says quietly, "The best friend of my best friend is a friend too. Even if Eden was lousy at sharing."

I plaster on a smile in case he's looking at me. The words both warm and chill me. "I'd like to be friends."

"Me too." Theo shifts onto his back, folding his arms behind his head. He stares up at a framed horror comic on the wall. "Between the two of us, we can hold space for her."

"Remember her? Like the art class did?" I don't think she would ever have expected that. I wish she'd known how much they cared.

"Bring her justice."

I mirror Theo. My left arm screams in pain when I curl it behind my head. The curtains in front of his open window sway gently in the breeze. "Speaking of justice, did you post that message about Mr. Lewis on the Puma Boards today?"

He shifts and props his head up on his hand, looking at me. "How do you know about that?"

I shrug. I fight to keep my voice steady. "Did anyone share anything helpful?"

"Maybe. There were two replies that stood out to me." Theo produces his phone from underneath his pillow and unlocks it. He holds it out to me. "I took screenshots in case the post got deleted. Here."

I don't take the phone. I can't make myself move. Fear sparks through me, and suddenly I'm afraid of what he'll find. I'm afraid of what I'll read.

Theo stares at me with dark eyes and a sad smile. "Go on," he says, mistaking my hesitation for concern. "I trust you."

I pick at one of my cuticles, slowly and meticulously peeling away the skin until it hurts. "You shouldn't."

"Why not?"

It's such a simple question that I can't help but answer. "Because I lie. I lie to survive. I lie to you so you won't hate me. I lie and tell people I'm fine. You shouldn't trust me because I don't deserve it."

To Theo's credit, he doesn't tell me I'm wrong. Instead, he puts down the phone and considers what I'm saying.

"It's not the same thing, but when my dad died, I told everyone I wasn't hurting. I felt like I was burning up from the inside out, and it frightened me to admit it, because that would make his passing real. It was easier to ignore the pain. But it wasn't just the grief I was pushing away—it was everyone and everything else too. Pain. Anger. Joy. Happiness."

I turn my head to face him. "What changed?"

He wiggles his fingers. "I broke my wrist, and I couldn't feel it. So I didn't tell anyone. Until Mom came home from work and freaked out. She dragged me to a doctor and then to a therapist. The therapist helped me open up, connect with my feelings. She taught me to approach grief as a friend instead of an enemy, and it helped. But it took time—a lot of time. So what I'm saying is, I understand that it'll take time for you too."

That's not why I'm lying.

That's not why I'm scared.

It's not the same thing.

He holds out the phone to me again.

I wince. "Thank you."

I take the phone and curl up with the dimly lit screen. There are two screenshots, and I read both the messages and the messages between the lines.

> [MESSAGE] I can't say I know what you're talking about, but if I did, I'd say it's lonely, carrying this secret with you. No one should have to deal with that. No one should have to go through it, especially not when abuse comes from people you're supposed to be able to trust.

And:

> [MESSAGE] I don't know why you're bringing this up now. Or at all. There's nothing to say. Everyone knows that Mr. Lewis is the perfect teacher and to think or say otherwise is unbelievable. Trust me.

[MESSAGE] I tried.

The usernames are ones I don't recognize.

I read the messages over and over again, and a whirlwind of emotions tears through me. Regret. Guilt. Hope.

Relief.

"You see it too, right?" Theo asks, staring at me intently. "What they *aren't* saying?"

I do.

"Does this mean you believe the graffiti in the classroom? Do you believe that Mr. Lewis assaulted students?" I try to keep my voice flat so Theo won't be able to tell how much his answer matters to me.

"I don't want to," he admits. "But... yes, I do."

"Good," I whisper.

I hand him his phone. I turn my head away. And I cry quietly so that Theo doesn't hear me.

For the first time since Eden died, I don't feel alone.

———

It's early. I blink against the sunlight and remember where I am. Theo's window looks out over the same tree as Eden's window, but his room smells different. It smells of ink and sweat and cologne. It smells of *boy*.

Dad will kill me if he ever finds out I was here.

The floorboards creak.

Without turning my head and indicating I'm awake, I try to figure out what's happening. Theo grabs a hoodie from his cluttered desk, puts it on, and slips out the door. It squeaks when he pulls it shut behind him.

I sit up and swing my legs over the side of the bed. Shirts and hoodies are draped haphazardly over his chair. I read the headlines on the walls and look at the old photos that line Theo's desk. One is of his mother at a military base. The picture of a tall, dark-haired man and a blond kid has to be of Theo and his father.

In front of the picture is a sparkly stone. Next to it, an award for best middle school newspaper article, as well as a wooden quill and inkwell.

My heart stutters when I see Eden's apple charm on the bedside table. Theo must have put it there for me.

I pick it up gently. I can feel the love Eden put in this gift. I tie it around my neck. I still don't feel like I deserve it, but I can wear it here, where Dad won't have questions.

It's strange, this freedom.

This room feels lived in, in a way that mine doesn't anymore.

Theo can keep all his meaningful belongings out. No one will break them or throw them away.

This is what Eden talked about: finding a place to belong. A place where you fit instead of being too much or not enough.

Raised voices drift up from downstairs, and a shudder goes through me. I crack open Theo's bedroom door.

Instead of anger, I hear laughter.

I grab one of Theo's hoodies too, because my arms feel naked and bruised without long sleeves to cover them, and quietly sneak out of the room to listen.

"It's early, Theo. I haven't even had coffee." Down the stairs, Mrs. Robinson's words are thick with sleep.

Theo, on the other hand, sounds entirely too awake. "How do you protect your sources, Mom? What if, by exposing injustice, you'll harm others who deserve to be protected?"

"Why are you springing this on me now? Did you find any evidence in your investigation?"

"No. Maybe. Not yet. But I didn't really sleep," Theo admits. "Payton needed a place to stay, and the floor isn't particularly comfortable."

His words are met with silence.

"Theodore Robinson."

Theo clears his throat uncomfortably. "Yes?"

"First of all..." His mother sighs loudly enough that I can hear it upstairs. "First of all, your question is both ethically and legally complicated. The station has a counsel, but a school newspaper doesn't. We *are* talking about the school newspaper, right?"

"You said you trusted me."

"God, Theo, I do. You're a smart and caring, and I couldn't be prouder of the man you're turning into, but I also told you I want you to be safe."

"Yes, but—"

"And I said absolutely *nothing* about girls sleeping over in your bed."

My cheeks heat, and I take a step back, hoping not to make the floorboards creak. It may be my first time in this house, but if I have one skill, it is being silent when I need to be silent.

"I just said I slept on the floor! You're making it sound like I—like I—like I shared the bed with her!"

I feel hot and uncomfortable, and laughter bubbles in my chest at the same time. By the sound of it, Theo is as embarrassed as I am.

"Besides, she needed a safe place."

I hold my breath, scared he'll say something more.

I hope he will, and I hope he won't.

He doesn't.

Theo's mother stays silent too.

I imagine her glaring at him. Or trying not to laugh. Dad would have exploded long before the conversation even got to this point, and Eden's mother would have walked away halfway through. I wonder if this is what it feels like to be cared for and trusted.

I've never wished that Mom had stayed. That Dad was different. Because she didn't. He isn't. You can't change your family. You can't wish your home away simply because you don't like it.

Still, I wonder what it would feel like for him to put me first and want to protect me. Maybe, in his own twisted way, he does, but that's not good enough. I want the father who shot hoops with me, who made me laugh, who I could confide in, who soothed my pain instead of causing it.

Maybe if more adults trusted us and listened to us, things would be very different now.

There's tenderness and exasperation in Mrs. Robinson's voice when she says, "We're going to have a long conversation about this after I've had my coffee and you've fed that girl some breakfast. Then we'll figure out what to do next."

"Yes, Mom."

"Insolent brat. I'm proud of you."

"I love you."

When Theo walks back up the stairs, I'm rooted to the spot. Underneath his oversize hoodie, I feel fragile.

Maybe he sees it, because he takes a gentle step forward and holds out his arms. When I nod, he wraps them around me and holds me close.

"Your mom seems great," I whisper.

He laughs and his whole chest rumbles. "She is."

"I'm jealous," I admit.

He only holds me tighter. "You're here, and you're safe. You can stay as long as you need to. I promise."

"Eden was right to trust you," I say into his shoulder, and I feel his breath catch.

Loss upon loss. Grief upon grief. Just for a moment, Theo circumvents all my walls like they don't exist and makes me feel like I belong. Then I disentangle myself from his grasp. "And you were right too."

He bites his lip. "About what?"

"About telling the truth together."

I take a deep breath. Theo's on the right path now. Once the story is out there, they won't be able to ignore it. Not again. Never again.

In the end, that's all we've ever wanted.

My heart hammers frantically. "I know where to start."

CHAPTER EIGHTEEN
PAYTON

THIRTEEN DAYS AFTER

I have to go." I hold out Theo's hoodie to him.

Theo frowns. He accepts the hoodie reluctantly. "I thought you just said—"

"Only for a little while. I have to go home first."

"Home?"

"I don't intend to stay." Nor am I planning to go there immediately. But I have to go back. One last time, to get what I need, and Dad shouldn't see me wearing someone else's clothes.

Theo's gaze turns inward, as if he's mentally taking inventory of the risks and wondering if there are any benefits. "I don't understand why you've stayed with your father at all," he says frankly. "He doesn't deserve you."

"He doesn't." A hint of anger at Theo's assumptions slithers through me, and the truth slips out. After our last fight, I started to believe it too. He *doesn't* deserve me. "But he's still my father." Not even Eden got that completely. "If I stay away, no one will take care of him. No one will make sure he eats. He'll be all alone. Besides, he's had time to calm down."

Theo doesn't say anything.

"Dad wasn't always like this," I continue, part of me feeling the need to defend him despite everything. Maybe I always will. "It's the alcohol and the pain. He's sick. He's not…evil. Some days he's *good*. Other days, I hope he can be."

Theo doesn't push harder than that, but I see the sorrow in his eyes. The difference is, this time it doesn't read like judgment, only regret that he can't help me more. "Is there anything I can do for you?"

I nod and look out his window at Eden's room. Someone—probably her mother—has closed the curtains, and for a brief moment, it makes me feel like I'm in two places at once. Like there's a part of me there with Eden, hidden away from the rest of the world. An imprint of the time we shared together, safe in our own small universe. A memory. Or just…me. Holding her. Feeling her skin against mine. Feeling her breath on my shoulder and her fingers in my hair and her love around me.

Despite everything, she always believed the world could be better, but the only way it can be is if we make it so. I tried to make a difference before. This time, I hope I can get it right.

"When I get back," I say slowly, "and I *will* come back, make me tell you the one story about Eden you haven't heard yet, and don't let me stop until I'm done. Just give me today to get ready."

One more day to get my affairs in order. One more day to talk to the people I've ignored. One more day to scrape together my fragmented bits of courage before I tell my story.

Our story.

I walk down the stairs and out the door. I get in my car and drive. Away from this neighborhood with its small but comfortable houses. To the north, where the streets are wider, the lawns bigger, the houses colder. These houses stand far enough apart that a tree wouldn't span the gap between two of them, but they're all connected in their own way.

Captain Steadman, Dad's former boss, lives on the north side of Fenix. Captain Steadman and his wife invited us over for dinner when Dad got out of the hospital. It was merely a courtesy, but Mrs. Steadman served us the fanciest home-cooked meal I've ever had, with multiple courses and different sets of cutlery for each. She told me that her twin daughters had gone to Pierce High School and that one of them was the cheer captain and the other was a star student. She said she hoped I had girls like that to look up to. She told me that every girl needs other girls to set examples for them, to be their confidantes and their sisters, whether related by blood or not.

I nodded politely. Even at nine years old, all I could think was that girls who grew up on the north side of town lived different lives from the girls I played with in our neighborhood.

I thought none of them would ever see me.

I was wrong, of course.

One of them did. She matched my anger and my pain, and she saw me. She told me we could make a difference in this town that is supported by Lewis Industries. I was foolish enough to believe her.

I pull into the driveway of a large white house with wisteria growing along the walls. Then I get out and knock on Kelsey Fink's front door.

CHAPTER NINETEEN
EDEN

12:57 A.M.

The storm outside worsens. If it goes on much longer, the roads will flood again, and we'll be stuck here. I check my phone, and the lack of reception bars makes me want to fling it across the hallway in a fit of anger.

I hate this town.

I hate how many of us hurt and feel trapped here.

The atmosphere inside the school feels charged as Oakley and Kelsey walk to Mr. Lewis's classroom. I don't want to draw attention to myself, so I can't move until they're inside. I have to get back to the parking lot. Payton will be waiting for me.

Oakley announces, "We brought more paint."

I hear the rumble of Cameron's voice, but I can't make out what he says.

Then a fourth person speaks up. "Good, I was running out."

I freeze.

My breath catches. Even my heart trips.

I'd recognize her voice *anywhere*.

I forget about being quiet. I cross the hallway.

When the lights flicker back on, I'm in the doorway of Mr. Lewis's chemistry lab.

There are regular desks here as well as lab tables with Bunsen burners and testing equipment. The shelves along the walls hold glass beakers, flasks, bottles, and test tubes, some empty, some filled with different-colored liquids. A laminated poster of the periodic table hangs on the far wall, and below it, there's another set of shelves with more equipment. The room smells off. Do chemistry labs always smell a bit like gas?

Perhaps it's the spray paint. All of the walls and several of the desks are covered in bloodred graffiti. Cameron is upending chairs and clearing space. Kelsey and Oakley are hard at work.

Criminal.

Pervert.

Rapist.

The red bleeds across the room. Mr. Lewis's papers have been tossed to the floor, and his desk is covered in spray paint. Cameron toys with his lighter.

I see all of it, and yet none of it matters, because there is Payton.

Payton, who is supposed to be waiting for me outside.

Payton, one of my best friends.

Payton doesn't see me. She's focused on spraying *pervert* on the linoleum floor.

I clear my throat, and the effect is immediate. Everyone stops and turns.

"Fuck, what is *she* doing here?" says Kelsey.

"What *are* you doing here?" demands Oakley.

But there's nothing from Payton, the girl I'm head-over-heels in love with. Her lips are drawn into a tight line, and red flecks of paint dot her hand and arm. She stares at me, hurt and furious.

CHAPTER TWENTY
KELSEY

SEVEN MONTHS BEFORE

Whenever I close my eyes, I see that wad of gum.

Whenever someone touches me, I freeze up.

I try to put my thoughts into words, but I struggle. I fade.

After a week of sleepless nights, not even my makeup can conceal the shadows under my eyes, and my chest feels hollow.

I know I should speak up. I know I should say something, *anything*, to someone, *anyone*. But there are a thousand ways in which you can tell a story—and a thousand ways in which you can fail.

"I—I want to speak to Principal Young."

After a week, I end up at the principal's office first thing in the morning. Her door is closed. Her secretary, Mrs. Matthews, squints at me through narrow glasses. "Ms. Fink, is it? She's not in today, but if you tell me what it's about, I'll see what I can do for you."

I grip the hem of my shirt. "I...I'd rather not."

"I can't schedule a meeting without knowing what it's about," she says, without mercy.

"Please? It's important."

Mrs. Matthews sighs deeply. "Ms. Fink, every student thinks they're important. It's my job to separate the wheat from the chaff, so to speak. We would never get anything done around here otherwise."

"I..."

"Speak up!"

I flinch. "It's about Mr. Lewis."

"James? If you want to transfer into one of his classes, there's a waiting list. Goodness knows, I love that man like my own son, but he makes life hard on the administration—" She shakes her head with a fond smile.

My stomach drops. The moment slips away from me—or maybe it was never there at all. "It's not that. It's...He...I..."

Mrs. Matthews turns to get a folder from her filing cabinet. "Ms. Fink, the work is piling up. I suggest you come back when you're ready to share what's so important to you."

"I don't want to... I want to talk to Principal Young about Mr. Lewis. He...last week..." I take a deep breath, and I push the words out with all my might. "He put his hand on my leg."

That's not all.

Of course it isn't.

But it's a start.

She has to hear me.

She *has* to.

The school secretary stills. She turns to me, and a look of distaste crosses her face. As if I've offended her.

"Ah," she says. She shuffles some of the papers on her desk. "Ms. Fink, listen to me. James—Mr. Lewis—is a good man. He's responsible for helping students get scholarships. He's responsible for finding students work. I don't believe he meant to make you uncomfortable. But good men can get burned by careless words like yours. I need you to understand that."

An emptiness opens up inside my stomach. I wonder if she picked those words on purpose.

I don't believe he would.

"Now, if you want me to, I will talk to him personally," she says, as if that's a solution. As if it's *enough*. "But it's best we agree that you misunderstood his intentions, don't you think?"

I don't believe he would.

Mr. Lewis's voice creeps into the back of my head.

Don't forget you came to me. You needed my help.

It would be my word against his.

Who would believe him?

Who would believe me?

"Ms. Fink?"

"I—yeah. Never mind. It's nothing."

"I do believe you have to get to class."

CHAPTER TWENTY-ONE
KELSEY

SIX MONTHS BEFORE

Senior year is unforgettable, but not in the way I hoped. Once you start fragmenting, all that's left are the broken pieces. I feel different, less connected, but those first days pass in a blur. The weekend comes and goes, and I barely realize it.

Freddie's birthday arrives, and I swing by Oakley's to have cake. I don't remember the taste. I don't remember if I brought him a present.

A week later, I freak out while I'm changing clothes for gym. I forget how to breathe. My head pounds.

Coach Mills sends Zanna with me to the nurse's office. I tell her it's not necessary, it's just stress, but she insists. I cling to the walls as much as possible. It's all I can do not to run away from Zanna. Everything about her is too familiar.

She doesn't know how I feel, of course. She's worried. She tries to distract me by asking me about volunteering at the shelter and my weekend plans. When I don't react, she hesitates. "It *is* just stress, isn't it?"

"Yeah, it's…" Everything hurts. "Today's not a good day."

Sympathy flickers across her features. "I know you've been struggling with chemistry. You had a test this morning, didn't you? Did Dad help?"

Bile rises up in my throat. When I shrug, she drapes her arm over my shoulders and squeezes. "I know he's my dad, but you can trust me. I've got your back."

The words wrap around my chest like barbed wire, and I pull away from her.

She's not quite fast enough to mask the flash of hurt on her face.

"I'm sorry," I whisper.

I tell Mrs. Nash, the nurse, that it's stress too. I need a moment to collect myself. She doesn't have to call my parents. And because I'm the perfect student, she doesn't.

Instead, she sends Zanna back to PE and gives me a pass for the remainder of the period.

She gets me a cup of tea and some painkillers for my headache, and I stare at myself in the mirror. I don't recognize the person who looks back at me.

After I spend a few minutes alone, Mrs. Nash comes to check on me. "Has this happened before?" she asks gently.

"I..." I force myself to smile. "No. It hasn't. Like I said, just stress."

She doesn't seem entirely convinced. "If it happens again, come to me, okay? You can trust me."

I thought I could trust Mr. Lewis too.

I promise I believe her.

It's a lie.

Instead, I simply fade further.

The fall colors are less vibrant than usual. Oakley's voice when she calls out to me or jokes about our Halloween plans is fainter. The air is heavier too. I go through the motions. I go to school early. I finish my homework when I get home. Sometimes I go to Oakley's house. I go riding on Thursday evenings and Saturdays. I volunteer at the animal shelter on Sundays. Every time I pass the sign at the entrance—a proud SPONSORED BY LEWIS INDUSTRIES—something inside me grows colder. Every other Friday afternoon, Cameron and I go running in the park.

Rinse, repeat.

When I stumble during a run, Cameron catches my arm. I recoil.

Instead of doing better at tests, I do worse. I start to fail all my classes except chemistry. Mr. Lewis makes sure of that.

The horses and the animals at the shelter become restless and easily spooked when I'm around, because I am restless and easily spooked. But no one seems to realize anything is different, that anything is wrong. Dad notices my grades, but to my surprise he calls it senioritis. He still lectures me and tells me he expects me to do better, but it doesn't feel like the end of the world. I wonder why I ever felt like it would.

How do you tell your friends and family, the people who are the most important parts of you, that you feel broken? How do you get them to believe the truth when all you have are careless words?

The more time passes, the more I don't know how to trust my own judgment. Did I say something to make Mr. Lewis believe I wanted this? Why me? Did I misinterpret the situation? Could I have done something? Why didn't I? Why can't I go back to the person I was before?

CHAPTER TWENTY-TWO
KELSEY

SIX MONTHS BEFORE

I try and fail again.

One Sunday, weeks after the assault, I make a plan to talk to my parents. I practice in front of the mirror. I wait until they get home from church. They gave me the choice to attend when I started high school, and unlike my perfect sister, I decided against it. Our church didn't feel like a place where I belonged. But we kept the Sunday tradition where Mom and Dad and I have coffee together afterward.

My heart flutters nervously. My palms are sweaty.

The car pulls into the driveway, and the doors slam shut. Mom's on the phone, and Dad's gesticulating wildly.

They don't see me standing in the middle of the living room when they enter, and the floor sways beneath me.

"Alice, *listen to me*. You are not a quitter. We'll find a solution, but dropping out is not it," says Mom. "Come home for Thanksgiving. We'll talk about it then. Do *not* do anything rash."

Dad fidgets with his Lewis Industries key chain, then drops the car keys in a bowl, where they rattle loudly. Mom drops her purse, then herself, onto the couch. Her face is blotchy.

"*No*," she says. "Columbia is your dream school, and we've already paid tuition for the semester. Go to your classes and keep up your grades. That's the deal." Her voice climbs higher. "Your dad and I are working very hard to give you this opportunity. We are doing everything we can to ensure that you and your sister won't be drowning in debt. I don't think completing your semester and getting these credits is too much to ask."

Alice foolishly presses on. I don't know what she says exactly, but she might as well have insulted generations of our family and brushed off all the sacrifices they made to get us here. Mom's face contorts with anger, and nothing Alice says can make it better. There's nothing I can say that won't make it worse.

"At least your sister is still working hard," Mom informs Alice, and that's when I back into the kitchen. I don't want to get dragged into this. Especially since I'm failing too. "She isn't constantly dealing with new *drama*."

I press my fingers into the palms of my hands, feeling smaller by the second.

Alice's reply is loud enough that I can hear her voice—though not her exact words—crackle through the phone.

Dad winces.

Mom starts to cry. Not her angry tears, but tears of genuine concern and disappointment.

I back away.

Dad catches my eye, and he must notice my hands are trembling. He must notice how pale I am. He must see that I'm not okay either, that I need him too.

Help me. Please.

He doesn't.

He sighs. "Whatever it is, can it wait?"

No, Dad.

It can't.

I breathe in and then out again. "Sure."

Mom cradles a pillow in her lap, staring into nothingness.

Dad takes the phone from her, covering the receiver with his hand. He raises his eyebrows in my direction.

I should ask about Alice. He expects me to.

I swallow and shake my head and leave them be.

Here's the truth about the moments that change you: You rarely see them coming. Sometimes you don't even notice how much they've changed you until long after they've passed.

And somewhere along the line, you lose yourself.

[MESSAGE TO: PUMA@SECRET.CO
MESSAGE FROM: SIERRA MORALES]

It's not that I didn't tell anyone. I tried to tell someone at a house party once. I saw another girl I knew who was being tutored by Mr. Lewis. So I approached her. I didn't know how to bring it up, but I thought we were in the same situation. So we should talk, right?

She looked at me like I was...*strange*. In that moment, when I wasn't sure what she was going to say, it felt like the loud music faded, rivers of sweat ran down my back, and I thought I was going to throw up. I didn't want her to experience what I had, but I'd hoped she would recognize me, validate me.

She only shook her head and backed away.

Turns out some tutoring sessions were just that. I asked myself: Was it me? *Why* was it me? Was this girl lying to me? Or did he plan actual tutoring lessons for plausible deniability?

It made me sick all over again. As far as I'm aware, he's been doing this for more than a decade.

CHAPTER TWENTY-THREE
KELSEY

SIX MONTHS BEFORE

By the time Halloween rolls around, I've perfected the art of pretending. We're going with a vampire theme instead of dressing as witches, an homage to our original vampire night, and Oakley and Zanna thought the three of us should get large bat costumes—wing-shaped dresses over dark leggings—and that Cameron should be covered in glitter. We're all meeting at Oakley's house to go to the dance that Lewis Industries organized for Fenix's teens in the park tonight while Mrs. Lewis-Walker takes Oakley's brother trick-or-treating.

Once I've changed, I look at myself in the large mirror in Oakley's bedroom.

Zanna twirls to show off her wings. High school swimming season starts next week, which means she's in her element. She's *happy*.

Her elbow brushes mine, and I flinch.

She frowns. "What's wrong? Are you hurt?"

We've had too many moments like this lately. Moments where she worries and fusses over me, and every time I turn away.

I shake my head. "It's nothing. No big deal."

Her frown deepens. "Kels, you haven't looked at me in *weeks*," she accuses. "Are you sure you're okay?"

I *can't* look at her. I can hardly stand to be in the same room as her. I know that's not her fault. I try to see her for who she is: ambitious, strong, ride-or-die for us. But I only see her for *what* she is. His daughter. Mr. Lewis's.

He's her *dad*.

A cowardly part of me hopes swim season will pull us apart. It happens, doesn't it? One day you're friends, and the next you've drifted in different directions.

Zanna steps in front of me, into my field of vision, and her eyes are the exact same shade of sapphire blue as her dad's, and suddenly I wonder if he'll be one of the supervising adults at the dance tonight. I don't want him to see me. I don't want his eyes to linger on me. It physically hurts. I take a step back. My breath catches. I don't want to be here. I don't want to go to the party tonight.

"I'm done with dressing up," I snap. "It's childish."

"You were the one to suggest it!" In the mirror, Oakley frowns, her eyes bright underneath the goth makeup she's wearing for the occasion. "Don't think we haven't noticed you've been quiet," she says. "Are you still worried about your grades? I've had to pick up my pace too. Senior year is hard for all of us."

"Besides, I thought you said Dad helped you." Zanna sighs. She turns away from me. She plops down on Oakley's bed and spreads her bat wings across the pillows. She plucks a little enamel spider pin from Oakley's collection of accessories and pins it to her dress. "Do you want to talk about it?"

"No!"

I can't. I didn't think they'd noticed I'd changed, and somehow that makes it worse. That I can't even pretend to be the person I was before feels like failure.

I tear off my bat costume and grab my hoodie from where it's lying across Oakley's desk chair.

Zanna stares at me, wide-eyed.

Oakley bites her lip. "Kels…"

I want to be here and belong with them, but at the end of the day, they're not just my friends. They're Mr. Lewis's family. How do I tell my best friends that this person they love and trust hurt me? How can I ask them to believe me and stand by me?

It's too much.

"I can't do this anymore," I snap. "I'm sorry."

I rush from Oakley's room before they can follow me. I turn off my phone, because it's not like anyone expects me home tonight, and

I run past haunted houses, past kids in all kinds of costumes, past the road that leads to my house.

I find myself—of all places—at Pierce High School. By now it's dark, and the only sign of Halloween is the toilet paper that covers the entrance. The field where we usually share lunch is pitch black and empty.

My lungs burn, and I double over, trying to catch my breath. As soon as I stop moving, my legs start shaking from the exertion. I usually drive to school.

I stumble toward our picnic table and sag down. I lay my head on folded arms and wish the world would disappear.

I don't know how to continue when everything hurts all the time.

Senior year wasn't meant to be like this.

—

Enough time has passed that I've grown cold all over when I hear footsteps.

My neck is stiff. My shoulders ache. I flinch at the sound of my name.

"Kelsey?" Cameron sits down next to me. His skin glitters despite the dim light and his thick hoodie. "Oakley told me what happened. She and Zanna are freaking out. They didn't know where to find you. It took me an hour, which is impressive in this hellhole of a place."

"I'm sorry I tore you away from the dance," I say. "I didn't mean to."

He sighs, air whistling through the small gap between his front teeth, like he's offended. "*Kelsey Fink.* You're more important to me than a dance."

I wrap my arms around my knees in response.

"We're worried about you." He pulls his phone out of his pocket and opens the group chat, but I place my hand over the screen before he can type anything.

"Tell them I'm okay, but not where I am, please."

He frowns. "Oakley is losing her damn mind."

She's going to want an explanation. Maybe... What if I explain it to Oakley? Not Oakley and Zanna, just Oakley? And Cameron came to look for me. He cares. I know he does.

I make a snap decision that I know I won't be able to undo. It's not fair, but ... "She can know. Just—not Zanna, okay?"

Cameron's frown deepens, but he nods. "Fine. Your choice."

He shows me the screen as he types out a message to the girls that I'm okay. Immediately after, he sends a private message to Oakley, asking her to come—and to come alone.

She replies within seconds. She's on her way. Cameron doesn't say what he tells Zanna, and I don't ask.

He puts his phone away and opens his arms.

I lean into him. He's warm.

"Did something happen with Zanna?" he asks.

I shake my head.

I don't know what to tell them yet. I don't know *how* to tell them yet. But when Oakley arrives twenty minutes later and wraps her arms around me, I feel safer than I have in weeks.

"You absolute fool," Oakley says, gently punching my arm. She doesn't even seem jealous that Cameron found me first. "You can't run away and turn off your phone and not tell us what's going on. I was *worried*!" She sounds like her mother when she rants like this, but I would never tell her that. "What if you got hit by a car? What if you planned to jump off a bridge or something? What if—" Her voice catches with emotion.

In that moment between breaths, with Cameron's arm heavy around my shoulders and Oakley's hands covering mine, I find careful words.

I try, and I don't fail. "Mr. Lewis assaulted me."

Cameron and Oakley freeze, and I curl up again.

I brace for doubt and cling to hope.

Cameron tenses, his arm around my shoulders tightening.

Oakley is the first to speak. "He did *what*." It's not a question. It's a cry of rage disguised as a sentence. She wraps her arms around me again. "Oh fuck. *Fuck*. I'm sorry. I—*fuck*."

"Bastard," is all Cameron says.

"You believe me?"

"Yes!" they chorus, as if the idea that they wouldn't is offensive, and I love them for it.

I *breathe*. For the first time in weeks, I breathe.

"Fuck!" Oakley says again.

"When did this happen?" Cameron asks. His voice is flat.

Now that I've said the first part, it's easier to share bits of the rest.

"When I went to ask him for extra credit." I stare off into the distance without seeing it. "He locked the door and…" My vision blurs. "He *touched* me." My cheeks burn. "I don't remember saying no. I—"

"He's your *teacher*," Oakley interrupts me fiercely. "He's a grown man. He shouldn't touch you. Nothing about this is your fault."

"But—"

"Nothing," she repeats, hugging me. "He's wrong. A teacher touching any student is wrong. It doesn't matter what you said or didn't say."

I turn to face her, and despite the tears on her cheeks, her eyes are blazing. "He never should have touched you," she says, enunciating clearly. "It's not your fault."

I sob.

"I'll murder him," Cameron says quietly.

Oakley pales. "I made that terrible comment about him being a silver fox. Is that why you didn't tell us? Fuck, Kels, you know I didn't mean that. I'm so sorry."

"I didn't know how to tell you," I admit. "He's your *uncle*. He's Zanna's *dad*."

She pauses as if she completely forgot about that, and then she laughs dismissively. "I don't care who he is—he's a pervert. Men are the worst. No offense, Cam."

He looks grim. "None taken."

"Do you want me to tell my mother? He should be arrested. She could probably sic the feds on him or something."

"He's her brother. I don't want…" My voice trails off. I don't want her to know before my parents do. I don't want to have to find the words to tell everyone. I don't want to face Zanna. Or the rest of the school. Or the person in the mirror I don't recognize anymore. "I don't want her to not believe me."

I turn to Cameron. "Please don't murder him. I need you here, not in jail."

Cameron's jaw is set, and he radiates fury. He looks at me like there's no one else in the world. "I'll do whatever I can to help you, Kels. Anything. Name it and I'll do it."

"Don't do anything rash." I'm not sure he won't. Because he's Cameron. That's how he is. "I don't know what to do from here. But I'm glad I told you."

We're a silent tangle of arms and comfort.

Then Oakley says quietly, "You *should* tell someone. Your parents. The school. The police."

"Yeah." I think about how I tried to have those conversations. "Maybe."

If I'm honest, I'm not ready to face that kind of dismissal again.

"I'll help you. We'll both do whatever you need us to do."

"Just be there for me?" I ask softly.

I feel her nod. Both of them.

"Always," she says.

"Always," he agrees.

Something curled up tight inside me unwinds.

For the first time since I walked into Mr. Lewis's classroom, I don't feel quite so alone.

CHAPTER TWENTY-FOUR
KELSEY

FIVE MONTHS BEFORE

We don't go to the Halloween party that night. Instead we stick together all weekend. We watch movies. We get pizza. The tight band around my chest loosens a little. Like maybe, with my two best friends by my side, things will get better. Maybe I'll find the words I need to tell others too.

But sharing doesn't get easier because you've done it once.

So many girls get assaulted and raped. So many boys and nonbinary students. But for some reason, that doesn't make it easier to talk about it.

Guilt and shame are twin emotions that aren't easier to carry because they're common. If you're not careful, they grow barbs and edges, and they morph into anger.

The anger comes on gradually. At least it does for me. For Cameron, it is immediate.

The Monday after Halloween weekend, Cameron and I arrive at school at the same time, but to my surprise, he doesn't acknowledge me. He legs it inside, hands balled into fists. I don't think he even sees me. He pushes through the crowd and disappears down the hall.

I freeze as realization hits me: Cameron is going to do something rash. After I explicitly told him not to.

I run through clusters of students, ignoring the grumbled protests and the snippy comments. One of the football players stops to shout something to a friend, and I slam into his shoulder. The closeness of people *everywhere* makes me feel faint, but I duck and swerve.

I know where Cam's going. I dash up the staircase to the second floor where the STEM classrooms and labs are.

Aaliyah, who takes first-period AP World History with me, calls my name from her locker. Something about our group assignment. I wave her off.

By the time I see him again, Cameron is already at Mr. Lewis's door.

"Cameron!"

He glances over his shoulder and shakes his head, then steps into the room and closes the door behind him.

I sprint. Like I can stop him. Like I can follow him inside. I can hardly stand to be in that classroom with other students.

I skid to a halt outside the room, and Cameron's voice carries even with the door closed. I lean against the wall right next to it.

"I know what you did to Kelsey."

I flinch at how harsh it sounds and how easily he shares what I've kept hidden. Blood roars in my ears, and my breath comes in short gasps. I don't hear what Mr. Lewis says in response.

"So you're a coward as well as a pervert," Cameron says. "You won't admit what happened."

Mr. Lewis's shoes creak on the linoleum. "Where is this coming from, Mr. Jenkins? *Cameron?*"

"Don't *touch* me. This isn't about me!"

"I'm concerned about you." Mr. Lewis sounds like he's the epitome of student care.

I thought he was empathetic. I was wrong. He is empty.

My head pounds.

Time distorts around me.

I don't want to listen.

I can't move.

The door swings open. Mr. Lewis's voice cuts through the white noise in my head, but he doesn't immediately step out. It gives me time to scamper backward.

"Mr. Jenkins, you cannot afford any more mistakes. Consider your next steps carefully."

Cameron laughs. "Are you threatening me?" He doesn't sound intimidated. He should be.

After the senior prank last year, Cam and his stepdad were called into the principal's office, and Principal Young told Cam that he was *this close* to being expelled.

Matteo was heartbroken. So this year, Cam's been toeing the line, more to preserve his relationship with his stepdad than for himself. I don't want to be the reason he crosses that line.

But I don't have the courage to intervene.

"Let's pretend this conversation never happened," Mr. Lewis offers. "I have prep to finish. We'll leave these baseless accusations in the past, where they belong."

I wish I could tell Cam, *Walk away. Please walk away. It doesn't matter. Leave it.*

He won't. Teachers may consider Cameron difficult and argumentative, but he's kind and generous, loyal to a fault.

"*No.*" Cameron's voice is strong. "These accusations *aren't* baseless. If you don't have the guts to admit—"

"There is nothing to admit," Mr. Lewis interjects.

"If it were up to me, she would tell her story herself. But I'll find another way to make sure the whole world knows what a creep you are."

This time, Mr. Lewis laughs, but there is nothing humorous about it. "Who would believe a failure like you?"

"I'm not a failure," Cameron snaps, and bangs his hand on a desk.

Slowly, the concerned voices of other students filter through my terror. The hallway is getting crowded.

"Is that Cameron inside fighting with Mr. Lewis?"

"I heard he kicked a teacher in middle school."

"What are they saying?"

"We should get Officer Parks."

Several students run to get the Pierce's SRO, while the others stay close for the gossip.

Two sophomores approach me. "Do you know what's happening?" one whispers.

I try to give some kind of reasonable explanation. But the words stick in my throat. *Do they know? How much have they heard? I can't stay.*

I duck behind the two girls.

Mr. Lewis's arm points into the hallway. "Leave. *Now*. You are clearly a troubled young man. Get to class, and do not come to me with these kinds of threats again."

Some of the students observing the standoff are recording with their phones.

"Now, Mr. Jenkins."

Mr. Lewis reaches into the classroom to grab Cameron by the arm, and that's when it happens. As Mr. Lewis drags Cameron out of the classroom, Cameron, his face pale with fury, tries to shake himself loose. "I told you not to touch me."

Then, "Let me *go*."

As he passes through the doorway, Cameron brings back his fist.

He punches Mr. Lewis.

There's a loud, resounding crack of bones.

Mr. Lewis howls and stumbles into the hall, his hands to his face, blood streaming from his nose.

Cameron stares at his fist, his eyes wide. "I didn't mean to. Fuck—"

Somehow, despite the crowd buzzing around us, he spots me. I back away, shaking my head. I didn't want this. I didn't want him to share my story. I didn't want him to fight for me. I didn't want this…

His face falls, but it hardly matters anymore.

Officer Parks comes stomping through the hallway with the entourage that went to find him. He snatches Cameron by his shoulder and cuffs him before I can do anything to stop him.

Cam lets it happen. He's gone quiet as students whisper around him. We both know context won't matter.

As Officer Parks drags Cam away, Mr. Lewis—playing the martyr and holding his bloody nose—shoos everyone off to class, and his eyes find mine. Not a muscle in his face twitches, and yet he looks triumphant.

Because he's right about one thing. No one will believe Cam. No one will believe either of us.

Mr. Lewis is in charge here. We're playing by his rules.

―

Still, I try. Once more. I run to the principal's office to explain to her that Cameron was provoked. Or rather, that he messed up for the right reasons.

If I explain, she'll understand. Right?

But Mr. Lewis is a good man, and I'm a failing student. Stop me if you've heard this story before.

I burst into the office and startle Mrs. Matthews, who nearly drops the coffee mug she's holding. Her gray-streaked hair is pulled back in a tight bun, and her mouth twists into a thin line. "Ms. Fink. I don't believe you should be here."

My mouth grows dry. I swallow hard. "Cameron…He didn't…"

"He did not *what*, exactly?" Mrs. Matthews demands. Large stacks of paper cover every surface of her desk, and she looks harried and overwhelmed, strands of hair escaping her bun. "He didn't *punch* a teacher? He didn't *threaten* him?"

She slams the coffee mug down on her desk, and fury floods her pale cheeks.

"In all my years at this school, I've never seen anything as disgraceful as a student attacking a teacher. I always knew that boy was up to no good, but poor Mr. Lewis has a fractured nose. He may be damaged for the rest of his life. If Officer Parks hadn't pulled that boy off of him, who knows what might have happened?"

"Cameron hit him once!" I shout. "Because Mr. Lewis—"

"Be *very* careful what you say right now. Mr. Lewis deserves respect and appreciation. Perhaps you should spend less time with kids like Cameron and more time at church with your parents."

I close my eyes—

And I see Mr. Lewis's face staring back at me.

You came to me. You wanted my help.

Everything I want to say turns to dust in my throat.

I give up.

"You're right, Mrs. Matthews," I manage at last. "I should be in class."

[MESSAGE TO: PUMA@SECRET.CO
MESSAGE FROM: IVEY MARTIN]

I fought him off, and he still made me believe I'd misjudged the situation.

    I was part of his Creative Science program, and between workshops, we ended up alone. It seemed accidental to me, but in hindsight, I'm sure it wasn't. I told him how I wanted to get a degree in aerospace engineering and how I dreamed of working for NASA when I grew up. I was so excited about it too. He smiled at me. He told me he'd put in a good word for me at Lewis Industries. He placed his hand on the small of my back and slid it downward. I freaked out. I jerked away and screamed.

    He flushed. He stammered that he had put a hand on my back in support. That it was innocent and he was proud of my work and my dreams, and he was so sorry that he'd made me uncomfortable.

    He *thanked* me for expressing my feelings.

    He looked genuinely upset.

I believed I'd imagined the extent of what happened.

I wish I'd told someone.

CHAPTER TWENTY-FIVE
KELSEY

TWO MONTHS BEFORE

I see things that I never saw before. Now I am paying attention.

Mr. Lewis rests his hand on Taylor's shoulder.

His gaze lingers on girls in tight outfits.

He makes students laugh so he seems less threatening.

No one sees what he's doing, or if they do, they pretend they don't notice. I try to catch Taylor's eye when he steps away from her, but she keeps on watching him with interest. I notice that some girls avoid him in the hallways though, keeping an eye on his movements and maintaining distance between them.

He's careful.

He sees me stare. I'm sure he sees me tense up whenever he takes a step in my direction, because the ghost of a smile will drift across his lips. His broken nose has somehow made him more popular.

Every time I see another teacher laugh or joke with him, I wonder how I am supposed to trust any of them. After his harrowing experience with Cameron, Ms. Thompson has begun to pick up coffee for Mr. Lewis at Bean There. Other teachers drop by his class to check on him. Coach Mills brings him some kind of homeopathic salve for his bruising.

Now that Cameron isn't in class, I make sure to stay close to other students. I stick by Elijah and Luis, who tolerate me because I'm friends with Cameron.

In the hallways, Oakley clings to me like a bodyguard. She's changed her usual routes between classes and even miraculously swaps one of them to be closer to me.

We keep an eye on each other, and we keep an eye on him when Zanna isn't there.

Zanna is hurting too. I know. She called me on Halloween after Oakley told her I was safe. I didn't pick up. I didn't pick up the following morning either. Then Cameron got into a fight with her father, and now I just try to avoid her. It's too awkward and painful.

When the three of us went to visit Cameron after he was expelled, Zanna asked him what had happened. He told her he'd snapped. No reason. Never mind. I knew he hadn't told his stepdad either, and he struggled to carry the weight of Matteo's disappointment.

Zanna insisted there had to be a reason, but Cameron said he didn't want to talk about it—couldn't talk about it since her dad was considering pressing assault charges. He glanced at Oakley and me, fidgeting with the dice on his desk. An awkward pause followed.

Zanna is a lot of things, but unobservant has never been one of them.

She looked at Oakley, then at me. "You know I'm not my father, right? Whatever happened between you, I'm not him."

It was an opening, and I should have taken it. She deserved as much. After countless sleepovers, trips to the mall, vacations, afternoons at the park, cheering her on at swim meets, and complaining about homework, parents, and crushes, she deserved more from our friendship.

But I didn't have anything left.

"Here I thought we were friends." She picked at her nail, then got to her feet. "You know where to find me if there's anything I can do, Cam." She narrowed her eyes at Oakley and me. "When you're ready to talk, let me know."

With that, she walked out. And while we've crossed paths at school, it hasn't been the same. A cold void is growing between us. I can't go back to the Kelsey I was, and we can't go back to who we were together.

More often than not, it's just Oakley and me.

I tried to apologize to Oakley for coming between them, but she wouldn't let me get past the word sorry.

She grabbed me by my shoulders so I had no choice but to face her. I tensed at the contact. "This is not your fault," she reminded me. "Not any of it. I will tell you that over and over until I get it through that thick skull of yours. I'll keep reminding you until you believe me. Got it?"

I do. Rationally, I understand that I'm not at fault here. I hold her words close to my heart, just like every way she shows she cares. The gentle step closer to me whenever we pass Mr. Lewis in the hallways. The way she brushes him off even when he tries to appeal to her as her uncle. The chocolate and coffee she brings to school for me. The way she lets me cheat off her if we have the same tests so that my grades aren't fully terrible. The college applications she fills out for me.

I'm pretty sure Oakley would do my homework if she thought it would make me feel better. She would do anything to make me feel better.

I know all of that. Rationally.

I wish it made a difference.

Instead I can't relax. I'm constantly on edge. I never knew your throat could get sore from not screaming.

So I see all the things Mr. Lewis doesn't want me to see.

The touches. The stares. The brushes of his fingers when he "accidentally" bumps into a student. When girls shrug him off, he's apologetic. When they don't, he lingers.

But as the weeks and months progress, I don't see him corner another student, and I'm simultaneously relieved and conflicted. Did Cameron's threats make a difference after all? Or am I the only one?

If I am, then why?

Why me?

That's what I keep coming back to over and over. What made me special? What made me vulnerable?

As time passes, it becomes easier not to say anything. Not to miss the old me. Not to feel. I ignore my parents' nagging, ignore Alice when she comes home for break and barely speaks to me. If I don't feel anything, I won't fall apart.

Until the last week of January. At the end of the day, as we're about to leave for the stables, Oakley remembers she left her knitted hat in biology.

"I'll go get it," she tells me. "Ms. Sanchez always stays late."

"I'll come with." I like Ms. Sanchez. I took biology last year. It was the only science class where I ever truly felt at home. Besides, I don't want to wait for Oakley on my own in the parking lot when it's so cold and gray. We jog through the hallways so we don't lose time. The school is empty around us.

When we get to the biology lab, Oakley knocks and dashes in to find her hat. I linger in the doorway.

Mr. Lewis's door is shut. I hope he has already left for the day.

"Kelsey?" calls Ms. Sanchez. "It's good to see you. I've been meaning to talk to you."

Her words root me to the spot.

Inside the classroom, Oakley looks up sharply from her desk.

I clear my throat. "Um, sure."

"I was very impressed by your work in my class last year," Ms. Sanchez says kindly. She's young, with bright colorful glasses and purple tips in her hair. She has a tattoo of Galápagos finches on the inside of her wrist. "If you haven't finished your college applications yet, I'd be honored to write you a letter of recommendation."

Her words tug at me. If she's any gentler, I will shatter. Maybe, *maybe*, she's one of the good ones.

Maybe she still sees the Kelsey I was before.

Then she continues, "I heard you were struggling in chemistry, but you've recovered admirably. Mr. Lewis told me. We all want to see you succeed."

Crash.

I jump when Oakley knocks over her chair.

"Oh, I'm sorry!" She apologizes to Ms. Sanchez, who shakes her head and laughs a little.

"It's just one of those days," Oakley rambles. "I don't know why I'm so awkward." Her eyes are on me, offering me a way out.

I take it.

I back away. "Thanks, Ms. Sanchez. I'll let you know."

I step into the hallway. I lean against the wall and force myself to *breathe*. Just breathe.

All I need to do is keep my feet on the floor and inhale and exhale.

Click.

Mr. Lewis's door opens, tenderly, quietly.

A junior girl walks out.

I don't know her name, but I've seen her around. She always carries herself like she wishes to disappear. She sometimes has bruises in odd places, like she's clumsy.

Today, though, she looks haunted.

She pulls the hood of her sweatshirt up over her head. Her shoulders tremble. Her breath comes in tiny gasps.

"Thanks, Ms. Sanchez! Come on, let's go!" Oakley flings herself out the door with her hat in hand, and she reaches for me. "Kelsey? Are you okay?"

She follows my gaze.

The girl outside Mr. Lewis's classroom startles. Her eyes widen when she sees me staring, and then she darts to the staircase like a deer escaping a hunter. Right there and then, I have the answers to the questions that keep me up at night.

It isn't only me.

Cameron's threat hasn't made a difference.

He was simply careful all that time.

"We have to go after her," I say.

Oakley's eyes darken. "Why?"

"Because I don't want her to be alone. Not like I was."

Oakley opens her mouth and closes it. She nods.

My numbness shatters into a thousand pieces. Hot, boiling rage cascades through me and threatens to overtake me whole. "We have to stop him."

A week later, I go see Cameron at his stepfather's restaurant, with its perpetual smell of yeast and tomatoes. Cam is sweeping the floor, and he looks tired, smaller somehow. Still, he smiles when he sees me.

"How are you doing?" I ask. It's such a nonsensical question. None of us are *good*. We're all hurting.

He shrugs. "Better now that Matteo is finally letting me work here. It's the first time I've felt useful in months, and it seems like maybe he's forgiven me a little. He tries to hide his disappointment, but I see the way he looks at me. I'm not sure how he's going to keep the restaurant going and pay legal fees at the same time." Cameron leans his broom against a table. "My lawyer says I can probably get off with community service. She says someone convinced Mr. Lewis to put in a good word for me."

"Zanna?"

"I think so."

"Good. That's…good." I can't meet his eyes. "Fuck, Cam, I'm sorry."

He grabs my hand and squeezes it. "Don't. I fucked up. It's not your fault."

"It's not your fault either," I say. "You were trying to help me. You were trying to protect me."

A blush colors his cheeks. He scuffs his foot. "Kels… I'm sorry too. I shouldn't have thrown your secrets around. I've had a lot of time to think about that these past few months. Anyone might have heard, and it wasn't my choice to make."

"Maybe it would've been for the best." I swallow. "There was another girl."

Cameron gasps. "Mr. Lewis *assaulted* another girl?"

"One of the juniors. We can't let this continue. We can't. I refuse." I've thought about this long and hard, and I'm done waiting for the right words to come. I'm done waiting for people to listen, waiting for an opportunity to speak. I'm done. Fury has become a constant, comfortable companion, and I have embraced it.

Cameron hesitates. "You only have a few months left before you're done with Pierce forever. You can leave this behind."

"No, I can't. Not if it means he gets to continue doing what he did to me. And her." My voice goes cold and flat. "Not until I tell my story so that *no one* can ignore it. So that they will have to hear me. So that *he* will have to hear me. I don't want anyone to be able to look away again."

"What can I do?" Cam asks without hesitation, like he's offering to pick up coffee or ice cream.

"No." I shake my head. "I don't want you to get involved again. Oakley is on the case too, and she's in organizing mode. I don't want to make things worse for you."

"I'm your friend, Kels. This is more important than what happens to me," he says. Like it's no big deal. Like it isn't everything.

Something clatters in the kitchen, followed by Matteo's warm laugh.

"Cam…"

"I do have one request. Talk to Zanna. Please. If it's going to come out, it's better if she hears it from you."

I flinch. "We don't really talk anymore. I can't stand the idea that this will break her too."

"Kels…"

"After, okay? After," I promise.

Cameron smiles. He's aged these past few months. He looks more serious. More weary too. "None of this should be on you, you know. Or on any of us."

I know. "But that doesn't change anything. It is. I will do what I have to do to stop him."

"Whatever you need, I'm there. Anything at all. I'm here."

CHAPTER TWENTY-SIX
EDEN

1:00 A.M.

I'm not angry that Payton's here.

I'm angry that she didn't tell me.

I trusted her with my heart. I told her everything.

We talked about my grandparents. About escaping. I told to her that I needed to find a home where people wanted to know how my day was, where they were interested in my carvings, where someone occasionally made me peanut butter pancakes because I love them. She held me tight and told me *she* would make them for me. Because part of her didn't believe such a place existed. But I knew she wouldn't stop me. She'd never stop me.

She wanted me to be happy.

I thought she'd leave me, let me go. In all the relationships I'd ever seen, someone always left.

But she whispered, if I did have a magic escape, she'd follow me, like she'd followed me the first time we met, when I was late for first period and I saw her standing outside on the curb, fidgeting with a scarf to cover a bruise along her collarbone. She looked weary and sad, and I don't know what possessed me, but hunger gnawed at me, and I didn't want to be at school either. I walked up to her and said, "Since we're both late anyway, we might as well skip first period altogether and get coffee."

To this day, I don't know why she said yes, but I spent money I couldn't spare on coffee and pastries for the both of us. She nibbled slowly on a pastry, and the terror on her face melted into wonder. "No one's ever done this for me."

They should have, I didn't say. And, *You deserve it*.

"I'm Eden," I said.

It was as simple as that. She followed me. I would happily follow her.

But now I wonder, was she ever serious about running away together? Was I naive to think she was different?

I know she doesn't trust easily. Payton has never truly talked about her father and his drunken rages. I don't know if that's to protect herself or him. Or both of them. The first few afternoons I spent at her place—and those times were rare—she told me he had terrible headaches, which was why we needed to be quiet. I pieced together what was really happening when I accidentally broke a coffee cup and he came storming into her room. The next day, I saw her bruises. The walls she'd erected around herself were a little higher.

The day after that, I first heard—or rather, first paid attention to—the whispers that followed her. The rumors everyone knew about Payton and Mr. Davis and that no one spoke out loud.

She only told me the truth because one night, I dragged her to my place, we snuck in through the window, and I asked. I told her I understood. That my mother brought home men who hurt me.

I naively believed that when she told me about her dad and when I opened up about my mother's useless boyfriends, there were no secrets remaining between us.

I want to believe she still plans to come with me and we can leave this mess behind. I want to live happily ever after together on a farm in a small town with our own orchard and miniature horses.

The only thing I've never told her is that I don't actually know if that's what my grandparents' farm is like, because the last time I was there, I was four. All I remember is this tall, misshapen apple tree whose branches reached up to the clouds. The apples were rosy pink and a little tart, and I ate so many my stomach hurt.

That winter, we went back. The branches of the tree were leafless and barren, and that was the last I saw of the farm. The next summer, barely a week after he gave me a little wooden horse for my birthday, Dad left and never returned. Mom packed us up and moved us to another town. She burned all the pictures she had of him, and by Halloween, her first boyfriend had moved in.

Dad never got in touch again, as far as I know. My grandparents didn't either. I don't know if they tried. I don't even know if they remember I exist.

They definitely don't know I'm coming, because I didn't call them—I didn't want them to say no. But I sent them a letter explaining. If I timed it right, the letter will arrive the day before we do.

And they won't be able to reject me once I'm there. I'm certain of it.

I need to cling to that hope right now. The idea that there's a future out there, waiting for us.

For me.

And now we're here, in the eye of the storm, and it's as if I'm looking at a stranger.

"I thought you trusted me. I could have been there for you." I take in the vibrant red words on the walls, and fury courses through me. Sadness too. "I could have *helped*. God, Payton, I'm so sorry."

She flinches like I've slapped her. "Eden…"

From the other side of the room, Kelsey bears down on me. Red paint stains her fingers and sleeves. "You can help by taking your pity away from here. Leave and pretend you didn't see anything."

In all my years at Pierce High School, I don't think Kelsey has ever said a word to me. But I saw her from a distance. Her life seemed perfect. She belonged to the popular crowd, rode horses, had a family—a *family*—who saw her and supported her.

At least, I thought so.

I thought it was enough.

"Fuck," I breathe. "I hate this place."

When I don't move, she gets up in my face. She has to stand on tiptoe to meet me eye to eye, but she looks so fierce that I take a step back. I don't want to fight her.

"Leave!" Kelsey's shout is punctuated by a roar of thunder. Storm winds slam against the windows.

I look past Kelsey at Payton, hoping she'll step in, tell me that she's coming with me. Because I know, with as much certainty as I know it's raining outside, that if we don't leave Fenix tonight, we won't have the guts to try again. Not anytime soon.

I—I should have made an alternate plan. Payton's the one with the car. I should have bought a bus ticket out of here, but I didn't. She's the one who asked me if she could come. I want her to. I want her with me.

"Payton, please. If you don't want me here, say so," I whisper, with every ounce of courage I have. "I'll wait for you."

She's silent.

Kelsey's breath is hot on my face. Cameron has narrowed his eyes, like he'll throw me out to protect his friends. Oakley has folded her arms.

Payton is silent.

So I do the only thing I can. I turn to leave where I'm not wanted.

"Eden. Stop."

CHAPTER TWENTY-SEVEN
EDEN

1:03 A.M.

> stop.
>   I stay.
>   For Payton, always.

CHAPTER TWENTY-EIGHT
PAYTON

THIRTEEN DAYS AFTER

The door opens before I have the chance to knock, and it's not Kelsey standing there, but Oakley Walker. She leans against the doorframe and folds her arms. "We agreed to stay out of each other's way, Payton. It's safer for all."

"We didn't agree to anything. You sent me a text." I immediately deleted it. I also purged Oakley and Kelsey's numbers from my phone so Dad wouldn't come across them, even by accident. But Oakley's exact words were: *We're the only ones who know what happened. Keep quiet. Keep your head down. Don't talk to us because people will notice. Forget it ever happened.*

"Same difference." She stares down at me. She's four inches taller than I am, and she's perfect in so many ways. Long, shiny hair. Subtly curved eyebrows. A straight nose no smile. "What are you doing here?"

"Do you want to have this conversation on Kelsey's doorstep where everyone can see us?" I shove my hands into my pockets to hide that they're trembling.

She narrows her eyes—and then she reaches for the door. "No, I don't want to have this conversation at all. I want you to leave."

I slide my foot inside before she can close the door. "For what it's worth, I don't want to be here either. But I also don't want to pretend that night never happened. My dad says there are security cameras at the school. There's *footage*." I'm building up to what I want to say.

Oakley huffs. "I *know* there are security cameras. The police know about them. The school board knows about them. Most importantly, *my mother* knows about them. Have you considered that the powers that be here in Fenix aren't asking questions because no one wants the answers?" She's flushed with anger, and I expect her to shove me out after all, but then a shadow crosses her.

"Let her in, Oakley." Kelsey appears in the entryway behind Oakley.

Oakley moves so I can step inside. "Whatever you want to say, make it quick. None of this would have happened if you hadn't got involved."

The words hurt more than Dad's punches ever have, but I'm good at taking pain without flinching.

Kelsey looks pale and lost. There are dark circles under her eyes.

The shirt she's wearing hangs loosely around her shoulders, like she hasn't eaten since the school burned. "What do you want, Payton?"

As I hear the door close behind me, some of my tension makes way for resolve. I take a deep breath. I dig my nails into my legs. And I speak as clearly as I can. "It'll be two weeks tomorrow. Two weeks without Eden. Two weeks without anyone asking the right questions—except for Theodore Robinson."

"Theo? The editor of the *Puma Press*? Is he the one who—*oh*." Oakley's lips disappear into a thin line. She steps in front of Kelsey.

"I want us to tell him the truth," I say, the words tumbling out, each of them louder and more determined than the last. "Together. Everything that happened between the moment you saw me outside of Mr. Lewis's room and now. The whole truth and nothing but the truth."

The words sit between us.

Then Oakley laughs derisively, and I feel myself grow smaller.

"*You* want to tell the truth?" Oakley shakes her head. "That's rich. You should be grateful no one is asking questions."

"Wasn't that the whole point?" I counter. "To get them to pay attention? To leave a message so loud—or bright—that it couldn't be ignored?"

"That was before," Kelsey says flatly. Her eyes are dull.

"Before what?" I ask, though I know the answer.

"Before your girlfriend *died*." She turns toward the back of the house.

Oakley follows, muttering under her breath.

Eden deserved more, I want to tell them. *We all do.* Instead, I awkwardly follow them, my footsteps echoing on the wooden floor.

Cameron sits in a corner of the sunroom, curled up on white-and-pink armchair, playing a game on a handheld console. He's pushed his large noise-canceling headphones aside, and he looks up when we come in. "Hey, Payton."

"Cameron." I nod at him.

"You didn't reply to my text. Are you good?"

I laugh at that, because I don't know how else to respond. "*No.*"

He manages a wry smile. "Yeah, okay." He rubs at his arm, and a bandage peeks out from underneath his sleeve. He tugs his shirt back into place.

Oakley folds her arms. "Payton wants the authorities to investigate what happened. She says the school newspaper is looking into it."

"That's not what I said," I protest. Not exactly.

"Am I wrong?"

I pull myself up taller. "No," I say. "I want the whole of Fenix to demand answers, if that's what it takes. I want people to acknowledge how much we hurt and how we were abandoned. All of us. Eden died, and everyone has decided it's better to pretend it was a tragic accident than to recognize what really happened that night. Why *we* were there. It isn't right."

It feels strange to be talking to them like this. Until a minute ago, Cameron was gaming. Kelsey has set her tablet aside, but the screen shows she was shopping for riding clothes and horse gear. Oakley was reading a college textbook. How are they all simply hanging out, living their lives?

Or are they only surviving too?

All three of them stare at me. It always felt like I was intruding on their friendship, but never quite so much as right now.

Oakley sits down in front of me and shakes her head like I'm a child who has misbehaved. "Let me explain to you what my mother told me," she says slowly and clearly. "The fire department found what was left of our work, and do you know what they did? They called my mother. The chief of police saw what was left of our work, and do you know what he did? He called my mother. That security footage you're talking about? It shows four teens breaking and entering into a school. It shows four teens vandalizing a school. It shows four teens who were involved in the death of a fifth. And one of those teens, involved in *multiple felonies*, is me." She points at herself. "The daughter of the most important woman in town. The heir apparent to the biggest employer in the region, which happens to be responsible for taking care of the vast majority of Fenix."

"So?" I need her to say it.

"So she's going to protect me. She's going to do what any loving parent would do—but it's not like you'd know anything about that, would you?"

I bring my hand up to my face. The bruise is still visible.

"I hate you," I whisper. I know the feeling is mutual.

Oakley shrugs. "I don't care. You should be grateful that we're protecting you too. Without the security footage, none of us will be implicated. What happened was tragic. The night destroyed one life. We don't want it to ruin others."

"She deserves justice. We all do." I turn to Kelsey. "That's what you *promised* me. That night was supposed to do *good*. It was supposed to make a difference."

"Well, it didn't," Kelsey says, her voice raw. "We tried. We failed. We lost more than we could have hoped to win."

"Eden deserves better than that," I snap. "Everyone who's ever gotten on the wrong side of Mr. Lewis deserves better. You know it isn't just us, right? What is going to make him stop?"

Oakley shakes her head. "God, you're naive. If the security footage can't go public, than neither can our graffiti. Mom made that very clear. She said a tragedy like Eden's death has the potential to bring a town together. Careless accusations would only drive us all apart." She sounds bitter. Kelsey flinches. But then Oakley presses on. "At the end of the school year, she'll talk Uncle James into taking a job at Lewis Industries HQ. He'll manage new scholarships for Pierce students, something like that."

"That will make a difference too," Kelsey says, though she doesn't sound convinced.

Oakley speaks over her. "Now we're not obligated to do anything more than take care of ourselves and survive."

"That isn't justice." I spit the words at her. "And you don't care about any of this at all. You're here because you have a crush on Kelsey and you want to protect her. But you're not protecting anyone by staying silent. You're a coward."

I wonder if I should tell them that Theo already has photos of the walls, that they're too late.

"You know what?" Oakley gets to her feet. "If you care so much about justice, Payton Davis, by all means tell your story. Become a martyr for a hopeless cause. But let me remind you of one thing: There still will be no footage. The three of us were never there. Our lawyers will attest to that. So will everyone in this town who owes my mom a favor. My mother may despise me now, but she'll back me up. Who will believe you, Payton, when it's you on your own? Will your father back you up? Will your friends? Oh, wait, I forgot—you don't have any. Isn't that why he chose you? Do you want to talk about cowardice? You're the one who ran away that night."

"Theo will believe me," I manage, though my throat is tight and every breath burns.

"Will he? You think he'll help you once he knows that you killed his friend?" Oakley asks me. "He'll hate you too. Everyone eventually does."

"I didn't…I…" I stammer. "We're in this *together*."

"No." Oakley shakes her head. "*We* aren't."

Cameron stays silent. Kelsey looks away.

"You promised me that it would make a difference." My voice cracks. I do feel naive.

Kelsey straightens, and for a moment I think she's taking me seriously, but then she grabs Oakley's hand. A cold and untouchable veil comes over her. It's like she physically takes a step back from me, though she's sitting in the exact same spot.

"You would have left us. You would have abandoned us without ever saying a word. I was wrong to include you. We're not responsible for what happened," she says quietly. "I don't feel guilty. I didn't light the fire. *I* didn't kill Eden. I'm not complicit. *We* are not responsible."

Oakley leans in to wrap an arm around Kelsey's shoulders in the same way Eden held me a thousand times.

"We're not," she repeats. "You are."

CHAPTER TWENTY-NINE
PAYTON

THIRTEEN DAYS AFTER

"No." The world sways under my feet. The glass of the conservatory ripples around me, and the white structure folds in on itself. I squeeze the wooden apple pendant so tightly it might leave a permanent indentation in my hand. "I never meant for any of this to happen."

I repeat the words when Oakley unceremoniously guides me out the door.

I repeat the words as she disappears back inside with Kelsey and Cameron in tow. Only Cameron looks back at me.

I repeat the words on my own.

Except it did happen. It's too late for regret.
We are not responsible.
I am, and I am alone.
I break.

CHAPTER THIRTY
EDEN

1:03 A.M.

Payton is quiet. She always is. She doesn't talk about the things that hurt because that makes them harder to ignore. But I can read her like my favorite comic. Her white knuckles betray her anger as she clutches a can of spray paint like she wants to crush it. The way her eyes dart back and forth shows her panic. She's afraid.

"Payton…" Oakley takes a step toward her and reaches out a hand.

It's the wrong move.

The fury Payton carries within her erupts. She throws the spray can at the glass-fronted cabinet where Mr. Lewis keeps beakers of chemicals for his labs. The glass shatters upon impact, breaking some of the containers within. Whatever's inside begins to pour out. The smell of spray paint makes way for the pungent stink of alcohol and something that reminds me of swimming pools. Bleach or chlorine or something.

Payton stares at me, trembling. "I wanted you to *wait*, but you *didn't*. I didn't want you to see me like this." She swipes some empty glass vials to the floor.

"Payton, please…" Cameron takes a step closer but freezes when she shatters more glass.

"Why didn't you want me to see you?" I try softly.

"I wanted a second chance, a third chance." She laughs, the sound full of sharp edges. "I don't want to feel broken. I don't want to carry this with me. I just want to forget."

Payton's despair hits me like a brick. "That's why we're here tonight," I say. "We can still go. We can leave this place behind and *never* look back. We can find a way to forget. I promise."

"Don't," she snaps. "Don't make promises you can't keep."

"I'm not—"

She laughs, and it's full of pain. "Look at me and tell me you don't see my scars," she demands.

I won't lie to her. "I see them. But they don't *change* you. They don't change how I look at you. You're one of my best friends. I love you. I'm *in* love with you."

Cameron takes another step closer and tries to pick up the flasks and beakers Payton has thrown onto the floor. He hisses when he cuts himself on the shards of glass. *"Ow."*

Payton clings to the edge of Mr. Lewis's desk. "How can you love me?" she asks, her voice small and vulnerable.

The words stab me like those shattered bottles.

Last night, when she came to my room to help me pack, she let me hold her. She had a soft, gentle light in her eyes that was only ever there for me. Despite all the walls she'd erected around herself, despite the anger she used as a weapon, she could still imagine place better than this. One where she could belong.

Now there is no gentleness. Only pain.

"I love you because you're brave enough to dream about leaving with me. Because you're strong enough to dance through the park at night even when you're hurting. Because you *see* me, and you make me feel less alone. Because I know you're an artist too, and I want to see you make the world more beautiful." I try to keep my voice from shaking, like Payton is a wild, skittish animal, as I count all the ways in which I love her. I'm terrified none of them are enough.

I look at Oakley, who is inching toward the doorway. Kelsey is crouched next to Cameron, tying a piece of her shirt around his hand. She mutters under her breath, and I purposefully don't meet her gaze so as not to set her off again.

Payton smashes her hands onto the desk. "I'm so tired of being strong. I'm so tired of being in pain."

"I know," I say. I do.

I take a step toward her. The smell of bleach is spreading through the room, and so are other smells. Acrid. Putrid. I can't place them, but they're sucking the oxygen out of the room. My eyes itch and burn. The stench does nothing to abate Payton's rage—or her fear.

"Everyone always looks away. Over and over and over again."

Payton reaches for the nearest shelf and throws flasks and vials to the floor. The liquids hiss and bubble. She doesn't seem to notice. She spreads her arms wide and indicates the classroom around her. "I wanted a safe place. I thought, at least when I'm at school, Dad can't touch me. They're supposed to take care of us here, right?"

Tears glisten on her cheeks. She looks exhausted, and I know she's not fighting me, precisely, but I'm tired of fighting too. We're all balancing on the edges of our fractures.

"We should go," Kelsey suggests quietly, and coughs. "We've done enough."

Oakley is already by the door. "Payton, stop."

Cameron frowns at the mess on the floor. "We have to get out of here."

We do. The rotten egg smell coming from whatever was in those last containers is vile, and the scent claws at my throat.

Payton's despair doesn't leave room for her to consider her destruction. She reaches for jar after jar, throwing them to the floor.

I push farther into the room, avoiding the broken glass. We need to open a window. Let in some air.

"I thought this place was safe. But then came Mr. Lewis. If there's one thing this fucking town is good at, it's pretending nothing bad ever happens in Fenix."

Payton shatters another beaker. With her rage comes power. I recognize that need to break something, *anything*.

Everything.

She pins me with a stare and her voice drops to a whisper, so I have to strain to hear it over the violence outside.

"Do you know what it feels like when everything you are gets broken into pieces and then, when it takes everything you have to cradle those pieces together and try to survive, someone comes along and breaks you all over again? Do you know how much it hurts?"

She snatches something from the lab bench: Cameron's lighter. She holds it beneath her thumb and shakes her head. "It hurts, Eden. And I want them all to feel it too."

CHAPTER THIRTY-ONE
PAYTON

THIRTEEN DAYS AFTER

I killed her.

Didn't I?

CHAPTER THIRTY-TWO
EDEN

1:05 A.M.

"Payton! No!"

It comes in a rush of sound from all around me.

From Oakley in the doorway.

From Kelsey, who's covering her mouth and nose with her sleeve, her words punctuated by coughs.

From Cameron, who scrambles toward the door.

The words come from me too. "Payton, please." I keep my focus on her face, not the lighter in her hand. Her eyes blaze.

There's a fire extinguisher at the back of the room, but none of us are close enough to reach it. There are water taps, but I'm not sure if that would hurt or help. Adding a spark to all that's been spilled would be disastrous.

"Payton, please." I take a step closer, ignoring the burning in my eyes and throat. I ignore everything else around me. I feel lightheaded.

"I know what it feels like to be alone and overwhelmed. That's why I came to you. I'm sorry that these men hurt you. It's not right, and it's not fair. You don't deserve to carry that pain with you." I nearly tell Payton I know how she feels, but that's not true. Our experiences may be similar, but they're not the same, and it's unfair to her to pretend otherwise. Her pain and my pain can coexist. Neither has to be diminished for the other to be real.

I reach out to her. "I see you. I'm here for you. I love you. I'll *listen*."

She blinks. I don't know if my words have reached her, but she hasn't flicked on the lighter yet.

"We deserve better than this. *You* deserve better than this."

Behind me, someone mutters. Kelsey. It occurs to me that now they *know* about us; for the past year, we've tried so hard to keep our relationship quiet for fear that Payton's father would hear about it and kick her out. But I'd rather leave telling the truth than carry more lies.

"We'll get through this together. We'll get to a place where we *are* safe."

That's the start. Healing can only come after the hurt has stopped.

Payton coughs, and she reaches for her throat.

"I'm so tired." Her eyes tear up, and my own vision swims. "I'm so tired of surviving."

I take another step closer to her. "You don't have to do it alone."

Her face twists. "I don't know how else to do it."

"Trust me," I say simply. "Trust me that I won't leave, no matter how broken you may feel. Trust me that I'll love you even when you're struggling to love yourself. We'll carry this together."

Her shoulders drop.

I reach out and fold my fingers around the lighter, gently tugging it out of her grasp.

A flash of lightning illuminates the classroom. When it recedes, the room seems dimmer than before.

Payton grabs my wrist. Her fingers twist around my bracelet, and the chain tightens around my wrist and digs into my skin.

I wince.

"Don't let go," she whispers. Her voice is raw with hurt and exhaustion.

I try to offer her the same smile she gave me when we first met. "I'm not going anywhere without you."

She coughs. "We'll go together," she says with more confidence. But the look in her eyes is empty. She doesn't move.

"We will," I promise.

She's pale, except for the rosy red blotches on her cheeks. Slow and steady does the trick. "Come, I'll open the window so we can let these vapors out, and then we'll go to your car and drive away. Our own happily ever after."

I give her my own confidence. My orchard and miniature horses.

Payton gives me a small nod. When I step back, she doesn't let go of my bracelet. A link breaks.

I curse, but it's drowned out by the storm.

Payton's hand slips away as she tries to catch the chain for me.

The air in the room claws at me. My lungs are on fire, and my eyes are burning.

Outside, lightning bolts and thunder make the whole building groan again.

I reach for the window and fumble for the latch.

Another flash of lightning cuts through the sky with a crackle. The air feels charged. Across the school's parking lot, one of the trees catches fire, the branches burning like a beacon.

Behind me, Payton coughs again.

"Hurry up! We have to get going," Oakley mutters from the doorway.

I push open the window.

The damp air rushes in around me.

Then lightning arcs down from the clouds, and I feel the static discharge crawl up from my hand through my elbow toward my shoulder, like someone has shocked me or hit my funny bone.

It arcs down the side of the school.

It sparks along the gutters.

The fumes that spill out of the classroom ignite.

For a heartbeat, the air itself *burns*. Like a fuse showing the fire the way in, forcing itself past the windowsill. The bluish-green flame doesn't look real.

The chemistry labs are filled with signs reminding students that a single spark can cause a fire. That even the controlled flames of the Bunsen burners need to be handled with care.

There is no controlled flame here. Just a mix of highly flammable chemicals. An endless supply of oxygen to keep the fire going.

A single spark.

Then the whole world explodes.

CHAPTER THIRTY-THREE
PAYTON

THIRTEEN DAYS AFTER

The guilt I've fought to suppress rushes over me like a tidal wave. Oakley's voice echoes in my head.

You think he'll help you once he knows that you killed his friend?

The three of us? We were never there.

Who will believe you, Payton, when it's just you on your own?

No one will. She's right. They won't be able to look past what I did—to Eden, to the school. None of the people who failed us will take the blame. That's never how it works.

But Oakley was wrong about one thing. Surviving isn't our only obligation. I've survived since Mom left, but I deserve more. Eden deserved more. The world *can* be better, and it's on us to make it so.

Perhaps that will be my way out of here. To prison or simply out. Gone.

Away.

I won't tell Kelsey's story if she doesn't want me to. But I'll no longer stand by quietly either.

I won't be silent.

I won't be silenced.

I don't know how I drive home, but I pull into the driveway and stare out at the unmown lawn, the flaking yellow paint on the house.

Home is the place where people miss you when you're gone.

Dad doesn't open the door when my car pulls up to demand to know where I've been for the past day and whether I'm okay.

This isn't home. It was never supposed to be. This is the place where I stored spray paint under my bed because I looked at the cans Oakley had brought to show us and for the first time—for the *first* time—I felt that pull Eden had when she looked at a piece of wood and wanted to find out what shape was inside it. I looked at the cans of spray paint, and I wanted to find out what I could make with it. What it could do—what *I* could do—outside of bleed accusations.

So I talked Eden into going to the hardware store with me, one of her favorite places on earth. She needed a new chisel, and with my savings she charmed Old Man Adams into letting her buy a few cans of paint. Green. Blue. Purple. The last remaining red. She was so excited that I was excited. She always loved to see me sketch. I sketched the characters in the comics she liked. I drew her tree house.

But I created only when she could see me—and only on the condition that I could destroy the sketches later. I didn't want anything to last and come back to hurt me.

Not until I saw the spray paint. She told me she could carve surfaces for me to paint. We could create *together*.

I had never before considered that a possibility, but I loved it. I wanted it.

I hid the cans under my mattress after the night the school burned, when I sneaked back into my room, my throat clogged with smoke, carrying a bag full of belongings that were never meant to return to Fenix. But today I need them.

I leave my key in the ignition. I leave the door to my car unlocked.

Whatever happens next, I do not plan to come back.

The house is quiet, but I don't risk entering through the front door. I circle around to the back and climb onto the trash can next to the back door. I reach for my bedroom window and pull myself up. I've done this a thousand times before on days when it was better to avoid Dad and on nights when I didn't want to be alone. I could do this with my eyes closed.

I know something is off even before I hoist myself into the room.

Though I hid most of my belongings, I kept one small token on the windowsill of my room. A small stress toy in the shape of a basketball. I thought it would be safe to keep because Dad bought it for me three years ago. He had a spell of good days. A week or two when he was sober and smiling and we even shot hoops together. He was the dad he used to be. Until someone set off fireworks in the neighborhood.

The only time I packed the tiny basketball away was the night the school burned, because I meant to bring it. It was the first thing I unpacked too, but it's gone now. The windowsill is empty, and when I climb into the room, I see why.

My entire room has been ransacked. The bed has been turned over, and the mattress is leaning against the wall. The closet has been turned inside out, with clothes flung everywhere. If I didn't know any better, I would think someone broke in.

I do know better.

This was Dad.

When I was eleven, Dad was convinced I'd stolen money from him to buy colored pencils I'd seen while we were out shopping. He combed through my entire room. My school bag. My closet. He broke whatever was in his way. When he didn't find anything, he cried. He told me he didn't want to distrust me. He didn't mean to hurt me. He still apologized back then. He bought me the pencils himself.

That night, he ordered pizza, and he tried to be a good parent. Until I accidentally dropped a glass of water and it shattered with a loud crash.

Then he snapped.

I never touched those pencils.

It's been so long since he had good days. Since it was him and me versus the world. Instead of him versus me.

I snatch a hoodie from the chaotic pile of clothes and slip into it, like it's a piece of extra armor, before I sneak downstairs. Immediately, I see the cans of spray paint on the dining table. The carvings Eden gave me. The birthday cards from Mom. A ticket stub from when Dad and I went to the movie together four years ago. All the mementos I kept hidden under my mattress and inside my closet.

Dad sits behind the collection, his arms crossed and his eyes hard. At his feet are the boots I wore the night the school burned, my singed shirt. I should have dumped them as soon as I changed out of them, but I didn't know if it was safe to do so.

My breath catches.

"I knew your friend was responsible for the destruction of the school. Tell me she didn't make you complicit in her criminal behavior. Tell me you didn't make her complicit in yours."

His voice is flat. He doesn't move. He just stares at me, and somehow, that makes me more scared than I've ever been.

Some days, fear silences me. Some days, it makes me want to flee.

But these past few days, when I knew I couldn't flee, when silence felt like it was choking me, when I had nothing else left, my fear morphed into anger. I feel it now, burning cold and bright. I step closer and place my hands on the edge of the table. "You have no right to my answers anymore, Dad."

He clenches his hands into fists. "I have every right to protect my daughter and my community. What are you caught up in?"

I laugh incredulously, and it's freeing. "You have never protected me."

"*Everything* I've ever done was to protect you," Dad snaps. "You're a stranger to me, Payton. I know I haven't always been the best father, but I did what I could to give you a home. I made sure you got to go to the best school in the district. I put a roof over your head. I taught you discipline. But I don't know this person who I'm looking at now."

He grabs one of the cans of spray paint. He holds it up to me, shaking it so the little metal ball inside rattles. "My daughter, a juvenile delinquent. These clothes… I've already called Derek. This will be enough to prove the fire wasn't an accident." His voice remains emotionless. "I don't know what you and your so-called friends were playing at, but I will see to it that you pay the price. I tried. I did. Perhaps justice can teach you what it means to be responsible."

"Justice? What do you know about justice? Or responsibility?" Anger claws at my throat like the smoke did. I push my hair out of my face so that he can see the bruises along my jaw. "You're not a great father, Dad. You put a roof over my head, but you never gave me a home."

He stands with a roar and upends the table, sending my belongings flying. The smallest carvings break. He hurls the can of spray paint he's holding against the wall, right next to my head.

"You ungrateful girl! Is this some desperate cry for attention? You have no idea of how harsh life can truly be."

I flatten myself against the wall, my feet surrounded by cans of spray paint with broken caps and fragments of Eden's carvings. "You have no idea what you're talking about!"

"I should have been firmer with you. Toughened you up for what the world can throw at you."

"You should have *loved* me!"

"What did you say?"

Now that I've said it out loud, I've forgotten how to breathe. I can't breathe. I can barely squeeze the words out again. "You should have loved me."

Dad steps back like *I've* slapped *him* and reaches for a chair to steady himself. His face goes pale, then reddens, and I'm almost relieved when I see the familiar rage return.

Almost.

Dad circles the fallen table. "You disrespect your family. You disrespect your father. You disrespect your school and your teachers. You dare to—"

"Yes." I put one of Eden's carvings in my pocket and snatch up two cans of spray paint. My hands tingle and my breath feels shallow, but I rise to my feet. "Yes, I dare to."

My hands curl around the cold cans of paint, and for a heartbeat, I'm back inside Mr. Lewis's classroom, the acrid smell of fresh paint curling into my nostrils and power filling me. Eden was nowhere to be seen yet.

"Yes, I dare," I say again. "Because you know what, Dad? I was at the school that night. The fire wasn't an accident. Tell that to Derek when you see him. If you see him. Tell it to the whole fucking world, for all I care. But when you do, be sure to ask Derek about the graffiti inside the classroom. And ask yourself why no one at the best school in the district ever noticed my bruises or my torn clothes. And then think about good Mr. Lewis, the teacher who assaulted me."

He reaches for the nearest chair and sits down hard.

I'm not done. "Maybe what happened at the school was a cry for attention. But ask yourself why I needed to cry out at all. Maybe it was disrespect, but I won't let anyone disrespect me any longer."

With the cans of spray paint in my hands, I turn on my heel and run back to my car.

CHAPTER THIRTY-FOUR
THEO

THIRTEEN DAYS AFTER

When Payton leaves in the morning, I retreat to my room. The blankets I used as a makeshift mattress are strewn across the floor. I leave them be. I grab my computer and go to the Puma Boards, placing my phone next to me in case Payton texts or calls.

I should have told her about Eden buying spray paint, but she looked so fragile already.

I trace my cheekbone, and I wonder if I did the right thing. Should I have let her go? Or should I have made her stay and demanded that Mom figure out a way to help? I know Payton didn't want me to tell her—she doesn't want me to tell anyone. Eden never did either. I let her sneak food from our kitchen and pretended I didn't see anything, but I never outright told her that she could take whatever she wanted, that I didn't want her to go hungry. I never outright told Mom that there were times when Eden's mother forgot to pay the bills so they had no heat or water. That her boyfriends were horrid and that Eden hardly ever had money for lunch.

Did I do enough?

I felt like I would make things worse if I told on them, that I would betray their trust. But I don't know if that's the right call anymore. Perhaps it *would* be better to tell.

People who don't ask for help can still need it, and needing help isn't a personal failing. It's just a fact of life.

But I can't very well run after Payton—and the only person I can help now is Eden.

I enter my login details and wait for the site to load. I have notifications that people have replied to my message but—

An error message pops up.

[MESSAGE] Login invalid.

I frown and try again, making sure to double-check the password.

[MESSAGE] Login invalid.

I hesitate, then register for a new account. I'll gather what information people posted and go from there. As long as I get screenshots, I can follow up. I can see if they want to talk to me, to the school newspaper, and help shape this story.

The site accepts my new login details, and I click through to the home page and—

Nothing.

My message is gone.

In its place, pinned to the top of the page, is a message from the admin:

> [MESSAGE] During these difficult times, we stand with the community of Fenix and the teachers of Pierce High School. Per our guidelines, hateful and divisive content will be deleted and the user(s) responsible for such behavior will be blocked. Any libelous or defamatory content will be shared with the authorities.

I reread the message.

As I watch, replies pop up.

> [MESSAGE] James Lewis is one of my neighbors. Do you know what these rumors are doing to his family?
>
> [MESSAGE] Free speech belongs to those who know how to use it responsibly.

[MESSAGE] Mr. Lewis should not be linked to that poor girl's death. He and his family have done too much for our town.

I stare at that last message. If the graffiti is true, doesn't he bear some responsibility for what happened in his classroom? Sometimes I wonder if anyone in this town cares about the truth when it's ugly.

As Payton told me, no one makes these accusations for fun.

I reach for my phone and shoot off a text to Payton.

THEO:

> My posts were deleted. I don't know if anyone else replied.
>
> I want to post the pictures from his classroom.
>
> What do you think?

I don't really expect her to reply. But a message pops up almost immediately.

PAYTON :

> Do it.
>
> Tell them everything.
>
> Eden deserves better than this. We all do. It's up to us to make sure we get justice.

I stare at my phone, slightly taken aback by her tone. Doubt and worry nag at me, especially because of Payton's promise to tell me a story about Eden I don't know yet. She told me she lies. What does she know that she isn't telling me?

But she's right. I've gathered leads. It's time to follow up on them and tie them together.

Amaya, June, Jalen, and I talked about setting up an anonymous tip line a while ago. We even registered an email account, but we've never used it, because there didn't seem to be anything that we needed it for.

I click to video call with the rest of the *Puma Press* crew. We set up a group chat—out of sight from Mx. Sousa—when we went through a period of virtual classes at the start of the year. We haven't used it a lot since, but I have to talk to them. I can't do this without them.

Amaya immediately accepts the call. Her face is flushed, and she's surrounded by trees. It looks like she's on a run. "Hey, T, what's up?"

June is next, large gaming headphones on her head and a large mug of coffee by her side. She rolls her chair back slightly so she isn't too close to her cam. "Wow, it's been a while."

"Are we finally writing an article about the fire?" Jalen's voice crackles through the call, though he keeps his camera off. He prefers it that way.

"Finally? It's only been two weeks." June sips her coffee and stares at me with large eyes. "How are you doing, Theo? Amaya says you've been investigating something?"

I stare at the screen in front of me—at my friends—and some of the tension in my shoulders relaxes. Seeing them makes me feel more normal. It's a reminder that I'm not as alone as I've felt these past few days.

"June wanted to send you a fruit basket," Jalen says.

I laugh and scratch my head. "You know I'm not ill, right?"

"We were planning to come by your house," Amaya explains. "We know you're hurting, and we don't want you to hurt alone."

"I appreciate you guys." I swallow hard when it occurs to me that Eden didn't have this. Payton doesn't have this. I glance through the window at Eden's bedroom and prepare to let it all tumble out. "I want you to know what I'm doing because it may implicate you too. I want you to be able to step away if you need to."

"We're in this together," Amaya says after they all share a look. "Go on."

I do. I tell them what I found inside the school. I show them the pictures of the classroom. I tell them that Eden didn't go to Pierce that night to jump—or to blow up the school—but to escape.

"Escape what?" Jalen asks.

Despite how easy it was to say everything else, I hesitate. "Home."

"Okay."

"And..." I steady myself. "And as for Mr. Lewis?" I tell them about the alumni group—"I knew that was you!" June says—and going to the hardware store. About Eden buying cans of spray paint. About the graffiti. About the assembly.

Amaya looks pale. "I have to talk to Taylor."

"She's in Mr. Lewis's class too, isn't she?"

Amaya nods. She accepts this so much more readily than I did, and it makes me feel slightly uncomfortable about my own doubts. Not quite guilty, but heavy regardless. I'm not sure I made the right decisions at any point, and I'm going to have to sit with that.

June scrunches her face. She's the youngest of us, a sophomore. "But if the accusations are there, why didn't we hear about them? Why didn't anyone investigate further? Oh…"

I can see the exact moment realization hits. After I broke into the school, I kept waiting to hear about the police investigating Mr. Lewis—trying to link what had been written about him to what had happened to Eden—but nothing showed up. Mom didn't hear anything at the station either.

"Because taking on Mr. Lewis will pit the whole town against you," Jalen says. "My brother works for Lewis Industries."

"My dad does too." Amaya grimaces.

"My moms as well," June says.

"But it shouldn't matter," Jalen puts in.

I nod. "I know. I don't know what the consequences will be. If any of you are uncomfortable with this, I'll keep you out of it. I promise. I'd rather face the repercussions myself than get you or your families in trouble. But Eden was my family too. I *am* hurting. I can't stand the idea of losing her friendship or breaking her trust in me, even after she's gone. I owe her this."

Jalen clears his throat. "What do you want to do?"

"I want to post the email address where people can send tips. The mods will probably delete my post, but once that email address is out there, it will spread. I know it will. If anyone has any information, we can listen. And maybe we can find the truth."

Something quiet passes between us four. Trust. Confidence. Then June nods. "Do it."

[MESSAGE] This message will probably be deleted, but the night the school burned, messages were spray-painted on the walls of Mr. Lewis's classroom.

[MESSAGE] The police know about it. I think the school administration does too. If you suffered at the hands of Mr. Lewis, you're not alone. If you know anything, if you've experienced anything, we want to hear from you. We'll listen. Email the *Puma Press* at puma@secret.co

CHAPTER THIRTY-FIVE
THEO

THIRTEEN DAYS AFTER

I set my phone to automatically download every email sent to the tip line. I know the others will keep an eye on the inbox too, but I'm worried about what the school will do once they read my message on the Puma Boards.

Identifying myself as part of the newspaper staff seems risky but worth it. It'll reassure people that I'm not some random person trying to get dirt on Mr. Lewis. I'm a reporter.

We *want* to hear what they have to say. We *will* listen.

My phone dings, and I snatch it from my desk.

It's an email, but not one I'm expecting. It's from the school administration, updating us on our return to classes.

[MESSAGE] After extensive discussions, Fenix Middle School has decided to allocate space for the juniors and seniors of Pierce High School so that they can resume in-person classes after the weekend. All upperclassmen are expected to attend an assembly on Monday morning at eight a.m., where we will inform you of the guidelines while we are guests at Fenix Middle School. Attached you will find your schedule with new room assignments and a school map.
Online classes will continue for the remainder of the students at this time.

I turn my phone to silent.

This is not a promise of normalcy but a threat. Everything will to go back to the way it was, which means I only have until classes start again to tell the truth about Mr. Lewis.

I can't wait for emails to come in—I have to get out and search for more information.

With Eden's backpack over my shoulder, I go next door to talk to Eden's mother. Mom and I went to offer our condolences the day after the fire and bring Mrs. Randall a casserole, and Mom has gone back twice to check in on her. I haven't talked to Mrs. Randall since. I didn't talk to her much before the fire either. Eden and I usually met in our tree. Or she would come over for dinner at our house. I've set the table with a third plate twice this week without thinking.

Before the fire, I knew grief as overwhelming emptiness. A void where a person should be. I was nine when Dad died. It felt like the world had shifted and tilted off balance, and I couldn't find my footing. I couldn't find my way forward. Later, when my therapist helped me reconnect with my feelings, even the smallest memory would be enough to make me burst into tears. Like when I stumbled across an old pair of Dad's shoes in our hall closet. Or when Mom made the strawberry and banana pancakes he usually made me when she was out of the country. The first time she got them just right, we both cried while eating them. It was almost like he was there with us at breakfast. There's an ache in my chest that's lingered. It hasn't stopped hurting, but I've grown used to it. The last time it threatened to overwhelm me was when I told Mom my name and I realized I'd never get to tell him.

With Eden, my grief is different. It's distant, clouded by not knowing what happened. I need answers so I can let go of all my questions and grieve her loss instead.

I place the backpack next to the door so Mrs. Randall won't see it immediately, and I knock. She comes to the door within seconds, and there's a brief flash of hope in her eyes, followed by a new stab of grief. I recognize that feeling well. For more than a year after his death, whenever the door opened, part of me expected Dad to walk in.

But it chafes to see her wait *now*. The first time Eden stayed over for dinner, Mom insisted on calling Mrs. Randall to let her know. Her boyfriend at the time was a trucker named Terry, who lived a few towns over. She'd gone to visit him for the weekend. She didn't even pick up her phone.

I remember thinking it was odd. Mom once promised me that she'd always pick up the phone, even if she was in the middle of recording, and she's kept that promise. When I told Eden about that, she shrugged. "Mom knows I can fend for myself."

It was her twelfth birthday that day, and none of us knew.

Mrs. Randall's auburn hair hangs messily on either side of her face. Her eyes are bloodshot and sunken. I don't think she's eaten or slept much these past few weeks. "Theo, isn't it?" She tries on my name like it's unfamiliar to her. She leans against the doorframe. "What do you want?"

"I wanted to know if you needed anything." I manage.

I want to know if you know that Eden planned to leave.

I want to know if Eden ever said why.

I want to know if giving you Eden's backpack will be healing.

She looks straight through me. "I need my daughter back, but I doubt you can help with that."

"I wish I could," I say honestly. I glance past her. There are takeout boxes and clothes strewn everywhere, across the couch and the dinner table. There are empty wine bottles and carvings Eden made that she didn't plan to take with her.

Her boyfriend, Arthur, is nowhere to be seen. Now that I think about it, I haven't seen his truck in the driveway since the memorial service.

"You were Eden's friend," Mrs. Randall says with a heavy voice. "Weren't you? I know I messed up. I wasn't there for her. I lost her long before I lost her."

"Can you tell me if she was happy?" she asks. "Is this my fault? Did I drive her to it?"

I shift uncomfortably. Is this how Eden always felt? Mrs. Randall is an adult. I'm Eden's friend. I can't comfort or take care of her the way she seems to need.

But at least I can give her *some* answers. "Eden didn't go to the school to jump." I pick up the backpack and give it to her. I removed the note with Eden's grandparents' address and the apple charm, but everything else is there. "She wanted to…" I don't know how to say this without hurting her. "She wanted to leave town for a bit. She never meant to leave forever."

Mrs. Randall takes the backpack. "Where did you *find* this?"

I wince and simply say, "I want you to have it."

She cradles the backpack like it can bring her closer to Eden. "Thank you. *Thank you*."

I wait for her to ask the questions I've been asking. If Eden was planning to run away, how did she end up inside the school? What happened to her?

She doesn't ask. She doesn't say anything.

I tug at the hem of my shirt. "Did Eden ever say anything to you about a teacher? Mr. Lewis?"

Eden's mother traces the zippers on the backpack.

She shakes her head. "We never really talked about school."

They never really talked about anything.

Mrs. Randall's hands tremble. "It's best if you go now, Theo."

I agree. Even without answers, I did what I came here to do.

"I am sorry," I tell her. But deep down, I know the words are meant for Eden. I'm sorry I never saw quite how lonely she was. How lonely they both were.

"Yeah," she whispers. "Me too."

I take the scenic route into town, my car windows down so the chilly spring air rushes through the car. I'm desperate to clear my head and dry my eyes. I watch the morning fade to afternoon, and the sunlight feels colder than it did before. I go to Matteo's, the best (and only) pizza place in town. The doors are open, but it's almost empty. The lunch crowd is nearly gone, and it's early for dinner.

A twentysomething girl with bright purple hair in long braids down her back and a Matteo's shirt is behind the bar polishing glasses. Her sparkly nails click-clack against the glass.

She looks up when I enter. "Can I help you?"

"I'm looking for Cameron."

She tilts her head. "Are you a friend?"

It's an innocent question, but it feels like a trap. I'm not good at lying. It doesn't come naturally to me, and I know she'd see through it.

Eden used to tell me that if I wanted to be a reporter, I'd have to learn to be diplomatic. But that's not how my brain works. I'd much rather be honest and kind.

So I tell the purple-haired girl, "I'm not. My name is Theo Robinson. I am one of the editors of the *Puma Press*, the school newspaper. I'd like to ask him a few questions."

She places the glass she was polishing on the bar and tosses the cloth next to it. "Sorry, can't help you. Cam doesn't have anything to do with Pierce High School anymore."

I lean in. "It's not about him. I mean, not really. I know he got expelled. It's about Mr. Lewis. Someone told me Cameron got into an altercation with him to protect a friend, and I…" I hesitate. "I would like to know if I could have protected my friend too."

A shadow passes over her face, and her mouth tightens. She glances past me at the occupied tables, where a handful of people are finishing their meals. Two men at the table near the window are wearing overalls with the Lewis Industries logo. "I'm sorry about your friend," she says, "but he isn't here. I don't know where he is."

She's lying. I'm certain she knows where he is. "If you see him, will you please tell him to get in touch with me? If he wants to talk? I would appreciate that."

She nods. "Yeah, sure."

"Thanks." I turn and walk out.

When I glance back through the window, she's pulled out her phone and I wonder if she's passing along my message—or warning him.

[MESSAGE TO: PUMA@SECRET.CO
MESSAGE FROM: KINGSTON SMALL]

I thought it was just me. Five years ago, after one of Mr. Lewis's Creative Science outings, I missed the bus home, so I had to stay at school until my sister could come pick me up. The weather was surprisingly bad for the time of year, and Mr. Lewis saw me sitting outside. He said I could sit and wait in his classroom, told me he wanted to hear about my college plans.

I had a bad feeling about it, but he insisted. He said I would catch a cold if I stayed outside.

The thing is, unless you've had Mr. Lewis as a teacher, I can't explain to you how popular he was on those Creative Science days. He let us make slime and throw it at each other. We experimented with fireballs and fluorescence. He was the cool parent at a kids' birthday party, and we behaved like seven-year-olds on too much sugar. Everyone loved him, so I told myself it would be fine.

It wasn't.

He assaulted me.

I blamed myself.

I was too scared to say anything. How do you tell on the teacher everyone loves?

CHAPTER THIRTY-SIX
THEO

THIRTEEN DAYS AFTER

I end up at Oakley's house midway through the afternoon with my notebook in my hand. I tried to find Kelsey, but she wasn't at home. No one was. Oakley lives in a veritable mansion. While most houses in Fenix are functional, this place belongs in an architecture magazine with its gray and brown stone, large windows, and huge porch. The driveway is probably heated.

It must be nice to be CEO of Lewis Industries.

I wonder what it's like to be the most important person in this town. To be responsible for so many homes and families and paychecks. If accusations had been made against any other teacher, the story would have come out already. But in Fenix, reality is manufactured by Lewis Industries. All it takes is a fresh coat of paint to hide the scars.

I knock and hear light footsteps run toward the door, followed by a voice. Oakley's voice. "Freddie! Wait!"

My heart leaps into my throat, and I suddenly feel unprepared to confront her. I hoped to have some sort of evidence. A story to get her to trust me. Instead, I have a weekend before Mr. Lewis goes back to teaching. But I'm here. I will.

One of the large double doors opens, and Oakley stands in the doorway with a kid at her side. "Can I help—oh." She stares at me. From underneath a beanie, her dark brown curls tumble over her shoulders, and I understand why Eden had a crush on her. "Theodore Robinson." She says it like she's been expecting me and like she's disappointed I'm here, both at the same time.

Oakley is one of those students who seems very comfortable with herself, but it's never made her approachable. She knows she's powerful.

"Oakley." I stand up straight and promise myself that whatever happens, I won't flinch. "I want to talk about Mr. Lewis."

Oakley's face twists with anger. The boy looks from me to her and back. "Uncle James?" he asks with a slight lisp.

Another voice comes from down the hallway. "Why?"

Kelsey Fink's arms are crossed and her eyes dark. She leans against a doorframe, soft music filtering out of the room behind her.

"School starts again in three days." This time, I'm the one whose gaze is bouncing between people.

Oakley sighs heavily. "Cam! Can you please take Freddie to the kitchen for some ice cream?"

Freddie's face lights up at the mention of ice cream. He runs through the hallway and past Kelsey. A second or two later, Cameron emerges from somewhere toward the back of the house and takes in the situation.

He nods at me. "Newspaper boy."

"Cameron."

Cameron glances at Oakley. "I told you." He sounds resigned.

I wonder what the girl from the restaurant told him, but I don't have time to think about it, because as soon as Freddie is out of earshot, Oakley rounds on me. Her gaze flares. "You have some guts to show up at *my* house to ask about *my* family like we're some kind of scoop. What do you want?"

I look at Kelsey. "Are you okay? I saw you have that panic attack during the assembly. Are you doing better?"

Oakley steps in front of Kelsey, blocking my view. "*No.* I don't want to be associated with your crusade against my uncle, and I don't want you here on our property. I will call the police if I have to."

"It's not a crusade, it's a quest for the truth," I say calmly.

"Is that why you're posting inflammatory statements on the Puma Boards?" As soon as the words leave her mouth, Oakley winces, like she didn't mean to bring it up. Something like fear flashes in her eyes. But she raises her chin, and she doesn't back down.

I was a fool to think I could get her to trust me.

"If you saw the post on the Puma Boards, you know your uncle's classroom was defaced with spray paint before the fire," I counter. Words are our only weapons in this fight, and I hope I'm wielding them right. "I saw you protect Kelsey from your uncle during the assembly. I want to know what you know. I want to know why you did that."

She steps toward me, and now we're close enough that we could touch. She's an inch or so taller than me, and she stares me down, her eyes blazing. "Fuck, do you make a habit of going to people's houses and asking intimate questions about their private lives? You don't see me coming to your house to ask if you still have nightmares about your father crashing his car, do you?"

I flinch.

How does she know that?

"How dare you?" My hands tingle, and the world sways beneath my feet. Fuck diplomacy. "Do you want to talk about personal? My friend *died*. No one knows how or why because your family is covering for your uncle like it's no big deal, even though he's *assaulting* students. And for all I know, he assaulted Eden too."

Kelsey pushes into the doorway to stand next to Oakley.

"Criminal. Pervert. Rapist." I spit the words at them both, but my eyes never leave Oakley. "You're a coward for defending him. You don't know how many people are out there hurting because all you care about is your family and your own safety."

It's cruel. It's conjecture at best. I brace myself for her to deny it. But she doesn't.

"You have no idea what you're talking about."

I throw my hands in the air. "Then *explain* it to me!"

Kelsey has gone so pale, it looks like she may faint. Her fingers curl around Oakley's.

"Theo." Kelsey stares at me. "He didn't assault *Eden*."

I freeze.

"Kelsey. No." Oakley steps between us again. Her expression grows cold. Then calculated. Then desperate. "Get out. If you want to know the truth about Mr. Lewis and what happened the night the school burned, you shouldn't be here. You should ask *your* friend. Payton is the only one who knows everything. But she hasn't told you, has she? She sent you on a wild-goose chase, and she hasn't told you the truth. So instead of coming here and accusing *me* of being a coward, maybe you should look a little closer at the people around you. Or maybe she knows that you're just in this for the story and she can't trust you either."

Before I can say anything else, she shuts the door in my face, and I stand there frozen.

Payton knows everything.

I knew she was keeping secrets, but—

Payton knows everything.

And she didn't tell me.

She didn't *trust* me.

I know she has told me she lies. I just never thought she would lie about this.

I walk back to my car in a daze.

I hear footsteps behind me on the driveway. I glance back over my shoulder to find Cameron walking up to me. He looks strangely sad. "Hold up."

"What do you want?" I demand.

"I want you to know something." He keeps his voice down. I can't help but glance back at the house and the large windows overlooking the driveway. Oakley and Kelsey stand next to each other, watching us.

"What?"

"I got into a fight because I tried to protect my friend. That's why Oakley fights. That's what you're doing too. I know what she said was cruel, but so were you." He breathes out hard. "Don't blame her for hurting, please?"

I hesitate, and then I nod. "Yeah."

He's not wrong.

Cameron looks like he wants to say more, but instead he turns on his heel and stalks back toward the house, hands pushed deep into his pockets, his head bowed.

I climb into my car, and I pull out my phone to see if Payton has left me any messages.

She hasn't.

Instead, I have notifications for *several* emails and—more importantly—three missed calls and several texts. All from Mom, telling me to come home *right now*.

[MESSAGE TO: PUMA@SECRET.CO
MESSAGE FROM: FENNA STEADMAN]

Dad taught my twin sister and me about the importance of dressing modestly. *The world isn't safe*, he would tell us. *Don't invite more danger onto yourselves.* So we didn't. We dressed carefully. We dressed to avoid danger, or so we thought.

There were days when I wore a stuffed puma head and knew no one could see me, and I felt so safe. Though I dreamed about being a real cheerleader.

My sister, meanwhile, cloaked herself in good grades and academic achievements.

We tried, you see?

But if someone wants to harm you, they're rarely stopped by outward appearances. I realized that when my sister told me about him. She always wore jeans and T-shirts, but Mr. Lewis looked at her like she wasn't wearing anything at all.

She made me swear not to tell our parents.

So I didn't. I didn't tell anyone.

Not until now.

But I swore never to dress as the mascot again. My school spirit—*any* school spirit—was dead and buried.

CHAPTER THIRTY-SEVEN
PAYTON

THIRTEEN DAYS AFTER

Thin clouds pass in front of the sun, casting shadows on the road and on Eden's house. From this perspective, I can see the back of Theo's house and the tall tree between their bedroom windows. I spent so much time there. Long afternoons doing homework with her. Long nights when Dad thought I was asleep in my own bed.

I was happy there.

I turn off the ignition and get out of my car. I have a note for Theo, and I want one last opportunity to say goodbye to the place I shared with Eden. I shrug my hood over my head and stuff my hands into my pockets.

I know exactly how to walk without attracting attention to myself. I duck underneath the kitchen window and dash through the backyard. Eden's house is quiet and dark, like no one's there. Arthur's truck isn't in the driveway, and I don't see the light of the TV in the living room.

These past few months, those have been the indicators that someone was home. The truck or the TV. Each of Mrs. Randall's boyfriends has had their own sign. With Arthur, it's his truck. For Wayne, it was the living room curtains being closed, because he hated daylight. If Eden came home to find a bike resting against the wall next to the front door, it meant Alexander was there.

I wonder—

I shake my head. It doesn't matter who's next.

What matters is that no one seems to be home now, including Mrs. Randall.

I dash to the tree. Wooden steps are nailed to the trunk, and I climb up to the platform amid the branches, worn down and polished smooth from all the people who've climbed and sat here.

From my vantage point, I can see Eden's room, and I expect the curtains to be drawn. They're not. The windows are open. The corners of the curtains sway in the breeze. The afternoon sunlight brightens the room, which looks exactly as it always has. Carvings line her shelves. A picture of Eden and her parents hangs over her bed, and on the other side of the room, a rusty spinning rack holds yellowed comics. It was the only thing one of her mother's boyfriends ever gave her that she wanted, she told me. Frank spent a whole year with them when Eden was seven, and he was kind to her. He took her out for ice cream every weekend during the summer. He built snowmen with her in the winter. When she broke her arm, he sat by her side and introduced her to his small collection of horror comics. He left them with her when he and Eden's mother broke up.

Last week, we sat in her room, trying to figure out what was important enough to pack and what wasn't. She took the comics out of the rack and held them close. Suddenly, she laughed. The sound was so full of joy it gave me goose bumps.

"We can bring only the happy memories," she said. "Leave the bad behind. That way, when we build something new, it won't be weighed down by disappointment."

She held out the comics to me. "After Mom and Frank broke up, I used to dream he'd come back for me. I used to dream Dad would come home too, though we'd moved twice since he left, so he wouldn't even know where to find us. When we start over again, no one will bring us down. Can you imagine, Payton?"

I smiled, but she grabbed my arms and shook her head. "No, imagine it. Close your eyes and imagine it."

Obediently, I closed my eyes, but I didn't know what to do—or how. So I thought of her. Her auburn hair. Her freckles scattered across her cheekbones and her collarbones. Her slender hands with all the tiny scars across her fingers from carving. Her dreamer eyes, brown flecked with gray.

I smiled.

She leaned in and kissed me. "Just like that."

I climb closer out of habit, and then someone moves inside the room.

My breath catches.

My heart skips a beat.

Someone rises from the bed. For a few moments, all I see is her shoulder-length auburn hair and pointy shoulders.

Then the afternoon sunlight catches on silvery strands. Mrs. Randall turns and stares out the window.

She doesn't see me in the tree.

She turns back to the room and picks two wooden roses off one of the shelves, and she cradles them in her hands, tracing the petals gently. They look so fragile between her fingers.

She looks so small and lonely.

She looks like she's lost all purpose in life.

I watch, because I don't know what else to do. I don't want to attract attention to myself.

I've always thought—like Eden did—that Mrs. Randall wouldn't mind if Eden left for her grandparents' place. She barely noticed when Eden was around.

Maybe I misjudged her. Maybe we both did.

Or maybe Mrs. Randall misjudged that Eden would always be there and took her for granted. Just like I did.

"I'm sorry," I whisper. I have so much more I want to tell her.

I'm sorry I failed you.

I'm sorry I never told you.

I'm sorry I was scared.

I'm going to make it better now. I'm going to get you justice, but I can't do that unless everyone knows the truth about Mr. Lewis. And that's on me.

Every time I close my eyes, I wonder what it felt like for Eden to fall. If she had time to regret jumping. If she was afraid.

Mrs. Randall buries her face in her hands.

There's nothing left for me to do here.

I clamber toward Theo's bedroom window and reach inside to place a note on his desk.

I'm sorry.

I do have to do this alone.

Then I slide out of the tree, and I run back to my car.

[MESSAGE TO: PUMA@SECRET.CO
MESSAGE FROM: NORAH COLE]
_____

I wish I could tell you. You're not alone.

CHAPTER THIRTY-EIGHT
THEO

THIRTEEN DAYS AFTER

Mom's psychic powers must kick in, because her name pops up on my screen before I can reply to her messages.

"Hi, Mom."

"Theodore Robinson, where on earth have you been?"

I wince. "I put my phone on silent. I'm sorry."

"I need you home immediately. Principal Young wants to speak to you."

I lean back against my seat. "Right now?"

"She called me at work, so yes, that's the implication." Some of the ice in her voice thaws. "This is about Mr. Lewis, isn't it?"

I balance my phone between my shoulder and my ear as I start the engine. "Probably," I admit.

She's silent, and I can picture her rubbing her eyes and squeezing the bridge of her nose. "Theo…"

"Mom…" I lean my head against the steering wheel. I thought I could do this on my own. Like Payton. Like Eden. But I can't. "Remember when you told me to ask for help when I needed it? I think I'm in over my head."

She breathes out softly. "I'm here for whatever you need," she says, "We'll get through this together."

It's the same thing she told me when Dad died, when the kids back in Flagstaff were cruel, when she lost her job, and when I didn't want to move here.

We'll get through this together.

We always have. Hearing her say it makes me want to cry with relief, pain, worry, grief, all mixed up in one.

"We'll go see Principal Young, and then we'll go home and figure this out. Okay?"

"Okay."

"Can you meet me at the middle school? Or do I need to pick you up?"

I raise my head and stare at the window, where Kelsey is watching me. "I'll see you there."

"I'll wait at the entrance," she promises. "We'll go in together."

I faintly smile at the idea of my mother hovering like a

fierce mama bear. It makes it easier to breathe. It makes me feel protected.

"Theo? I love you."

"I love you too, Mom."

On my way to Fenix Middle School, I try to call Payton several times, but the calls all go to voicemail. Her silence leaves me uncomfortable. But I wouldn't know where to start looking for her. And right now, I have to meet Mom.

I leave Payton a message, asking her to please call me back as soon as she can.

As promised, Mom is waiting for me. Most of her work these days is research instead of on-camera reporting, but she's wearing her studio look: her dark blue jacket and a white blouse, her hair pulled back, and a thick layer of makeup. Her mouth is set in a stern line and there are questions in her eyes, but she opens her arms and holds me for a full minute.

Fear, worry, safety, and heartbreak all clash against each other.

"It'll be all right. We'll get through this."

"I wanted to understand why Eden died," I admit softly. "But everything I learn just makes it more complicated."

"Oh, Theo." She runs her fingers through my hair, pushing a stray strand out of my face. "Stick to the facts. Don't admit to anything you didn't do. Don't share anything that may incriminate you in any way. As soon as we get out of here, we're going to get takeout and have a long conversation where you tell me everything that's going on, and we'll figure out our next steps."

I nod. That sounds sensible. It sounds like something I can manage.

But when we walk into Principal Young's temporary office, my hands grow sweaty. Mrs. Matthews, the principal's secretary, notorious for fiercely guarding the principal's office and schedule, glares at me over sharp red glasses. I once got into an argument with her when I tried to get an appointment to interview the principal for the *Puma Press*. When she told me Principal Young didn't have any open appointments, I went over her head to Mx. Sousa, who arranged a meeting. Ever since, Mrs. Matthews mutters disgustedly every time she sees me.

Today having an appointment doesn't feel like a victory.

Mom clears her throat. "Mrs. Matthews, I believe? We spoke on the phone. We have a meeting with Principal Young."

"Theo is to go straight through," Mrs. Matthews says with distaste. "Principal Young and Officer Parks are expecting him."

A surge of panic courses through me. Officer Parks, the school resource officer, is responsible for safety inside the school. He's called into meetings when the school thinks there's been potential criminal misconduct.

Mom squeezes my hand and nods at Mrs. Matthews. "Thanks. We'll both go in."

Mrs. Matthews half rises from her seat. "I don't think that's—"

"No one is speaking to my son alone," Mom says, her tone brooking no argument.

When we go inside, it's worse than I thought. It's not only Principal Young and Officer Parks. Mr. Llewellyn from the school board is also present. They all look up when we enter. Mr. Llewellyn wears the same grave expression he had at the assembly. Officer Parks hooks his thumbs around his belt. Principal Young frowns at my mother.

The three of them look like my judge, jury, and executioner. But I can use this meeting as part of my investigation too. I push my shoulders back and keep my head high.

"Mrs. Robinson. Theo." Principal Young points at the chairs in front of her desk and introduces the others. "Please, sit down."

Mr. Llewellyn takes the seat next to the desk, but Officer Parks stands comfortably behind Principal Young like a menacing shadow. At the start of every year, he tells the students that he's here for our protection, but no one wants to get on his bad side.

"Principal Young. What is this all about?" Mom keeps her voice neutral.

Principal Young takes a manila folder off her desk and opens it. Gingerly, she takes out several papers and spreads them out in front of her. I recognize them immediately. They're printouts of my photos of the school and my posts on the Puma Boards. "We're here to talk about your son trespassing on school property and maligning a celebrated teacher in the wake of a tragedy."

To my right, Mr. Llewellyn shifts and crosses his legs. He takes a pen out of a cup marked WORLD'S BEST MOM and taps it against the desktop. He looks like it offends him to even acknowledge me. Then he says, "We are willing to make allowances for the fact that Theo has lost a friend, but we cannot let this type of criminal behavior stand."

"I—"

Mom places a hand on my arm to silence me.

"Hush, Theo." She looks at the printouts one at a time. She reads the messages, takes in the details of the photos, and I see her put the pieces together.

"I don't see any proof that my son posted these pictures or these messages, Principal Young. I do see some very disturbing allegations."

Principal Young snatches the printout of today's message from her and points at an underlined sentence. "You can see here that the poster of this message identified himself as a current member of the *Puma Press* editorial board. That narrows it down to only four students."

She flips pages. "Furthermore, the username on this first post is one Theo has used on other occasions, most notably as part of the *Puma Press*. Our IT department informed us that both usernames are attached to the same IP address, implying that after the first was banned, Theo simply created another."

Mom opens her mouth, but Principal Young raises her voice and bulldozes on. "*In addition* to this evidence, we have reports from multiple sources identifying your son as the ringleader responsible for this malicious behavior. If the rest of the editorial board is also involved, they will be dealt with."

"They're not responsible." The words tumble out before I can stop myself. I know Mom said not to incriminate myself, but I won't let Principal Young pull my friends into this.

"Theo," Mom says. "Be quiet."

"No." I shake my head and bite my lip. The atmosphere in the room is oppressive. I push on. "Amaya, Jalen, and June had nothing to do with this." It's as far as I can stretch the truth without lying.

"So you admit that you are responsible?" Mr. Llewellyn asks sharply. He looks at me like he's already made up his mind.

I glance at my mother. "No. I'm just saying they aren't."

Mr. Llewellyn slams the desk, and I startle. "These messages are libelous, young man. You've defamed a respected teacher *and* the school administration. We will not sit by and let it happen."

His tone needles me. Mom probably wants me to shut up, but I can't. "If Mr. Lewis preys on students, he doesn't deserve to be a teacher, let alone a respected one."

Mom raises an eyebrow. "Theo makes an excellent point."

"In all my years at Pierce High School," Principal Young says coldly, "I have *never* heard any complaints about Mr. Lewis's behavior. If I had, believe me, we would have investigated immediately, as is our obligation by law."

Something inside me, tender from my confrontation with Oakley, *snaps*. "So... the messages on the walls were...decorative? Art?"

"An act of *vandalism*," Mr. Llewellyn fumes. "Do you not recognize the seriousness of this situation? The damage you have done to this school and its reputation? It is my recommendation that the school should press charges and have you *arrested*."

I've been perched on the edge of my chair, entirely tense, but at those words, I fall back.

Mom's holding one of the photos I took inside the classroom, one where the word *rapist* is very clear. "Forgive me if I'm missing something here," she says in her reporter voice. "It seems to me that the most important consideration is in fact not whether my son broke the law, but these accusations in one of your classrooms, seemingly about one of your employees who is entrusted with the care of young people. I would like to understand what you're doing to follow up on this besides harassing my son."

I could hug her.

Principal Young leans forward, tenting her fingers. "Mrs. Robinson, I respect the work you do as a reporter, but believe me, there is no story here." She indicates one of the photos of the classroom. "The police and the Fenix Fire Department alerted us to the graffiti on Mr. Lewis's walls after their investigation of the school. Everyone involved took the accusations seriously, and I immediately reported them to the appropriate authorities. As far as I'm aware, neither the police nor the school board uncovered any evidence to support the graffiti."

"It's been thirteen days," I say. "Do you even know who was

responsible for the messages? Is there any security footage? Did you figure out who bought the cans of paint? Did you speak with anyone aside from Mr. Lewis?"

Maybe, *maybe*, they did investigate and conclude that the accusations were baseless. Maybe this is all some big misunderstanding. But an unreadable expression passes over Principal Young's face. She glances over at Mr. Llewellyn, then blinks her mask back in place. "No."

"But you did look into these allegations?" Mom prompts. She reaches for her phone and opens her voice notes app. "Would you be willing to go on the record about that?"

She places her phone on the desk, but Mr. Llewellyn picks it up and turns it off, then hands it back to her. "No, we would not. With no evidence to substantiate these claims, we consider it a private matter to be kept *out* of the press."

Mom squeezes her phone, and the veins on the back of her hand bulge. It's the only outward sign that she's growing angry. "Principal Young, I will ask you again: Did you look into these allegations?"

Principal Young shares a look with Mr. Llewellyn before she nods. "The school board spoke to Mr. Lewis. They concluded that he's not aware of any wrongdoing."

My own phone burns in my pocket with half a dozen emails I haven't read yet screaming at me to open them.

"What about any of his current students?" I demand. "Did you speak with any of them? Any of his former students?"

I'm not sure what fuels my discomfort most, Principal Young and Mr. Llewellyn's false arguments or Officer Parks's silent presence. He stares stone-faced from behind Principal Young. As far as I can tell, he doesn't even blink.

Mr. Llewellyn laughs softly. "We have better ways to investigate than posting on the alumni board, son. Unless your attention-seeking, unsanctioned behavior has turned up information we might have missed?"

"I—"

"*Not* another word without a lawyer present, Theo," Mom snaps.

I suddenly see the trap—if I tell him what I found, I have to admit to posting the messages. So I clamp my mouth shut and swallow what I meant to share.

In the silence that stretches between us, I feel the tension in the room shift. If I'd been here on my own, I would have said far more than I should. I assume that's what they were hoping for. Mom's presence, not just as my mother but as a local reporter, shouldn't be the deciding factor in whether my school treats me fairly or not, but it is.

Principal Young takes back control of the conversation. Her voice is loud and clear and offers no room for argument. "Neither the school board nor the police found sufficient evidence to necessitate further investigation of Mr. Lewis. In the years he's taught here, he has received only commendations. Whoever defaced his classroom must have had cruel intentions. In the meantime, this community is in *pain*. Your actions have only exacerbated that pain, and I'm most disappointed in you."

It's the strangest thing. Despite the fact that I know she's lying to me—whether on purpose or because she doesn't know the full story—those words hurt. It's as if Principal Young is pressing on the emotional bruises Oakley left.

It's not fair.

She glances at my mother before she adds, "Still, I understand that you're grieving too. We...should make allowances for that."

In other words, she doesn't want to antagonize the local media.

Principal Young continues, "We want our community to heal. Mrs. Matthews tells me that her church intends to look after Eden's mother. Lewis Industries has already—quite graciously—committed funds to start rebuilding the school while our insurance claim is processed. We want you all to have a chance to thrive."

Her saccharine smile and diplomatic words aren't convincing, but the bit of information she just let slip is. I don't know how long an investigation into a teacher's misconduct normally takes, but I bet it's longer than two weeks. I don't know how much time big donors need to allocate funds, but I bet that's longer than two weeks too.

No evidence of wrongdoing, no security footage, no concerns about the money needed to rebuild the school. They may even make a profit after the insurance pays out.

Mom's so still that I know she has noticed this too. She sounds pensive when she says, "We all want a healthy, beneficial, and safe environment for our children."

"Exactly." Principal Young nods. "So please do keep that in

mind, Theo. Let us all work together to that end. Stop your witch hunt."

Mr. Llewellyn glowers at me. "If you don't, the school board *will* press charges for trespassing and ensure that you're prosecuted to the full extent of the law. Do you understand?"

I stare at him for what feels like ages, then turn to Mom, who gives me a slight nod. I plaster on a fake smile and hope he doesn't see the rage that burns behind it.

"Yes, sir. I understand perfectly."

CHAPTER THIRTY-NINE
THEO

THIRTEEN DAYS AFTER

The drive home is silent. Mom told me to leave my car in the middle school parking lot and that we'd pick it up later. She wants to keep me close.

I don't mind. It's a privilege to go to a home that feels safe.

But once we leave the school grounds, I take my phone out of my pocket and frown. "It's true, you know. All of it."

Mom glances over. "The allegations?"

"He's been sexually assaulting students for years." I tap my phone screen to make it light up. My number of email notifications has grown to eleven. At the same time, there are no missed calls or messages from Payton. "Can we go to Payton's house? I need to know she's safe."

"Is she involved in this too? And Eden?"

"Eden got caught up in it, I think. Payton..." Oakley's words echo in my head. "Payton hasn't been responding to my texts. I want to know she's okay."

"Do you know where she lives?"

"Yeah." I give Mom the address, then open up my inbox. My breath catches. While I can discount several of them as hate mail, most of the emails...aren't.

Scrolling through them one by one, a chill runs down my spine.

[MESSAGE] Mr. Lewis offered to tutor me.

[MESSAGE] I blamed myself.

[MESSAGE] I thought it was just me.

[MESSAGE] He assaulted me more than a decade ago.

A decade.

A decade of silence.

"When we get home," I say quietly, "we need to talk about what's next. Because we can't let this slide. *I* can't let this slide."

Mom's quick, proud smile warms me. "I know. We won't. But I do want to get a lawyer involved, and we need to gather all relevant information before we bring this to the studio."

The idea that my mother could really get people talking is appealing, but... "We can't bring it to the studio. Not yet."

"Why not?" Her voice holds no judgment, just curiosity.

We turn onto the street where Payton lives, and I recognize the twin Green girls playing with a Frisbee in their yard. They attend Fenix Middle School and are part of the school newspaper there. If I'm not mistaken, they're off to Pierce High School next year, and that makes me want to scream.

"The station can report the story," I say, "but it's ours first. Payton's. Mine. *Puma Press*'s too. The rest of the editors know what I've been doing, and they support me. The station can have the story, but I want us to be the ones to tell it."

Mom pulls in front of Payton's house and parks. Since Dad died, it's been the two of us against the world. We make it work. From the very first day she told me, all we have is the love that makes our family and the trust that keeps us strong. I've always felt like I could talk to her, and in return she gives me more freedom than most of my friends have. Mom never just says no. She always explains why.

But now, for the first time, she hesitates. "I get it, Theo. I do. But I don't know if that's the right way to go. I don't know if it's safe for you. For any of you."

"Do you only report on the things that are safe to talk about?" I counter.

"Of course not." She shakes her head with a faint smile. "But that's my job."

"And these are my friends."

She pinches the bridge of her nose. "Let's go see if Payton's home first."

"Mom?" I know what else I have to tell her. She has to understand what's going on. And it's easier to have this conversation here, in the car, with our eyes on the road. The words don't quite feel as hard. "Before we go in, you should know that I think Payton's father is abusive."

Mr. Davis pulls open the door with force. His eyes are wild and bloodshot. He reeks of beer, and his hands are balled into fists. "Who are you? What do you want?"

Mom clears her throat. "Mr. Davis? I'm Haley Robinson, and this is my son, Theo. We're looking for Payton."

He zeroes in on me. "Theo. What do you want with my daughter?"

Payton says he has good days too. That there are times he takes care of her. I just see an angry, pitiful man who hurts the girl I've come to consider a friend, despite all the secrets she keeps.

"Nothing, sir. I just want to know where she is."

"Well, that makes one of us," he scoffs.

Mom places a steady hand on my shoulder. "Mr. Davis, are you okay? You don't look well."

"It's nothing I would care to share with you, a *vulture* of the media. Ma'am."

"Mr. Davis, where is Payton? You're not holding her here, are you?" I would try to push forward if it wasn't for Mom holding me back.

He spits on the ground. "Don't—do *not* take that tone with me, boy. I told you, I don't know where my daughter is. She's a common criminal, and when someone finds her, I hope it'll be the police."

"What do you mean?" Mom asks, slipping into reporter mode. Calm, neutral, inviting. The only evidence I have that she's as angry as I am is how hard she's squeezing my shoulder.

"What I mean is, she and that freak friend of hers blew up the school because they felt slighted. I found the evidence myself, and instead of admitting to what she did, my daughter tried to shift the blame. Then she ran off. But believe me, I've already called the police. I will *not* let this stand."

I'm raging inside. Maybe I should pity this man. Maybe he's hurting and sick. But the more he says about Payton, the less I want to try to understand him.

"What kind of evidence?" I ask through clenched teeth.

"Spray paint. She took some of the cans, but I kept the rest to turn over when an officer gets here."

I take a deep breath to steady myself. My ears are roaring. My heart pounds.

"Mr. Lewis, are you certain—" Mom tries, but he cuts her off. He jabs a trembling finger in my direction.

"And *you*, boy. I don't know what your intentions are with my daughter, if you fancy yourself her boyfriend, but you should know she is a nothing. You should steer clear."

"You could have protected her," I snap. It takes everything I have not to scream at him.

He turns bright red. "What's that?"

"Never mind." Mom yanks me back before Mr. Davis can lunge at me. "Theo, we're leaving. Mr. Davis, thank you for your time."

"Now *wait a minute*—" he roars.

Mom is already marching me back to the car. "No, we're leaving. Theo, come on."

"Mom…"

"Now."

—

My hands shake.

I hate him.

"Can we go by Eden's grave?" I have to focus on finding Payton, because if I allow myself to think about her father's comments—no matter how drunk he was—I will rage or cry. I want to slam my fist into the car's dashboard. I want to break something. I want the world to not be so fucking unfair, especially to the people I care about.

Mom's lips press into a thin line. She nods. "We can do that."

When we reach the church, I dash between gravestones.

Payton is nowhere to be seen, but I linger for a second. The earth on Eden's grave has settled.

I'm not sure if I believe in a life after death, but this is the closest I can get to Eden now. So I promise her, "I'll do what I can to protect her. I wish I could have protected you too."

She doesn't answer. Of course she doesn't. The only sound in the graveyard comes from the wind rustling through the trees. A small bird chirps and takes flight, and the same breeze that plays with the leaves cools my cheeks. The setting sun colors the sky red, and this moment could be meaningful. Maybe. Honestly, it's just lonely.

By the time I get back to the car, I'm chilled through. I shake my head to let Mom know Payton isn't here, and the frown she's been wearing deepens. I slip into my seat and hug my knees.

"Would she do something foolish?" Mom asks.

I shrug helplessly. "She's hurting. I don't know what she'd do. But I told her she could always come to us if she needed help."

"Oh Theo." Mom reverses the car and begins the drive home. "She's always welcome if her home isn't safe. All your friends are. *Always*."

"I should have told you about her father, but it felt like betraying her trust. It still does."

"Did something happen between her and her dad last night? Is that why she stayed over?"

"Her father freaked out at her, and she needed a safe space."

"We can set up a temporary bed in my home office. We can talk with her when we find her, call social services about what to do next. In the meantime, is there anything else you want to share with me?"

I shake my head.

She sighs. She places her hand on mine and squeezes. "Next time, tell me, okay? Next time, you tell me."

For the first time, there's an edge to her voice. I feel on edge too. While Eden taught me it was naive to think all families are loving and caring, I want to cling to the fact that *most* are. I hope they are. I hope the little girl we pass who is playing ball in her yard while dressed as a princess has parents who love her unconditionally. I wish the same for the purple-haired kid with the rainbow shirt who's walking five dogs at once. I hope they have a family who protects them and fights for them when they need it.

But as we drive by house after house, I can't help but wonder how many secrets are kept inside, how much pain and sorrow hides behind closed doors, how many of my friends in Fenix have had to rise from the ashes and remake themselves over and over again.

I wonder what on earth I can do to keep the people I care about safe.

When we get home, I find a note on my windowsill, and I know whatever I've done isn't enough.

[MESSAGE TO: PUMA@SECRET.CO
MESSAGE FROM: ALICE FINK]

Mr. Lewis offered to tutor me.

    I always got good grades, but I found myself struggling with my chemistry homework, and he offered to help. He started with brushing my hair out of my face while I was reading the textbook, putting a hand on my shoulder when I aced a test. The attention made me feel more secure and confident, so I didn't push back. I wondered later if I should have, if that would have made things better. I thought it was my fault.

    I've carried that with me into college.

    I'm only now realizing how much I hurt.

CHAPTER FORTY
PAYTON

THIRTEEN DAYS AFTER

Mr. Lewis's house is smaller than Kelsey's but quite a bit larger than where I grew up, larger than any of the houses in my neighborhood. The siding is a subtle gray blue, and the porch spans the entire width of the house. There are patches of clover in the grass, and bright, colorful curtains peek out from behind the windows.

There's a sign with their names next to the front door. James Lewis. Claire McNally-Lewis. Zanna Lewis.

In a strange way, the house looks so mundane. An upper-middle-class house for an upper-middle-class family with 1.9 kids and a dog. There's probably a dusty set of bikes in the garage from when the family tried to live healthier. The kids' artwork stored in boxes in the attic. A pool, apparently, or so the rumor goes.

Harmless.

That's what it looks like.

There's nothing at all scary about Mr. Lewis's house, and yet facing it fills me with dread.

His classroom once seemed safe too. A place where I could go for help because I didn't want Dad to freak out over a failing chem grade. I should have dropped the class and filled my lab requirement some other way.

I should have known not to trust Mr. Lewis, but he smiled and told me how proud he was of me for asking for help.

No one had ever told me that before.

I should have seen right through it.

But I basked in the kind words. I didn't shy away from that first soft touch, even though I should have.

Until one day, it became more than that. Until that care turned to pain as well.

In a way, the worst part wasn't how much it hurt physically. Or how empty I felt afterward.

The worst part was when Kelsey Fink found me. She'd never spoken a word to me before, but she looked at me with blazing eyes and said, "I know what he did to you, and I'm sorry. I'm so sorry. I want to find a way to stop him and make him pay for what he does to us. Are you in?"

She didn't look at me with pity. She looked at me with understanding.

Briefly, I thought someone would believe me and fight for me.

But now I have a series of texts from Oakley.

OAKLEY:

> That school newspaper reporter friend of yours was here. We sent him back to you.

> If you say anything, if you tell anyone what happened to Kelsey, if you imply we were there with Eden—you won't like what happens next.

> Kelsey is moving on. She tried to make a difference, but she has to take care of herself now.

> Leave us alone.

> Don't talk to us.

> Don't talk about us.

> Or we'll make sure everyone knows who started the fire.

My hands shake. I lie. I keep secrets. I would never share Kelsey's without her permission. But I hoped *she'd* be willing to share her story. To stop him. How can they talk about moving on?

And how can they talk about being blameless? I'm guilty, but aren't they also to blame?

Everyone who was there in the school with me.

Everyone who stood aside and did nothing.

Everyone who stood by amid the pain,

the loneliness, the abuse.

I'm tired, and I'm guilty, and I'm so angry it will tear me apart. Let it.

I won't stay silent any longer.

I won't let anyone cover this up.

I'm done being afraid.

This isn't justice, like Kelsey promised.

This isn't vengeance.

This is me screaming my throat raw until someone hears.

I stuff one can of spray paint in the pocket of my hoodie and shake the other one.

Then someone places a hand on my shoulder.

[MESSAGE TO: PUMA@SECRET.CO

MESSAGE FROM: AMEENA SADER]

We're stronger together. I wish I'd known that sooner.

    This is a reminder, should you need it.

    I see you.

    I believe you.

    I support you.

    I am you.

CHAPTER FORTY-ONE
KELSEY

ONE DAY BEFORE

The night before we put our plan in motion, I call my sister.

"Alice, can I tell you something?"

"Is it important? I'm studying for midterms." Her voice is flat. She sounds exhausted, but I need her.

"You were too busy when you were home for Christmas too."

"Because I have a busy life." Sarcasm seeps in as she says, "Can't disappoint the family, what with all the money they're investing in my future."

"Alice, that's not fair. They want what's best for you." I wince at how empty those words are coming from me.

She groans, "God, you sound like Mom."

"Ugh, don't. If there's something *better* for you, I'm sure you can convince them of that."

"Right. Because the last few times we talked about college, that went *so well*. Speaking of—have you heard back about your applications?" she asks, not-so-subtly changing the topic.

I grimace. "Uh…not yet."

"Should've gone early decision, kid."

"Now who sounds like Mom?"

"Don't throw my words back in my face!" she snaps. A year ago, she would have laughed at that. Now she just sounds angry.

"Then don't change the subject. Isn't Columbia everything you wanted?"

"Past Alice lived a different life. Can we not talk about me? Tell me about whatever high school drama you've got going on. I miss those days when everything felt massive but none of it mattered."

Her words are a gut punch. I need her. I need her to be my big sister, because a storm is coming, and I'm scared. "Whatever. If you're not going to take me seriously, I'll hang up and leave you to your midterms."

She sighs and softens a little. "Kelsey. Kels. Kid. My very favorite baby sister. I never take you seriously, you know that. With all the wisdom of my advanced age, let me tell you that high school isn't the end of the world. One day, you'll look back at what felt like a struggle, and you'll laugh." Her words have a teasing lilt, like she's trying to tempt me into one of those fights we used to have for days on end.

I respond in kind, but my heart isn't it. "First of all, I don't think so. Second, you're the worst."

"You still love me."

"I just...*fuck*. Can you stop being so condescending and tell me everything will be all right?"

"That *does* sound important."

"*Alice.*"

"Fine. What's up?" She isn't joking anymore, and it takes my breath away. I want to tell her, but now I don't know what to say. Not over the phone.

"I...We... Something happened at school. My friends and I are planning to stand up to the administration."

"Are you being vague on purpose?"

"Yes?"

"Are you going to break the law?"

I try to smile. "Have you met me?"

"You didn't answer my question. Is it dangerous?" Alice sounds more concerned with every question.

It warms me. "I don't think so. But I'm worried we'll be ignored. It matters. I don't want to mess it up."

"Hm. It's hard to tell you what will happen without knowing exactly what you're planning to do. But if you're doing the best you can, that's important. You won't change the entire world and you don't have to. You can affect change in small ways. My—Amina is part of a climate activism group on campus, and she always reminds me that change starts with one choice, one decision."

I perk up at that, grasping at the distraction because her words are suddenly too close, too real. "*Your* Amina? Do you have something to tell me?"

"Gotta go. Gotta study." I can hear my sister *smirk*.

"Alice, wait!"

"What?"

I have to ask, "What if we don't change anything?"

"It matters that you tried. I meant what I said. The world outside of high school is so much bigger. Once you're out of there, you can follow your own path. It doesn't always get easier, but—"

"It gets better?" I make a face.

"It gets different. *You* get better. What's going on, Kels?" Her voice has grown quiet, and I can picture her now, worry lines between her eyes. It wouldn't surprise me if she's nibbling her lip. She used to do that whenever she was studying or worrying about a test.

I push my nails into the palm of my hand. Perhaps I can build my way up to this. "You're the second person to tell me that the world outside of high school is better. Do you know who was the first?"

"I forgot to enroll in Telepathy 101. Enlighten me." She has to be rolling her eyes.

"Mr. Lewis. Do you remember him?"

"Yeah, sure. The chem teacher."

"My friend Cameron got into trouble for fighting with him. He got expelled. Because Mr. Lewis is *a good man*. Cam made a mistake, but Mr. Lewis... The administration loves him. I'm sure his connections with Lewis Industries help too. And the scholarships for the best chemistry students—"

I'm rambling when Alice interrupts me. "Kelsey. Focus. Why are you telling me this?"

"I just thought that...maybe you'd remember him. I..."

"Believe me, I remember Mr. Lewis," she says, and she sounds as tired as she did when she picked up the phone. I remember Mr. Lewis mentioning her, but she has never mentioned him.

I hear rummaging on the other end, and Alice says something to someone. Her attention slips away.

"It's just—"

She coughs and interrupts me again.

"Kels, if you're not going to be straight with me, I have to study. I'll be thinking about you. Stay away from Mr. Lewis and you'll be fine. We'll talk soon, okay? Love you."

With that, she disconnects.

"Alice? Wait! Alice!" *Fuck*. "Love you too."

CHAPTER FORTY-TWO
KELSEY

THE DAY OF THE FIRE

Oakley leans against the tree where we're gathering just outside the school grounds. We agreed to meet after dark to go through the plan one final time. Tension knots my stomach. We're so close now, but part of me wishes we could just be home. Somewhere safe and comfortable. But Oakley insisted on meeting here.

"She doesn't want to be seen with me," Payton noted when I told her. "I don't belong with you."

"That's not true," I said, not entirely convinced.

Payton smirked. "Yes it is. You didn't even know my name. Besides, you're seniors and I'm not. It would look strange."

I didn't fight her. The Kelsey from before would have stood up to her—or *for* her—or known how to get along with her. Me, I only know that we have a common enemy and that's enough. We exist in different worlds.

I used to think girls like her were more likely to be victims. The weird, quiet, vulnerable types.

I was so wrong. It's girls like us. All of us. He has made us all vulnerable.

Our pain and hatred are magnets, pulling us toward each other. But Payton's made it clear she's not here to be friends. Neither am I.

Oakley has taken charge, because that's what she's good at. Schedules. Lists. She's been planning tonight with a vengeance. She's been *protecting* me with a vengeance.

After college applications were in, she started showing up at the stables to watch me ride. She spends long afternoons and evenings with me at my place, watching this quirky TV series about a vet in an English village. It's one the few things that makes me smile—and *that* makes her smile. She's ditched some of her own after-school activities and her mother's events to spend time with me. We're constantly in each other's orbit. We are each other's gravity. I love her for it.

Oakley made a whole list of pros and cons for water- and oil-based spray paints before she ordered them online. She bought different cans of paint and showed them to us. She even demonstrated them for us. In the end, toxic fumes and environmental hazards won out, but that's my fault. My one demand was that the paint wouldn't be easy to remove.

We have our story to tell. I want to make sure it lasts.

"We have to wear gloves," Oakley said last night as she went through her notes one last time. "Paint stains on our hands are going to be a dead giveaway."

I shrugged. "If the story is going to come out, I *want* him to know it was me. That it was *us*."

But nerves have wormed their way into my throat. I haven't been this nervous or scared since that day in Mr. Lewis's classroom.

Gloves are a good idea.

The spray paint is a good idea.

This is a good idea.

Right?

"What if it doesn't change anything?" I ask. "What if it doesn't make a difference?"

Cameron jogs toward us and waves hesitantly.

These months have changed us all. He's grown taller, and he's been working out. His soft lines have given way to hard edges. He's grown more cautious, and it's not a good look on him. Even when he got into fights at school, it was never malevolent. He'd lose his temper when someone bullied a kid or he couldn't handle the injustice of some decision. But as soon as his temper fled, he'd scratch his head and look remorseful. Lashing out wasn't right, and he knew that, but he never truly harmed anyone either.

Now he's the one who looks hurt. If he gets caught breaking into the school with us...

"What if we make matters worse for Cam?" His lawyer and the school's came to a settlement of sorts, but I don't know what will happen if they think he broke the law again.

Oakley reaches out a hand, waiting for my nod before she places her fingers on my arm. "He chose to be here. We all did."

She rubs my shoulder with her thumb, but I can't look at her. I don't want to be responsible for their choices. Am I?

"We want to do this for you. You deserve to be free from him. Whenever you need me, I will be there. I will do *anything* to keep you safe."

"What's going on?" Cameron asks, frowning. The hoodie he's wearing pulls on his shoulders, proving he's filled out. His voice is different too. It holds a new sadness.

"Kelsey wants to know if we're doing the right thing."

"We are," he says simply.

"It's not just about me," I argue.

Cameron drops his backpack onto the grass. The cans of spray paint, which he kept safe for us, rattle inside. "You're right. It's not just about you. It's about all the other girls he did this to. Everyone he'll try to assault. We can't undo what happened, but we can stop him from ever doing it again."

Oakley nods fiercely. "We have to keep him from harming anyone else."

"Once they see what we've done, they'll have no choice but to listen." Cameron looks at me intently. "Are you ready?"

I try to let their confidence fuel me, and I plaster on a smile. "I'll have to be."

Cameron's gaze drifts over my shoulder as Payton approaches. She has her hands pushed into her pockets, and her shoulders are pulled up to her ears.

She doesn't look ready either. She always looks like she's balancing on the edge and expecting the world to reach out and punch her.

But despite her nerves, she's determined. She brought her own cans of spray paint after she saw Oakley's samples. She has a core of steel and anger. When Oakley and I found her that day after she left Mr. Lewis's classroom, she wasn't puking out her guts in the bathroom. She was standing under the bleachers, away from prying eyes, punching the wall of the school over and over and over again. Her skin was torn to shreds and her knuckles were bloody and bruised.

She didn't let me touch her. She flinched away from sympathy. She just told us, "I'll do whatever you want me to do to bring that bastard down."

She lifts her chin and stares at us now, her eyes flashing. "Right, so are we doing this?"

Cameron picks up his bag, jingling the cans. "Every assault, every bit of pain he caused, we'll make sure his classroom bears witness."

"We'll go in through Mr. Bradford's computer lab," Oakley says.

She produces a small key. "I stole this when I went to see Zanna after class yesterday. Mr. Bradford won't notice it's gone."

Infamously, at the start of the year, he didn't even notice when two entire classes didn't show up. He sat at his desk playing solitaire or online poker or something like that.

"The wind picks up around us, and it starts to rain.

Cameron licks his lips. "No one should be around tonight. We'll be in before midnight and out before one a.m."

"Good," Payton mutters.

Oakley raises an eyebrow. "Should we keep in mind your one a.m. curfew? Do you have somewhere else you need to be?"

Payton doesn't respond. She never seems fazed by Oakley's snarky remarks.

Oakley stares at Payton. If I'm completely honest, Payton is right to think Oakley doesn't want her here. Oakley doesn't trust her.

"We don't know her," she told me. "She's weird and too quiet. She never seems to tell the full story."

"She's hurt," I argued.

Oakley shrugged. "What if she's dangerous?"

I only told her, "I know she keeps secrets. I also know how hard it is to speak up." So I don't blame her. She promised to be here tonight, and it matters that she is.

In another life, we wouldn't have been friends either. We don't have to be more than coconspirators. But I do need her here. Her cold rage fuels my own. Together, we're not alone.

I clear my throat. "Tomorrow morning, as soon as Mr. Lewis's classroom is discovered, we'll go to see Principal Young. Oakley and me. You too, Payton, if you want. Mrs. Matthews won't be able to stop us this time. I will tell the principal what Mr. Lewis did. We'll take pictures tonight, and if anyone tries to dismiss us, we'll post them on social media, we'll send them to the police, to the local newspaper, to everyone. We'll be so loud they can't ignore us."

I glance at Payton, whose mouth is pressed into a thin line. While she's here tonight, she couldn't promise to help us tomorrow. Apparently this is her limit on *whatever you want me to do.* I try to respect that, though it's hard to accept. She's part of this. She should want to fight too.

At least it helps to know that I'll have Oakley by my side. My own immovable force.

And Cameron, who always has my back. He smiles. "Good. Are you ready?"

"Yes," I say, shoving away my nerves. My voice comes out loud and clear.

Payton usually keeps her emotions guarded, but tonight I can see them all in her eyes.

Loneliness. Fury.

Hope.

"Are you ready too?" I ask. "I know this won't be easy."

She nods. "Tonight will change everything. I refuse to carry this pain with me," she says carefully, as if she tastes every word. "I don't want to give him—give any of them—that satisfaction. I deserve better than this. *We* deserve better than this. We'll stop him once and for all."

I hold out my hand, and she slides hers on top.

"Together," I whisper.

Oakley places her hand on top of ours.

Cameron adds his hand to the pile. There are tiny scars from working in the restaurant's kitchen across his fingers. "Payton is right. Tonight we make this school safer for everyone."

"For all of us," Oakley and I repeat at the same time. We share a smile, I feel the comfortable pressure of her fingertips against my wrist.

Payton doesn't say anything, but she lets out a deep breath.

For all of us.

CHAPTER FORTY-THREE
EDEN

1:07 A.M.

Everything is loud and quiet all at once.

Everything hurts.

My ears are ringing. My head is pounding. I'm going to be sick.

Something heavy pushes against my chest, and something sharp digs into my leg. I claw at it, but I don't find purchase.

I'm cold and wet, and I feel wind on my skin, though I'm inside.

There's fire and rubble. Thick smoke rolls across what I can see of the floor. The smoke is oily and bitter and disgusting.

I don't know how to breathe.

I turn toward my face toward the harsh air and let the freezing cold suffuse me.

I reach for the heaviness on my chest again, and my fingers curl around concrete. Part of the wall?

The classroom around me is unrecognizable. When I look to my left, I see a void where a wall should be.

When I look to my right, I see flames.

Ms. Ruiz taught us about fires in elementary school. Heat, fuel, and oxygen. All the chemicals and the lightning were good fire starters, and the flames have nearly endless fuel and oxygen.

Fire laps at what remains of the drop ceiling above me, and water rains down from a twisted, burned sprinkler head.

It's not the smoke that's choking me. It's terror. Pure, breathtaking terror.

In the distance, someone calls my name.

I try to lift the weight off my chest. My ribs protest the movement. But I have to get out.

"I'm here!" I push the concrete block to the side, inch by excruciating inch.

"Eden? Can—ear—ee?"

"I'm *here*!"

"Payton?" It's Kelsey. "Cameron?"

With strength born of desperation, I shove at the concrete block, and I feel my ribs snap and shift. My head feels light, like I'm going to faint, but the piece of glass I can see in my leg refuses to let me drift.

I take a deep breath, roll onto my side, and I stay low.

Pain courses through me. The meager dinner I ate earlier tonight claws its way up my throat, and I vomit. My vision twists.

I wipe my mouth with my sleeve and try to ignore the disgusting taste, the way even my teeth are sour.

I force myself to keep close to the floor, where the air is clearer, and orient myself.

"Payton? Kelsey!"

A wall of smoke and flames separates me from the others. In the opposite direction is the gaping hole where walls and windows used to be.

The wind fights to push into the room. The smoke tries to spread out. The fire just consumes it all. It's everywhere.

I cannot see a way through.

I don't know how to get out.

I would give anything to be home with my mother now.

I didn't even say goodbye because I figured she wouldn't miss me. And if she did, well, we could talk on the phone. There'd be time.

I should have waited in the parking lot in the rain.

Help me get out, I plead.

"Eden—where's Payton—where are you?" Kelsey's voice is a lifeline. I cough. "I'm here! I'm here!" Then, "I don't know where she is!"

Amid the smoke and the flames, I glimpse figures. Kelsey is visible and then gone again. When she reappears, she's clinging to another taller figure. Cameron. Their shapes change and morph, like some twisted sort of shadow puppetry.

Cameron ducks low, shielding his eyes with his arm. "Payton!" His voice cracks and trembles.

I try to crawl closer, but I have nowhere to go. Now that I know where the others are, it's almost easier to understand them. Kelsey stands in what had been the doorway. She keeps trying to venture inside, but the heat pushes her back. "Payton, come on!"

"I can't see her!" I shout.

Our gazes connect across the chaos, and the bright glow makes her look ghastly white. She reaches out a hand. "Eden! Can you make your way here?"

I don't know.

I don't know.

The floor around me is slick with rain. My leg throbs from the piece of glass in it. I'm perhaps a foot from the outer wall. Everywhere else is fire and flames that are growing closer.

"I don't think so…"

Her face twists.

Oakley wraps her arms around Kelsey's waist from behind. Despite the growling of the fire and the high-pitched whistling of some of the gas containers, I hear her. "If we can't find Payton, we have to go!"

"*You* said this was a good idea," Kelsey snaps, looking back at her. "*You* convinced me to be here!"

"I didn't mean it like this!"

"We have to get out!" Cameron reminds them urgently.

I freeze. "What about me?"

"Run through?" Cameron suggests. "Or jump?"

Through the flames? Or out of what used to be the window? I can barely stand. Panic floods through me. I can't. I *can't*.

"Please don't leave me." It's the closest to begging I've ever come.

"We won't," Kelsey shouts. "We'll get you and Payton out."

But I know she's lying. They are no match for the fire. If they don't escape, it will consume them and the rest of the school.

Oakley grabs Kelsey's arm. She will leave us without a second thought if it means keeping herself and Kelsey safe. "Come on. We never should have involved her."

Her.

Payton.

Right now, I hate Oakley with the same ferociousness as the flames around me, as the storm at my back.

Kelsey pulls her arm free, but Oakley grabs hold of her again. "She did this. You know that, right?"

"She's a victim too," Kelsey shouts at her.

"I'm not going to die for her!" Oakley screams. "And I don't want *you* to die in here either!"

She drags Kelsey out of the classroom.

Leaving me to burn or jump.

[MESSAGE TO: PUMA@SECRET.CO
MESSAGE FROM: LYDIA OLSON]

After Mr. Lewis assaulted me, I demanded to see the principal. Mrs. Matthews said he had meetings, so I camped outside Principal Grall's office for the rest of the day.

The wooden bench was so uncomfortable, and Mrs. Matthews spent most of her time staring at me with this mixture of disgust and fear. Like I was some kind of ticking time bomb. If people constantly look at you like you're the problem, it gets under your skin. It plants seeds of doubt, and pain is such a fertile environment.

She even called the SRO on me. He wrote me up for missing classes. He tried to drag me out of there. I wouldn't leave.

Eventually Principal Grall appeared. He was a tall, lanky man with a deceptively kind face. Everyone at school—at least when I was there—knew him as tough on rule breakers. That's why I hoped he'd do something. But when I tried to tell him why I was there, he pursed his lips, looked me up and down, and made me feel so small.

He asked me if I had proof of my allegations.

I didn't, of course.

I was suspended for a day for, in his words, "behavior unbecoming to a Pierce High School student."

CHAPTER FORTY-FOUR
THEO

THIRTEEN DAYS AFTER

I place my hand on Payton's shoulder. When I read her note, I realized there was only one place she could go. Seeing her now with two cans in her hand, I realize she is carrying so much more than grief alone. "Hey."

A can of spray paint clatters to the ground, and Payton flinches. "*Fuck.*" Her voice is as sharp as the rattling cans. "Theo?"

I pull my hand back. "I'm sorry. I didn't meant to startle you. Breathe, please. *Breathe.*"

She's trembling, and her breath rasps. "You scared me," she manages half-heartedly.

I see her claw at her defenses, trying to get them back up. I stare past her at Mr. Lewis's house. "I got your note," I say. "You're not alone. And he's not worth it."

"I hate him," she whispers. "He destroyed everything. And no one will listen to me. The others…" Her voice trails off. She shakes her head. "There are no others."

There are, I want to remind her. Not just the people she clearly doesn't want to talk about, but the ones who send me messages. The ones who saw the pictures of the walls and felt seen.

Payton deserves to be seen too. And heard.

"I will listen." I speak gently. "He assaulted you too, didn't he? You meant to stop him, to tell everyone what he did, but somehow things got out of hand. Eden was there with you, to help or support you, but then the fire overwhelmed you both. Is that more or less what happened?"

She shakes her head. "She didn't know. Eden. She didn't know."

I bend down to pick up the fallen can of paint and place it out of her reach and out of sight in case someone drives by. I sit down at the side of the road.

"What happened?"

She sinks down next to me. "I was so angry. I felt so lost. I wanted to do something right. To stop these men from hurting us." She closes her eyes, but behind her eyelids, they move rapidly, like she's reliving every moment. "I didn't want her to see me differently."

Tension ripples across her shoulders, and then panic overtakes her.

She breaks.

"I'm sorry," she says. "I never meant to put her in danger. I never meant for her to die. She died because of *me*."

She sways, and I catch her in an embrace. She doesn't resist. I have so many questions, but asking them now would be cruel.

"Do you hate me?" she asks in a small voice.

"I don't," I say. And that's the truth. "Why didn't you tell me?"

"You wouldn't have believed me." Payton shakes her head. "I wanted you to believe me. I wanted you to understand. Leading you to find the truth was all I could think of." She keeps muttering the same thing over and over again, as though she's breathing the words in and out. "I'm sorry. I'm so sorry."

Somewhere across the road, Mr. Lewis is probably at home with his daughter and his wife, and they have no idea this is happening.

Somewhere across town, others feel the same pain as Payton, and they don't know this is happening either.

The same words, like a prayer to hold on to. "I never meant for this to happen."

I would have believed you, I want to tell her. But would I have? A week ago, Payton was a stranger to me. In most ways, she still is.

So instead I hold Payton, and she clings to me like I'm the only thing keeping her upright in the middle of a raging storm that never let up. I pull her closer, and her shoulders shake.

My heart squeezes, and I feel a heady mixture of pain and anger and loss. I want to tell her I don't blame her, but I'm not sure it's the truth. I'm not sure it matters either. It's not for me to judge. So I say the only thing that does matter: "Come home with me. Mom will take care of you. And we'll bring him down. Together."

She takes a deep, shuddering breath, and she *pushes* the words out like she will drown in them if she doesn't. "It's just me, Theo. I'm no one. If it's my word against his, everyone will side with him. They'll side *against* me. You can't fix that. Not even with your newspaper." She glances at the spray paint. "They'll probably arrest me, but Eden deserves my truth. I'm tired of hiding it."

"It isn't just you," I say slowly. With clarity, I know what our next steps must be. I pat my phone, thinking of the messages that have been sent to our tip line. "It isn't just you, Payton. I know of a better way to get everyone's attention so no one can ignore you anymore."

She looks up at me with a glimmer of trust and hope. "Do you promise?"

I do. "I promise."

She sobs. "I'm sorry."

I am too.

CHAPTER FORTY-FIVE
THEO

THIRTEEN DAYS AFTER

Mom isn't the best cook, but she makes chicken soup from scratch. She tells us she's made up a bed for Payton in her office, and she's called a lawyer friend who'll come talk to her in the morning.

Payton nods and takes it all in, but her eyes keep drifting to me, as though she needs the assurance that this is real. On my way home, I told her what my plan was, and she agreed to it immediately. Wholeheartedly.

When we've finished eating, I show Payton to my mother's office and dig up some comfortable T-shirts and pajama bottoms from my dresser. Once she's changed and has everything she needs,

I go to give her space, but she holds out a hand to me. "Theo? Can I tell you what happened?"

It may not be the smartest move. Maybe we shouldn't talk details until Mom's lawyer friend gets here in the morning. But she's had to stay silent for so long.

She reads my hesitation. "Not as a newspaper editor or a witness or anything. Just—as a friend. You…deserve to know. I'm so tired of carrying this alone."

I understand that. I nod slowly. "Okay."

"Yeah?"

I sit on the floor next to the fold-out bed, look up at her, and *listen*. "Tell me the one story about Eden I haven't heard yet. And more importantly, tell me about you."

So she does.

—

Once Payton has told me about the night the school burned, I tell her about all the messages sent to the anonymous tip line. She reads them. Quietly, On her own. Then she helps me draft a response to all of them, asking for permission to share. I send them out one at a time, and then I walk downstairs. I sit down at the kitchen table, grab the notepad Mom uses for groceries, and start sketching out an edition of the Puma Press with all the pent up fury inside me. When I realize Mom is looking at me, I still.

I clear my throat. "I know you think this may not be safe, but I can't stand by and let Mr. Lewis assault more students. I can't stand by and let the school ignore what happened. They probably won't let me edit another school newspaper after this, but someone has to report what happened. For Payton. For everyone he hurt. For Eden too, because she didn't deserve to get caught up in this. Without him, she would be alive." And happy. And free.

Perhaps Mom recognizes the truth in my words, because she nods. "What do you need?"

I bite my lip, wary for some way she might turn this around. I get wanting to protect me. I do. But I need to protect my friends too. "Your office when Payton isn't sleeping. Food for the *Puma Press* crew for the whole weekend."

She looks a little sad and a little proud all at once. "Done," she says. "On one condition: We talk with Robert in the morning, and you follow his *exact* advice. Deal?"

"Deal."

Everything goes into overdrive. The following morning, Mom's lawyer friend shows up, carrying an obscenely large cup of coffee and a briefcase. Robert wears a blazer over a band shirt, and his green-rimmed glasses stand out neon bright against his dark brown skin. He puts the briefcase on the table and takes out a laptop, but he seems to have newspapers and comics in there too. I like him immediately. He's younger than I expected, but if Mom recommends him, he knows what he's doing.

He tells us that he's going to handle any and all communication with the authorities from this point forward. We're not to talk to the police without him there, and it's best if we don't talk to anyone from the school without him or a parent present either. Payton winces at that, but Mom reassures her that she's happy to step in for her dad if it's needed. In a twisted kind of way, I'm not sure if that makes things better for Payton or worse. I remember what she admitted when she left here.

I'm jealous.

But then she looks at both of us in wonder and I hope the good outweighs the bad.

Strangely, she *isn't* worried about her father having called the cops on her. "I know I'll have to pay for what I did one way or another," she says like she's accepted it as fact.

Robert nearly chokes on his coffee when he hears that. "Let's settle matters of guilt and culpability in an appropriate manner. From where I'm sitting, you're a victim and a survivor, not a criminal," he says carefully. He takes out two old-fashioned business cards. "So you know how to call me."

Despite the situation and all his extremely justified concerns, Robert agrees that as long as we keep Eden's name out of the piece and don't share anyone's story without their permission, we can publish a special edition of the *Puma Press*. "I could advise against it, but I know better than to tell Robinsons what not to do," he says with a wry smile in Mom's direction. She blushes.

"I will remind you," he points out, "that school newspapers do not legally fall under protected speech. Your principal can—and very likely will—prohibit you from writing about your teacher."

I nod noncommittally. "I know. Our adviser always reviews the *Puma Press* before it goes to print. But we have to try."

It helps that I don't intend to print this edition at school. Or let Mx. Sousa read it.

Robert raises his eyebrows.

I keep my face blank and smile at him.

He sighs.

Still, there is comfort in knowing he's here for us.

Once Robert is gone, Payton expresses the same thought. "I'm glad to have him in my corner, but I can never pay for any of this, and I can never repay you."

Mom, who's sitting on the other side of the kitchen table, reaches out a hand to her, and when Payton reaches back, she gently squeezes her fingers. "Never worry about repaying us in any way other than by thriving," she says simply.

"And helping me with the newspaper," I add when the heavy emotion become too much to bear. "I've already invited the rest of the crew over to help, and I'd like you to be a part of it."

Payton blanches at the mention of the others. But she breathes out hard through her teeth, and she nods. "Okay."

Which means that two hours later, when Amaya and the others show up, Payton doesn't flee like Eden used to flee. We push her bed to one side and cover it with pillows so it can be used as a makeshift sofa. Amaya brings a large box of donuts. June looks a bit nervous but intensely determined. Jalen immediately plops down on the pillows. Payton perches on a chair.

"So, what's the plan?" Jalen asks, tugging at one of his braids.

I pass around bottles of soda, then place my computer in the middle of the sofa. I open the tip line inbox and point at the screen. "This."

Jalen and June lean in to read.

Amaya looks at my mother's bookshelf, pulling books out and pushing them back in. "I've already read the emails," she says softly when I ask. They drafted responses together.

"How's Taylor?" I ask.

The books in Amaya's grasp slips. Her shoulders drop. "She's fine. She's safe. He never touched her, and I've been struggling with how relieved I'm feeling."

"You shouldn't be," Payton says, observing her quietly. "You shouldn't feel guilty. I'm glad he didn't harm her. I just..." Her mouth works. "I wish I could understand why he picked us. I wish I knew what we did."

Amaya walks over to Payton and—when Payton nods—grabs her hand. "You didn't do *anything*. None of what happened is your fault. His choices were fueled by cruelty and selfishness, and you bear no responsibility for them. Do you hear me?"

One corner of Payton's mouth pulls into a half smile of appreciation. "Maybe."

I hear what she isn't saying. That she still feels responsible. If not for Mr. Lewis's actions, then for her own.

"So this is what we'll do," I say, when everyone has finished reading. "We need to bring Mr. Lewis down. I have reached out to everyone who emailed our tip line, and I've asked for permission to share their stories—ideally with their names, but anonymously if they prefer. Six have already agreed. They're prepared to talk to the police as well. Once we've broken the story, the local media can have it too. Mom promised she'll do everything she can to make sure the station features it. But since this happened at our school"—I glance at Payton to make sure my wording's okay—"since this happened to *students*, I want us to be the ones to tell these stories first. We'll make sure neither the district nor the administration is able to dismiss us, ever again."

They all nod.

I spread my arms out wide, as if to encompass the whole office. "We have one weekend to put together a special edition. June, can you do the layout? I have pictures of Mr. Lewis's classroom after the fire for the front page. I'm under strict instructions not to mention Eden in any of the articles about Mr. Lewis, but I would like to add a short obituary on the back page. Payton can help with that, maybe." I tap my leg. "Amaya and Jalen, I'd love for you to write a reconstruction of Mr. Lewis's time at Pierce from the moment he started working here nineteen years ago to now. Anything you can find. Remind readers that a lot of people stood by and let this happen."

"Do you want us to hack into the school computers to see if there are any complaints in his file?" June suggests. "Because I'll do it."

"I would rather you not do anything illegal while we're using my home Wi-Fi," I remind her with a faint smile.

She scratches her ear. "Right. Yeah. Layout it is."

"I'll work with the information in the emails and keep an eye on what comes in. I'll find a way to include all the stories that we're allowed to share." Reading them once was bad enough. Going through them over and over again to make sure everything aligns will be worse. I don't want that to fall on the others. Or on Payton.

I clear my throat. "I need you all to know, we're probably going to anger a lot of people in Fenix. Including people at Lewis Industries. I don't know how involved they've been in covering this up, and I'm not sure how to find that out."

Payton coughs but doesn't say anything. She's carefully avoided saying that anyone else was present the night the school burned. She has never mentioned names. But it doesn't take much to guess. Based on what Kelsey said and how Oakley responded to my questions, I have an inkling who the others are—and why the school board and the police department have stayed silent.

"I have reason to believe Lewis Industries has been very involved," I say. "And I don't know what that means for your family members who work there. The company might retaliate." I want to give my friends an out. One last chance. "We're not showing this edition to Mx. Sousa for approval. We're not sharing it with any of the teachers beforehand, and we're likely going to get into a lot of trouble for it. After this, I don't think there'll be a *Puma Press* anymore. So if you'd rather I do this alone—"

"Stop," Amaya interrupts me. "Stop trying to scare us away. We're doing this together. This is too important."

"Exactly," Jalen says. The three exchange meaningful looks, and it's clear they've talked about this. Jalen bumps my elbow. "We've got you."

June nods, her pink-tipped ponytails bouncing. "If we go out, we go out with a bang."

As soon as she realizes what she said, she looks at Payton in apology, but Payton says, "I'll help you with the obituary. But if you all let me be a part of this—"

"You *are* a part of this. You're a friend of Theo's, which makes you our friend," Amaya interrupts. "I'm sorry, but you're stuck with us now."

"Thank you." A blush crawls onto Payton's cheeks. She takes a deep, shuddering breath. "Then we'll do it right, which means you have to let me tell my story too. Not about the night the school burned. But about what happened with Mr. Lewis."

I lock eyes with her. "Are you certain?"

"No," she admits. "Yes."

I hesitate. It's a brave thing to do, and it's not on me to take that away from her, only to support her. "Then we'll include your story too."

She manages a smile, and she doesn't flinch when June pats her hand awkwardly.

Amaya looks at her with bright, shining eyes. "Can I hug you?"

"Me too?" June asks.

They let Payton think about it. They let her decide. When she finally, cautiously, nods, they both wrap their arms around her tenderly.

Payton's eyes find mine, and I see a flicker of surprise and discomfort before she settles into cautious joy. "Is this what a *Puma Press* group hug feels like?" she asks.

"Not quite yet." Then, making sure she's okay, I wrap my arms around all three of them. A moment later Jalen follows too, though like always, his arms end up twisted with Amaya's.

"This is," Amaya says. "Once the *Puma Press* adopts you, we take care of you."

"Isn't that also what you said about the fish in the tank in our classroom?" June says with such sincere confusion that I can't help but snort. Amaya giggles. For a brief, magical moment, laughter bubbles up around us and between us, and when I look at Payton, she's laughing too. It makes her *shine*.

We work through the rest of Saturday and all of Sunday. Mom makes us homemade lasagna and provides us with ample ice cream, coffee, and snacks. I like the food, but our determination to finish this newspaper could have sustained us. Amaya works with a drive I've never seen before. She didn't even study this hard for the SATs. Jalen disappears to the town library twice for research. June hums while she's working, and because she has the loveliest singing voice, we let her.

But no one works as diligently as Payton. It's like she needs this to *be*. It's catharsis, perhaps, a little.

When the sun sets on Sunday evening, the three of them go home. I send the file to Mom's printer, and I let myself fall back on Payton's bed as the printer begins to spit out our special edition of the *Puma Press*. Payton looks as exhausted as I feel, but she's focused on the printer. She's more present than she has been for as long as I've known her.

"We're doing this," I tell her. "For Eden."

She nods. "For all of us."

[MESSAGE TO: PUMA@SECRET.CO
MESSAGE FROM: PAYTON DAVIS]

I always wondered if Mr. Lewis preyed on the girls who had no one to talk to. Girls like me. If that's what made him feel safe.

Admittedly, I never thought I would tell anyone what happened. I wouldn't have told anyone if it weren't for friends who reminded me I'm not alone. Isn't that the most harrowing thought? That assault is easier to talk about because it has affected many of us?

I didn't want to bring home a failing grade, so I asked Mr. Lewis for help. He did what he apparently does to most of his victims. He invited me into his classroom and locked the door.

I froze.

CHAPTER FORTY-SIX
EDEN

1:08 A.M.

The last thing I hear is Kelsey's strangled cry as Oakley pulls her out of this mess.

The hungry roar of the fire overtakes all sound, all thought, everything.

I thought I felt stuck in my life before, but this is completely different. I lie on my stomach with my head in my arms to protect myself from the heat.

But then—

Someone groans. A chair scrapes across the floor.

My heart trips.

Smoke fills my lungs, but I manage to keep my voice steady as I shout, "Payton? Talk to me. It's just us."

Nothing.

Nothing.

I don't know how much time has passed since the explosion. It feels like we've been here forever—standing in the parking lot in the pouring rain seems like a distant memory—but it can't have been more than a minute or two.

Your whole life can change in two minutes. Or in two moments. Opening one window—and then opening another.

"Payton?" I try again.

The gas canisters that fuel the Bunsen burners whistle and make weird sounds, and I wonder how long it will take for them to explode.

Then,

"I'm sorry. I didn't mean for this to happen."

Payton's voice. Soft. Raw.

I would recognize it anywhere.

I crumple. Suddenly, all that's left is fear and loss. I didn't know it was possible to grieve something that hasn't happened yet, but I do. I want to get out of here. I want a chance at a better life. I grieve the lives we might have had.

I still believe we deserve them.

"Me neither," I say.

"I just want the pain to stop."

I'm trying to figure out where her voice is coming from. Near—or maybe behind—Mr. Lewis's desk?

Perhaps that's our only luck. The wind is blowing the fire deeper into the school, away from the corners of the classroom. I have no way out unless I run through the inferno, but the fire isn't coming for me yet.

Not yet. I will bargain with the universe itself.

Not yet.

Give me more time.

"Payton, listen to me." Flames are licking at the wall around the doorway, but they haven't covered the opening completely. It's an escape. "You have to get out of here."

"I don't want to go back to the way things were."

I look out at the dark night through the hole where the window used to be. That will be my escape. It's only two high floors, and the drop will surely be better than staying here.

But not yet.

Not until Payton is safe.

I shift closer to the thunderstorm, and I breathe in the fresh air.

"So don't go back. I promise there are places out there where your dad can't hurt you. Places where you can trust the people who are supposed to protect you. Places where you're loved. You just have to get out of here. *We* have to get out of here."

She doesn't reply.

"Payton! I won't jump until I know you're safe. I won't leave you!"

"Maybe you should."

"I *won't*." If it's the last thing I do, I will make sure she gets out of here. "We're in this together, right?"

"Eden…" The finality in Payton's voice makes me want to claw at the flames that separate us. Any tears I might cry evaporate in the heat.

"Payton, I need you to trust me."

"I love you," Payton says in reply. I can hear the emotion in her voice, and I hate that this is the first time she's said this. I want to hear her say it again and again and again.

"Tell me you trust me." I wait for her to say she can't, that it's hopeless. "Try, Payton. For me."

I shift closer to the outer wall and the air outside. We're up higher than I thought it would be. "Run, Payton. *Please*. I'll meet you outside."

Then, like a miracle, a tall figure appears in the doorway. It can only be Cameron. Smoke is swirling all around him, and he coughs, then holds up something.

"Eden!" he calls out. "I have a fire extinguisher. Just hold on."

Cameron Jenkins, Fenix's resident bad boy, who's never up to any good. Pure relief washes over me.

"Payton is near Mr. Lewis's desk! She's closer!" I shout with all the breath I have left in me. "Get her out. She needs to run."

"Eden…"

The first of the small gas canisters explodes with a scream. Shrapnel flies past me.

"Eden!" The fear in Payton's voice rings out over the sound of the fire.

"Go."

Cameron points the nozzle of the fire extinguisher in the direction of Mr. Lewis's desk, where Payton must be crouching. It wouldn't be enough to tame the inferno between us, but he can carve a path for her.

Another canister explodes, closer to me this time. The force pushes me forward. The flames spread faster now.

"I love you. Run."

"Run!" Cameron echoes.

I hold my breath and will her to go.

There's shadowy movement beyond the flames. Payton stands. She doubles over and coughs loudly. She looks desperately in my direction—and she runs.

She runs along the pathway Cameron created through the flames. I hope she keeps going. To safety.

She runs, and I breathe.

Until it hits me: I'm truly alone now.

I thought I knew every thread and barb that kept me tied down, every cruelty, but I only accounted for my own secrets. Not those of others too.

I shouldn't be here. I know that.

But I am.

I'm here.

I could wish I'd never entered the school, but it made a difference, didn't it? Payton got out.

Love amid this destruction. At least it made a difference.

I push myself up despite the fact that everything hurts, and the heat immediately envelops me, but I only half notice it. Even the roar of the fire disappears into the background.

I fold my hands and curl my fingers, rubbing at the nail of my thumb with my other thumb. When I carve figures out of wood, I let the grain guide me to find what's hidden within. I hoped running away would feel the same way. Like letting the path ahead guide me.

With the heat of the flames at my back, I face the night. Thunder rumbles in the distance, and the rain is slowing to a drizzle.

I'll wait outside.

I'll meet up with Payton.

We'll make a new home, a place to belong. A place to matter.

I close my eyes.

My foot slips.

I stumble forward.

Before I can jump—

I fall.

CHAPTER FORTY-SEVEN
PAYTON

EIGHTEEN DAYS AFTER

When we sneaked into the school two and a half weeks ago, the mood was dark and tense. A storm raged outside, and the electricity inside was struggling. With the lights flickering on and off, the school alternated between existing and fading away.

By contrast, Fenix Middle School is an explosion of color. The walls are painted in soft pastels with brightly colored tiles. Several have motivational quotes decorating them, reminding students to be honest, curious, and kind.

Half of the school is cordoned off for Pierce's juniors and seniors, and I've never felt older than when I see the first middle school students arrive. I clutch my bag to my chest and nudge Theo. "Look how young they are."

Theo's lugging a heavy backpack, and he grimaces. "I swear they get smaller every year."

I hope that by the time they get to Pierce High School, it'll be a safer place for them.

Theo's mother dropped us off early, and she's waiting in the car, because she knows our plan. She reminded us again this morning over breakfast that she is proud of us and that she has our backs. It's weird how those words warm me. I don't know what to do with that feeling or how to hold on to it.

But I try.

We're among the first to slip into the gym, which is once again set up for an assembly with long rows of folding chairs. It won't be as crowded as last week's assembly, when the whole student body was invited.

Amaya leans by the door and propels herself forward when she sees us. She's carrying a shoulder bag. Jalen has already found a place in one of the rows on the left side of the gym, a cotton tote bag under his seat. Because the middle schoolers are using all the lockers, we have to carry everything we need for school with us—and today our bags are filled with copies of the *Puma Press*'s special edition.

Amaya's hand brushes my arm. "Are you ready?"

"As ready as I'm going to be." I'm not as nervous as I expected. Sure, my stomach is in knots. My story might as well be written on my skin. I can feel the words seared into me. But if I have one skill, it's surviving pain and discomfort. I've let fear guide me for so long, and now I let courage take the lead.

"Good. June texted to wish us all good luck."

As a sophomore, she's starting her day with online classes. Theo is confident that when the story breaks, it will reach the rest of the students swiftly.

Amaya finds a place on the right side of the gym, opposite Jalen. She pushes her bag under her seat too.

Theo looks at me. "Right in the middle of the room, then?"

The largest block of seats is in the middle. Other students are filtering in, talking loudly. Worry zings through me, and I push it down. "Sure. But somewhere near an aisle, if that's all right with you."

"Of course." Theo gives me an understanding smile, and I'm grateful he promised to sit by me.

We talked long and hard about how to get the *Puma Press* into the hands of readers. Amaya suggested distributing the newspapers to the classrooms before students arrived. Jalen rightfully pointed out that teachers would confiscate them before anyone had a chance to read them. It's the same reason we opted for spray paint in Mr. Lewis's classroom instead of posters: We wanted to make it impossible to get rid of the evidence quickly.

June suggested folding the papers and pushing them into the middle school's lockers, but that felt like too much work to do unnoticed.

So in the end, we settled on boldly handing out the papers during the assembly. Hopefully by the time the teachers realize what we're doing, it'll be too late to stop us. Even if we get caught, there are four of us and a lot of papers.

Theo takes a seat, hiding his bag underneath his chair, and I do the same. We're in sync without thinking about it. I wonder what Eden would think if she could see us, her two best friends, working in tandem. Two parts of her world that she kept separate because she was so terrified to lose them—to lose us.

I hope she would understand. I hope she'd be proud of us.

More of the juniors and seniors start coming in, and the teachers find their places at the front of the assembly. My heart leaps into my throat. I struggle to breathe. This time, however, it isn't smoke clawing up my lungs but panic.

I jump when Principal Young taps the microphone. A few of the lights around us dim, leaving a spotlight on the makeshift stage. "Juniors and seniors of Pierce High School—"

As she welcomes us, Theo elbows me. He's holding a stack of the papers. "Ready?" he asks softly.

I touch Eden's necklace, and I nod. "Let's do it."

Fumbling quietly with the zipper of my bag, I pull out my stack. The top edge of one sheet slices my finger, and I hiss at the paper cut, nearly dropping and scattering the pile. Dad would say I'm so clumsy. I don't listen to his voice in my head.

Principal Young drones on at the front. From behind me comes a whisper. "What's that? Give me one."

I turn and pass a few papers to him. He's one of the guys from the football team. Dave, or David, or something. He's not someone I'd normally talk to. Now I whisper back, "Pass these on."

He takes them and does what I ask. I swallow down the panic clawing at my throat. The girl in front of me only takes one copy of the *Puma Press*, but she must read the headline, because she turns back for more to pass out. Then the boy behind me taps my shoulder for more too. Once I've started, it becomes easier to let them go, knowing the articles will take on new life as they are shared.

Next to me, Theo passes out papers with gusto, tapping people's shoulders. As the assembly progresses, he gets increasingly careless, his whispers louder, his movements less controlled.

From the corner of my eye, I spot Amaya. Where Theo is determined, Amaya is graceful.

On the other side of the aisle, a student calls out softly, "Hey, can I have one too?"

I recognize Nafisa from Eden's art class. I nod. I grab a fistful of papers and glance at the stage to make sure Principal Young isn't looking in our direction.

In the front row, one of the teachers—probably alerted by the rustling and the voices—turns to us, and I freeze.

Mr. Lewis's eyebrows are up near his hairline, and it's as if he's staring straight at me. His mouth slowly slips from a surprised gape into an angry frown. A big part of me wants to crumple up the pages and pretend they never existed.

"Payton!" Nafisa's whisper sounds too loud.

I press back against the chair.

His stare displaces more oxygen than the smoke did.

Without breaking eye contact with Mr. Lewis, I reach over and hold out more copies of the *Puma Press* to Nafisa.

Maybe that's the turning point. Or maybe we reached it already and I failed to notice, because all of a sudden, the gym is quiet. I look from Mr. Lewis to Principal Young. She's paused her speech and holds the microphone, looking confused. The rustling of paper gives way to whispers and protests. Doubt and outrage.

In the void of Principal Young's silence, several things happen at once.

Mx. Sousa, the history teacher and adviser of the *Puma Press*, gets up from their seat and legs it toward Theo. They hold out a hand to him. "Give me one, Mr. Robinson. *Right now.*"

Theo—who has moved down the aisle and is handing papers to a member of the chess club—yelps. The noise is followed by a shout from the other side of the room.

"No!" Zanna Lewis grabs her purse from her seat. She faces Kelsey and Oakley, who sit side by side a few rows down. Her other hand clenches at her side. "Is this it? Is this what you couldn't tell me?" Her shrill voice breaks and her shoulders slump. "I thought we were *friends.*"

She storms out.

"Good riddance!" someone calls out.

"She isn't responsible for her father's actions, you ass," Amaya calls back. Then she covers her mouth with her hand and looks wide-eyed in my direction.

Oakley gets up out of her seat and runs after her cousin. The door slams behind her as chaos descends on the gym. Shouts. Arguments. Students are muttering in disbelief, and others are sobbing.

"What is this behavior?" Principal Young calls out. "You are high school upperclassmen, not middle schoolers. Silence!"

One of the senior boys—I think his name is Luis—grabs a paper and brings it to her personally.

Mr. Lewis snatches one of the papers out of the hands of an unsuspecting student.

In the aisle, Mx. Sousa has finished scanning the first few pages of the *Puma Press*. They've gone pale.

"Why didn't you consult me?" Mx. Sousa asks Theo. "I'm your *adviser*." There's a mix of anger, hurt, and fear in their tone.

"Payton?"

Kelsey timidly stands next to me. She holds a copy of the *Puma Press*. The photos on the front page are a tangible reminder of what we did—of what we *tried* to do. She's shaking. She's as lost as I was.

"Did you...?" she starts, gesturing to the paper in her hand.

"Only my story is mine to tell."

She nods. "Thank you."

Others crowd around Amaya and Jalen, who still have copies of our printouts. Some of the teachers join the line.

Two rows down, a girl sits with her head in her hands, friends flanking her on either side. Several people have pulled out their phones, either to call someone or text pictures of the paper. A few teachers and Officer Parks try to confiscate the newspapers, but for every one they take away, another finds its way into students' hands. The story is out.

If we had told one person at the time, no one would have believed Mr. Lewis was capable of assaulting students. But there is no way to dismiss our accusations—*my* story, *our* stories—now. The whispers of doubt in the gym make way for disgust. Disgust morphs into anger.

I'm certain some doubts and denials will linger, but they're not the loudest voices. They have no room to grow.

Kelsey retreats to a corner, where she sits on the floor with the newspaper in front of her, her chin on her hands. I don't know if she's reading or simply taking it in. This. All of it.

There's a commotion at the front when Mr. Lewis crumples up the paper he's been reading and throws it onto the floor with force. He sees us and stares daggers, his trademark smile gone.

"Lies!" he seethes, heading for us. "These are terrible lies! How *dare* you? You will pay for this, all of you!"

But when he nears, something miraculous happens. Two boys from the football team step in front of Theo and me. Other students follow, one at a time, without flinching, creating a protective shield around us. The football players. The chess club members. The popular kids. The history geeks. The band. The field hockey team. The rest of Eden's art class, with Nafisa and Morgan holding hands tightly, both wearing bracelets with the same stone hearts they placed on Eden's grave.

One by one, they take out their phones, filming Mr. Lewis's rage.

The senior who stepped up first says, "We won't let you touch them. Ever again."

The fury in Mr. Lewis's eyes is terrifying, and I shrink back, but Theo places a reassuring hand on my arm.

A tall senior who I've seen hang out with Cameron pushes his phone into Mr. Lewis's face. "Pervert."

The words from the graffiti are taken up by the people around him. "Criminal."

"Rapist," I whisper.

Mr. Lewis looks like he wants to shove the students aside, but the chant around him grows louder, and he shakes his head.

Then he does the unthinkable. He turns and stomps out of the gym.

We all let him, because there is no real escape. The truth is out there. It's everywhere.

I pull free from Theo's grasp and take a deep breath. "Now he knows what it means to be afraid."

Principal Young pushes her way toward us.

"To your classes, all of you," she orders weakly. "Theo. Payton. With me."

Everyone stays where they are—until I nod.

And I am overwhelmed by something I rarely felt before. Something I will never forget.

Support.

It's hard to read Principal Young's expression. We know now how many people support us, but I don't know if she's one of them.

I glance at Theo. We discussed what might happen after the paper went out.

The three of us walk down the hallway toward the office Principal Young is using temporarily when Theo speaks first.

"My mother should be waiting for us in your office. We would all love to know why the administration sheltered a predator for so long."

Principal Young, to her credit, replies, "It seems like we have a lot to talk about. Far more than I've been aware of. Please, join me."

She guides us into the small office, past Mrs. Matthews, who's already claimed a desk in the administrative den in front of Principal Young's workspace. She's nearly apoplectic, waving at the door. "They—they just walked in! They insisted on seeing you! I—"

Principal Young cuts her off. "Matilda, please cancel my meetings for today."

Principal Young enters her temporary office, and Theo drops a paper onto Mrs. Matthews's desk before we follow the principal in and she shuts the door.

Inside, Theo's mother is waiting for us with Robert, the lawyer.

I reach for Theo's hand and squeeze it while Mrs. Robinson introduces Principal Young and Robert.

"A lawyer?" Principal Young looks taken aback. "Is that necessary? Surely we can have this conversation amongst ourselves first."

"If I may remind you," Theo's mother points out calmly, "I told you the last time we spoke that my son would not have further conversations about this without a lawyer present. The same holds true for Payton. It *is* necessary, Principal Young. We are going to do this properly or not at all, because someone has to protect these teens after so many have failed to do so."

Theo smiles at his mother.

I settle into one of the chairs. Principal Young holds the newspaper as she sags down into her seat. "I understand. Please, tell me."

"What do you want to know?" Theo counters.

"Everything." Principal Young places the special edition of the *Puma Press* on her empty desk. On the front page are photos Theo took of Mr. Lewis's classroom after the fire. On the back page is a picture we took of Eden's carvings, the ones she made for us and would want to be remembered by.

I reach for the necklace she made me, and the small wooden apple feels warm to the touch. I hold it gently.

I'm not alone.

I clear my throat, and one word at a time, I tell my story of the night the school burned, of trying to find justice, and of the girl who believed in me and the future we wanted to create together.

[MESSAGE TO: PUMA@SECRET.CO
MESSAGE FROM: EMMY MCNEAL]

He wasn't the first.

    I hope I was the last.

CHAPTER FORTY-EIGHT
EDEN

~~Dear grand~~

~~Hello~~

Hi,

I'm not sure if you remember me. I'm Eden. Eden Randall, Scott's daughter. You're my grandparents. I hope you remember me. I know it's been a long time, but...well...

I need you.

When Dad left, I thought it would be my mother and me against the world, like in stories or movies. I thought things would be okay. Sometimes they are. Most of the time, they *aren't. There's always someone else here. Boyfriends are easier to manage that daughters, Mom said once. Easier to cast aside when they don't fit anymore, too.*

I don't fit anymore.

I can't stay here.

I love to carve wood figures. I like to think I inherited that from Dad. Or maybe from one of you?

Anyway, it's not just me who needs help. It's Payton too. Payton's my... Payton's the girl I'm madly in love with. She doesn't really have a home yet either. Not one where she can breathe and sing and dance without fear of being hurt.

Not one where she—where either of us—can be.

We both need a safe place. A place where we're wanted. I hope your home can be that safe space. I dream about your farm, you know? I remember visiting with Dad when I was tiny. Do you still have animals? Do you have an orchard, or just an apple tree? Do you have a spare bed or two?

By the time you read this, we'll be on our way.

We won't stay if you won't have us, I promise, but we need a destination. We're not running away. We need a place to run toward. Because that isn't cowardice. It's hope.

I hope you'll open the door for us.

I hope I'll see you soon.

All my love,

Eden

EPILOGUE
PAYTON

AFTER

Theo sent me a set of paint markers. Amaya added watercolor markers to the care package. She sends me small colorful bits of stationery every so often too. She meant it when she said the *Puma Press* crew would be there for me. I don't have words to tell her how much I appreciate that friendship.

I wake up early and sketch the horizon on thin wooden planks. There's something more durable about wood than paper. It reminds me of Eden. I'm not very good at sketching without hiding it yet. But Elisha, my therapist, reminds me that I don't have to be. She tells me creative work is therapeutic.

And I do like it.

Making art feels so much better than scrawling words with spray paint on Mr. Lewis's walls. It isn't just the feel of the markers in my hands or the way every sketch is a little different. The world changes around me, and I try to reflect that on the page. The sky here is endless, with farmland for miles. Unlike Fenix, where every familiar turn and every familiar landmark was a shackle that bound me to home, here is nothing. The open space makes it easier to breathe.

I wish Eden was here beside me, making one of her carvings. Like we planned.

Theo sends me updates from Fenix.

Mr. Lewis has been fired and charged with multiple counts of assault and rape. The school administration didn't file charges against Theo for trespassing, and Principal Young is trying to make amends. She claims she didn't know what was happening. Rumors are that Mrs. Matthews kept students from speaking up in the past. I'm not sure that's an excuse.

After the story broke at school, it was impossible to contain. Pierce High School and Fenix have been at the center of a handful of news cycles. The *Puma Press*, to everyone's shock, *hasn't* been disbanded, and the special edition found its way to local and regional newsrooms. It was national news for a hot minute. State media kept on it for a few days until a freight train derailment took over the headlines. Theo has promised his mother will keep checking in on the school for the local station, at least.

Lewis Industries came under fire for trying to protect Mr. Lewis, but it didn't last long. In the end, money speaks louder than truth. Half of Fenix needs Lewis Industries to pay their bills. But mercifully, Amaya's father, June's mothers, and Jalen's brother weren't fired Mrs. Robinson thinks the company couldn't afford more bad press.

I stayed with Theo and his mother for about a week after we released the special edition. Theo continued attending classes—or what passed as classes. The whole school was in disarray. Teachers wanted to give students the opportunity to talk, and they needed the space to work out their own feelings too.

But I didn't go in. I couldn't face them. No one outside of the *Puma Press* crew missed me anyway.

Oakley ignored me. Cameron checked in with a handful of texts. Principal Young rescinded his expulsion, but I don't know if he decided to go back.

To my shock, Kelsey dropped by Theo's to apologize. She told me she was sorry about everything. She's trying to heal. Her sister flew back home, and they both had a long conversation with their parents. They're planning to spend some time together, the four of them, to reconnect. She told me her parents had agreed to pay for therapy for both her sister and her. What we did made a difference for her, and I'm relieved.

I am.

She doesn't deserve to carry the burden of what happened forever. Elisha would remind me that that's true for me too.

I'm not there yet, but it's getting easier to think that one day I will be.

Dad called me twice. The first time, I told him I was safe and I didn't want to speak to him. The second time, I let it ring.

I haven't spoken to him since.

I have spoken with the police on several occasions, always with Robert present. Not just about what happened with Mr. Lewis but about what happened the night the school burned. Robert's unsure if they're going to press charges against any of us for breaking and entering and recklessly causing the conditions for the fire. For being involved in Eden's death. If they do, he thinks the charge will be something called negligent homicide. He talks about mitigating circumstances. Circumstantial evidence. The security footage simply never showed up. But Lewis Industries has provided Oakley and Kelsey with the best legal team money can buy, and Robert says they'll make it look like I'm solely responsible. Cameron refused their legal help, but he's the one who tried to save us. He shouldn't get caught up in this.

Then again, a little voice that sounds remarkably like Elisha tells me, neither should we.

Neither should I.

Still, I *feel* responsible. I am responsible in so many ways. I won't blame the prosecutor for pressing charges if they do. We just have to wait and see.

After the truth about Pierce came to light, Theo's mother brought me to the hospital to get me a chest X-ray and have me checked out for any lingering damage from smoke inhalation.

When we got home with a fancy new inhaler in tow for me, I had a voicemail from an unknown number. The crackling voice introduced himself as Gary Randall, Eden's grandfather. He told me Eden had sent him and his wife a letter. It had arrived two days after the school burned, and that was how they'd learned of her death. They were devastated by what had happened, and it had taken a while for them to figure out how to get in touch with me. He said her letter had mentioned me. "I know it may be a small consolation," he said, "but we would have welcomed you both. There's a place for you here."

When I returned the call, he told me, "We know what happened from the news. It may seem strange to you, but we don't blame you. If there is blame to go around, it belongs squarely on the shoulders of the people who should have protected you and our granddaughter. It falls on us too. We should have been there."

Something in his voice cracked. "We can't undo that. But we can be there for you, for as long as you need a place away from Fenix."

"It might be forever," I said, uncertain of what else to say.

"Then forever it is. We'll figure it out somehow. Eden would have wanted us to help you."

It felt like too much to accept. "But I..."

"Eden would have wanted it," he said again, emphasizing every word. "It's the least we can do to help you both."

Help me.

Eden *would* have wanted it.

Run, Payton.

I love you. Run.

I'm here now.

When the sun has risen well above the horizon and I am done with another sketch, I hear the back door of the Randalls' farmhouse creak open. The chickens in the yard cluck. There are no horses here, and very few fruit trees except for one big, gnarly apple tree, but in so many ways it's as special as Eden's carvings and as idyllic as she hoped it would be.

I miss her. I miss her so much it hurts. There are so many times I want to talk to her and the realization that she's gone hits me all over again. The pain is overwhelming. The grief is overwhelming. Still, facing my feelings is better than the numb emptiness.

Sometimes I make sketches for her. I won't ever be able to share them with her, of course, but they're tangible reminders of all that she gave me and all that I took from her.

Elisha reminds me every session that I never meant to hurt Eden. She's right. I never intended to hurt her, but the choices I made did exactly that.

Am I guilty despite my best intentions? Am I less responsible because I never stopped being in pain?

I'm not sure there's a right answer.

Footsteps crunch through the yard.

"Payton?" Gary calls out to me.

I turn from my spot beneath the tree and wave at him.

His face lights up. "Dot made breakfast. She sent me to find you."

"She noticed I wasn't inside?" The words feel strange and uncomfortable. Dad only ever noticed my absence when he was angry with me. Gary and Dorothy are different. We're figuring each other out. We're getting used to each other. They're gentle with me, kind.

I am trying to be good back.

Gary scratches his ear and offers me a lopsided grin. "Truth be told, the house is quiet when you're outside. It's nice having you here."

Eden once told me that a home is a place where you belong, a place that isn't complete unless you're there.

I stare at Gary, and after a moment where I feel everything all at once, I nod. "I'm coming."

I place the markers in their box and gather my sketches. I straighten my shoulders, take a deep breath, and turn toward the house.

I'm not happy yet.

But right here and now, I know that one day I will be.

ACKNOWLEDGMENTS

Thank you to everyone who helped me figure out this book, who read it and provided invaluable insight, who listened to me struggle, who asked the right questions, and who cheered me on.

Thank you to everyone at New Leaf Literary & Media for being fierce supporters of this book.

Thank you to everyone at Sourcebooks for handling this story with such passion and gentle care.

And thank you, dear reader, whether this is the first of my books that you've picked up or the tenth. Thank you for letting me tell stories with a sprinkle of hope—and with the reminder that every one of us deserves to have a place where they belong, a home where they're protected, a trusted friend who will fight for them, and a vast horizon.

ABOUT THE AUTHOR

Marieke Nijkamp (she/they) is the #1 *New York Times* bestselling author of *This Is Where It Ends* and many other novels for young adults and young readers. She lives in the Netherlands. Visit her at mariekenijkamp.com.

sourcebooks fire

Home of the hottest trends in YA!

Visit us online and
sign up for our newsletter at
FIREreads.com

....

Follow
@sourcebooksfire
online